His gaze was repeatedly drawn to her—after all, he had been given a glimpse of what she looked like without clothes and it was a sight that would not be easy to forget.

He clenched his fist on the table. What was wrong with him? It was not as if he hadn't seen a mostly naked woman before. He'd seen far too many, by most people's standards. And yet, when she had risen out of the water, like the Norse goddess Ran, confounding him, pinning him in place with a challenging stare and then her knife, his mouth had dried and his throat had constricted. A sudden dart of desire—something he hadn't felt in a very long time—had taken him by surprise and his heart had begun to pound in his chest.

It was ridiculous and most inconvenient. He had traveled here to meet his new bride—to agree to the terms of their arrangement—and now he couldn't take his eyes off this other woman...

Author Note

Thank you so much for choosing to read *Claimed by the Viking Chief*.

Wren has always despised the Danes of the north, since they seized her and took her captive in battle when she was just a girl, tearing her from the arms of her mother. Gifted to the enemy chieftain's daughter to be her companion and servant, she is now the thrall of Earl Ingrid, the ruler of Boer. Wren has vowed that one day, she will be a free woman.

Jarl Knud, the Chief of Nedergaard, knows he must make a marriage alliance with neighboring Earl Ingrid of Boer to keep his people safe from attack. However, his first experience of marriage, when he was a younger man, has left him ashamed—and determined never to fall in love again. On his way into Boer, Jarl Knud catches a servant woman bathing in the moonlight—Wren. Seeing her at the mercy of Earl Ingrid and his men the next day, he is disturbed he wants to rescue her from her plight and claim her for himself. But does he dare to love and risk losing everything again, especially when he knows he stands for everything Wren despises?

I loved writing this love story, creating these characters who are perfect for each other despite their very different stations in life. They have both suffered so much pain in the past that I had a great time setting them on a path of adventure to achieve their happy-ever-after.

You can contact Sarah via @sarahrodiedits or sarahrodiedits@gmail.com or visit her website at sarahrodi.com.

SARAH RODI

—

Claimed by the Viking Chief

Recycling programs
for this product may
not exist in your area.

ISBN-13: 978-1-335-72394-9

Claimed by the Viking Chief

Copyright © 2023 by Sarah Rodi

For questions and comments about the quality of this book, please contact us at CustomerService@Harlequin.com.

Harlequin Enterprises ULC
22 Adelaide St. West, 41st Floor
Toronto, Ontario M5H 4E3, Canada
www.Harlequin.com

Printed in U.S.A.

Sarah Rodi has always been a hopeless romantic. She grew up watching old romantic movies recommended by her grandad and devouring love stories from the local library. Sarah lives in the village of Cookham in Berkshire, UK, where she enjoys walking along the River Thames with her husband, her two daughters and their dog. She has been a magazine journalist for over twenty years, but it has been her lifelong dream to write romance for Harlequin. Sarah believes everyone deserves to find their happy-ever-after. You can contact her via @sarahrodiedits or sarahrodiedits@gmail.com. Or visit her website at sarahrodi.com.

Books by Sarah Rodi

Harlequin Historical

One Night with Her Viking Warrior
Claimed by the Viking Chief

Rise of the Ivarssons

The Viking's Stolen Princess
Escaping with Her Saxon Enemy

Visit the Author Profile page
at Harlequin.com.

For Aldo and Claire,
for all your love and support

Chapter One

Boer Fortress, the Kingdom of Denmark—
9th century

The longhouse was a flurry of activity. Wren watched as the other thralls placed the last of the clean tankards, bowls and spoons on the tables. They scurried around her, sweeping the floor, laying out furs on benches, preparing the hall for Earl Ingrid's guests the next day.

The warrior chief of the neighbouring settlement was coming to visit—and there were rumours Jarl Knud of Nedergaard had marriage on his mind.

Another Dane to despise, Wren thought. Another Dane who no doubt took whatever he wanted from unsuspecting villages, leaving homes destroyed and devastated families in his wake. Wren knew all too well what these ruthless chiefs were capable of, since such a man had seized her and taken her captive in battle when she was just a young girl, tearing her away from her home, ripping her from the arms of her screaming mother.

Gifted to the Earl of Boer's daughter, Ingrid, to be her bond servant, the two of them had grown up together, becoming companions. But while Ingrid was the sole survivor of her family and had gone on to become the Earl of Boer herself, Wren was still trapped in a life of servitude, in a place she could never call home.

She raked a hand down her face, trying to cast aside her bleak thoughts. Things weren't so bad. Earl Ingrid treated her as well as could be and she'd learned to find happiness in her daily tasks and comfort from her friendships with the other thralls here. When Wren had shown promise and a passion for combat from an early age, Ingrid had even allowed her to train alongside her shield maidens, sparring with the sentinels of Boer. And Wren served her ruler loyally. In return, in private, Ingrid sought out her company and often listened to her counsel. But not a day went past when Wren didn't long to prove her merit, to be rewarded for her service and finally set free.

This rumbling of a union between the chiefs of Nedergaard and Boer troubled her mind, like a storm encroaching on an already overcast day, for such an alliance would affect them all, she thought, glancing around the hall again. If Earl Ingrid married, they would have a new master and Wren had heard just how formidable Jarl Knud could be. Famed for his imposing height and great strength, descriptions of Jarl Knud's striking appearance and tales of his prowess on the battlefield had been relayed to them time and again and Ingrid had already begun to imagine herself in love with him.

He was known for his ruthless raids in faraway lands west of the ocean and it was said he had fought numerous tribes in the North before rising to be the powerful leader of Nedergaard—the centre of trade at the mouth of the Vesterhavet. But as to whether Jarl Knud's character was to be as admired as his warrior reputation, they had yet to find out.

Wren swiped her hand across her damp forehead. Despite darkness descending, it was still warm for a midsummer night here and a sliver of moonlight spilled through the door, enticing her outside. Reckless rebellion darted through her and she excused the other thralls, bidding them goodnight. Surely no one would notice if she disappeared by herself for a while? After all, Earl Ingrid had already retired to bed and the work was done for the day.

Everyone knew war was coming to the shores of their lands, as the Earl of Forsa in the south was making plans to attack, wanting to claim the coastal settlements as his own, but there were as yet no signs of their enemy encroaching on their borders tonight. All was quiet, the settlement was safe.

Slipping out of the hall, Wren walked calmly across the square, so as not to draw any particular attention from the guards on the ramparts. She stole past the farmsteads, smoke billowing out from their rooftops, and through the fields of rye, gently swaying in the evening breeze. Then, glancing all around her, checking no one was about, as she would surely be punished for her disobedience, she prised open the little gap in the wooden fortress walls, as she'd done so many times before. On the other side, she took in a deep breath of freedom before charging across the flatlands in the light summer cloak of darkness.

The tide had retreated, exposing the vast expanse of mudflats and deep rivulets winding through the dark, craggy humps and out to the churning sea. It was a dangerous, oppressive place, yet with each stride Wren shrugged off more of her invisible shackles. She took one last look back at the stronghold before breaking out into a swift run, making sure she kept within the shadows of the moon.

She didn't stop until she reached the tidal pool, her one and only sanctuary. Tearing off her threadbare tunic and her tattered boots, stripping down to just her undergarments, she leapt off the bank in wild abandon, as if she were still the young girl who was just five winters old when she was last free, and sank with delight into the freshwater bath. She relished the feeling of the pool washing away the chores of the day, soothing her tired, aching muscles.

It was only when she surfaced, wiping the water from her eyes, that she saw them—and she froze. There, on the outskirts of Boer, were twenty or so white tents lined up on the northern border, small campfires burning, and the distant, muffled tones of men talking carried across to her on the wind. Wren's skin prickled—a sense of duty and a fierce need to protect the people of Boer tearing through her.

How had she not noticed them before? If she had, she would never have been as foolish as to come here alone. She would have returned to the hall and sounded the warning horn instantly. Were these men from Forsa? Straining to hear the low tones, she realised the men were laughing heartily, some even singing. Strange—that wasn't something they'd do if they planned to make a surprise attack.

In alarm, she turned to wade back to the muddy dunes where she'd so carelessly discarded her clothes—and the small wooden knife she carried secretly in her boot, for she was forbidden from having a weapon of her own. When she heard the snapping of a birch twig and two male voices drawing closer, her blood ran cold.

'You know, it's not too late to change your mind…'

She ducked lower in the water, backing farther into the long reeds of grass. If she were to be caught, if she were to be found here, there was no telling what these men would do to her.

'We've come this far,' the taller of the two was saying. In the pale glow of the moonlight, she could just make out his incredibly broad shoulders and dark blond mane of hair, just long enough for it to be fastened at the base of his neck in a band. He had a thick, well-groomed beard and full lips.

'This woman may be able to patch up the cracks in Daneland, strengthen our borders, even, but can the same be said of your heart?' The blond's companion was dark, with a deep scar etched through his brow.

They matched each other in height and, going by the look of their armour and weapons tucked into their belts, these men were definitely of the dangerous, fighting kind. She swallowed. She was a fool. She should not have left her lookout post at the entrance to the longhouse.

'I appreciate your concern, but I care not for matters of the heart, you know that,' the blond one said dismissively. 'Her status and her army, those are the only things of importance to me. You may have married for love, Rædan, but I will only suffer the bonds of marriage again for something far more important—power.'

Typical Dane, she thought scornfully.

'This calculated selection of a wife sits uncomfortably with me,' the one named Rædan continued, sounding troubled. 'It reminds me too much of the rulers of my past.' At least that one seemed to have some sense.

'And I, like them, must think of the strategic gain. It is a legacy I need, not love.'

'A legacy. You mean your reputation, children— or both? So you do at least plan to consummate this marriage, then?'

'I have bedded enough women in my time—I can't imagine I shall find that part a hardship.' He grinned. 'And if it is, I shall only need to share her bed long enough for her to produce an heir.'

'You sound as if you would turn her into some kind of concubine, or an animal kept to breed from.'

The blond one laughed and Wren bit down on the inside of her cheek in disgust. His open assault on those of a lower position in life made her seethe with anger. She pitied the poor woman this man was planning to wed. How could he think so little of his future bride and of women in general? The thought had her ducking farther beneath the water. A man such as he would not treat her kindly if he were to discover her hiding here, listening.

'I hope you know what you're doing.'

'Trust me, I do...'

'Then let us join the others and have some ale, for this could be one of your last nights of freedom, my friend,' the one called Rædan said, cupping the other's shoulder.

Wren's heart lifted in hope. Were they leaving? This could be her chance to get away, to warn the people of Boer that an army of men was at their gates.

'You go ahead. I'll be along shortly.'

No! She pressed herself farther into the reeds, not caring about the sharp rocks grazing into her skin as she watched in dismay as the dark one strolled away, heading back towards the camp, while the other took a few steps closer towards the marsh pool. His brow was furrowed as if deep in thought as he stared down into the water. Soft shadows fell across his face and he momentarily took her breath away. He was a lion of a man, beautiful but robust, and yet, she reminded herself sharply, his words had been so ugly and unfeeling.

It was only when he cast off his animal pelt from his shoulders and began to pull off his chainmail that she started, aghast. Blind panic took over at the sight of him tugging up his tunic, revealing his bare, taut stomach. His broad chest was covered in dark streaks of dramatic ink snaking their way over his shoulder, and scars—lots of them. His large muscles in his arms flexed as he discarded the material and one thing was suddenly very obvious—he intended to enter the pool.

There was no way she could cry out to stop him coming closer, because what would he do, a red-blooded warrior, upon finding a woman out at night, all alone, barely wearing anything? A woman with telling short, cropped hair and a slave collar around her neck… She would be fair game to him and his men. And yet she couldn't not warn him she was here, as right now he was kicking off his boots, reaching for the tie on his trousers, and within moments he would be joining her in the pool, completely naked.

'Stop!' she cried, fear charging through her, forcing her to speak out, as she thrust herself forward, making sure to keep her body and her neck beneath the rippling surface. 'Don't come any closer.' She needed to get to her clothes and her weapon. She needed to get to safety.

He balked, his hand halting. 'What the—?' he muttered, his brows knitting together as he searched out the owner of the voice in the darkness, his gaze skimming across the water. Finally, his deep brown eyes collided with hers in the moonlight, and her breath hitched.

'Who are you?' he barked. 'And what the hell are you doing out here?'

'I was about to ask you that very question,' she snapped back.

'Are you…bathing?' he asked, incredulous, his piercing eyes narrowing. 'This late in the evening?'

'I didn't know there were rules about what time you could bathe…'

'There should be!' He bent over, swiftly snatching up his tunic from the ground.

'That's strange. It looked like you were about to do the same,' she said, fiercely treading water.

He pulled the material back over his bare skin, tugging it down, and she let out a slow, relieved breath.

'I'm a man, you're a woman. Are you out here all alone?' he asked, glancing around. 'And at night?'

'I *thought* I was alone. I came out here for that very reason. I didn't know anyone would think to intrude—especially not an army of monstrous men!'

'Monstrous?' he mocked, his lips twitching. And she felt a dart of annoyance slice through her. 'We're hardly an army. This is Jarl Knud's camp,' he said, motioning with his head to the tents behind him in the distance. 'We're visiting Boer on the morrow.'

Relief swept through her that this wasn't one of Forsa's men, but one of Nedergaard's soldiers instead. 'Well, you can tell your chief you're early,' she said. 'Earl Ingrid isn't expecting him till the sun is at its highest point in the sky.'

'What can I say? He's keen.' He grimaced, raking a hand over his hair while peering down at her in the water, as if trying to get a better look at who he was talking to. 'Are you from Boer?'

'What's it to you?' she said rudely, her legs beginning to tire now.

'If you are, then you definitely shouldn't be here,' he said. 'This is no man's land—between Boer and Nedergaard. You should know it is inhospitable. Unsafe. And word has it that Forsa's men are on the move. They could attack any day.'

'Exactly. No *man's* land. Like you stated so obviously, I'm a woman.'

He raised an eyebrow. 'Not that you're behaving like one. Come, now, get out of there.'

'Not a chance, for how do I know you won't attack me when I get out?'

'Believe me, I have better things to do than attack wild, sharp-tongued women! Besides, I doubt you have anything worth looking at, let alone pouncing on.'

'Then perhaps you could take your leave?'

He folded his arms over his chest, suddenly grinning. 'I don't think so.'

She scowled at him, taking the opportunity to look him up and down again. He was infuriating! There was no denying he was an incredibly attractive man, but she had heard his unkind words about his future bride, practically likening the woman to chattel, and was now bearing witness to his beastly behaviour.

Still, she didn't think he would hurt her. He hadn't called to his men to show them what he'd chanced upon and he'd reinstated his clothes, not carried on removing them. No, if anything, he was just mocking her. He didn't seem to think she was worth attacking, but by the looks of it, he wasn't planning on leaving her be, either.

Well, she refused to let him intimidate her. This was her place, where she liked to come to be alone, and he had interrupted and then insulted her. Glowering, stubborn pride overtook all reason as she waded to the other side of the pool. Wanting to jolt him into moving, and desperate to reach her weapon and her clothes, she launched herself out of the water, making sure her dark hair covered the metal around her neck.

'Við hamri Þórs!' he muttered in shocked surprise, holding up his hands in defeat as he swiftly turned his back on her. 'I was teasing you. I didn't expect you to take me at my word!'

She felt a shaft of triumph shoot through her, before it was wiped away by the sudden blast of cool night air hitting her damp skin and she forced herself to hold back a little squeal from escaping her lips. Instead, she strode over to the few things she owned in life, telling herself not to run, to keep calm. She did not want him to know she was deathly afraid of him.

'Your civilities are severely lacking—just like your clothes!' he said, although seemingly unable to help himself from glancing back over his shoulder.

She stole a look at him in return as she swiped up her tunic and began pulling it on over her wet, cling-ing underclothes as fast as her trembling fingers would allow, tugging it firmly into place. She wrapped her hand around the handle of the hidden knife.

'As are yours, talking about a woman in such a hate-ful way. I feel sorry for the poor lady you were discuss-ing,' she said, stealthily crossing the distance between them.

'Were you spying on us?' His back was still turned, his hand braced on his hip.

'No, but perhaps someone should be, to keep *your* civilities in check,' she said, gently pressing the tip of the knife into his back.

He sighed and gently raised his hands in defeat.

'Who are you?' he asked, sounding irritated now that she had caught him off guard.

'I am none of your concern. Now close your eyes and say the runes out loud…' And, just like that five-winters-old girl she still longed to be, she stuck out her tongue at his broad back in defiance, tucked her boots under her elbow and ran.

Wren stood behind Earl Ingrid in the square as the gates to Boer slowly opened the next day, to welcome Jarl Knud of Nedergaard and his men. Sweat licked Wren's brow and she was unsure if it was due to the midday sun burning down on them or the unease tearing through her body. All at once, her panicked gaze took in the number of horses and their riders, surveying their armour and weapons, assessing the danger, the risk. Were they to be trusted? And yet she was distracted, she couldn't stop herself from searching out the man she had encountered last night. Was he here? And if so, would he realise she was only a thrall and reveal her crime?

The moment her eyes fell upon him her heart sank, sickness churning like the ocean waves in her stomach. No! She did not expect his to be the first face she came across, heading up the convoy as the riders trotted their horses forward through the archway. Surely the man she'd had the unfortunate chance of meeting at the tidal pool last night wasn't the Danish chieftain himself? No, no, no…

Wren wanted the ground to swallow her up. She wanted to be back in the flatlands, sinking beneath the water, washing her discomfort away. She shook her head slightly, trying to make sense of it all. How had she missed the signs?

He had, after all, been talking about making an advantageous marriage. An alliance to strengthen his rule. He was a man of power and raw ambition. He wanted to create even more of a name for himself— a legacy. Of course it was him! How could she not have pieced it all together when she'd heard him talking? Because all her thoughts had fled when she came up against his impressive looks and his wide-grinned mockery, that's why!

He was not what she'd thought he would be like. She'd been expecting someone older—someone far less pleasing to look at. But he was larger than life itself, a man at his best, cocksure, today ornamented with chunky gold rings and silver arm and wrist bands that showed off his status and wealth. He drew the eye like a dazzling polished jewel, making his presence known—and she had never seen a man look so perfect.

His golden mane was neatly fastened and he wore chainmail and a leather vest over an exotic blue silk tunic with a trim of gold thread. A red cloak, lined with thick fur, was fastened tightly over his right shoulder with a brooch. He was a man who wanted to stand out, she realised, and she knew why—because power and status were the only things of importance to him. He'd said so himself to his friend. And as for the words he'd spoken about his future bride… *About İngrid*… Now Wren knew, despite all that they had heard of his impressive warrior reputation, his character was clearly lacking.

But if his raiding triumphs and trading routes in the west were to be believed, they could certainly do with an ally such as he right now. And stealing a glance at her leader's face, she could tell Earl Ingrid had already been won over by his good looks. Wren tutted—Earl Ingrid was almost slavering.

'Earl Ingrid, it is an honour to meet you at last. Thank you for allowing us to visit you,' Jarl Knud said, descending from his magnificent horse and approaching them with an easy smile. Wren's stomach flipped at the flash of his straight teeth, the sound of his smooth, deep voice, and apprehension had her lowering her gaze to the floor. She couldn't acknowledge him—if she did, he might recognise her and there was no telling what Earl Ingrid would do if she knew Wren had left the settlement last night.

She tried to calm herself...it was almost unheard of for Danish chieftains to meet the eyes of a thrall, or even talk to them—their only uses being their ability to work, as a commodity to trade...or as a bed wench. She swallowed. No, she was worrying for nothing— he wouldn't even notice her.

Her ruler stepped forward to greet him. 'Welcome to Boer, Jarl Knud. We have heard so much about you. I trust you had a safe journey?'

'We did. Thank you. Fascinating scenery you have here.'

'Yes, and so tricky to navigate! But I see it didn't hinder you.'

'Of course not. It would take more than a bit of mud to hamper us.'

Wren tried not to roll her eyes at his arrogance.

'The rain has at least held off for you. You and your men must be hungry. We have a feast prepared, just as soon as you've settled the horses.' Earl Ingrid turned to her. 'Show our guests to the stables and then to the longhouse, would you, Wren?'

The chieftain turned to look at her and Wren nodded, holding her breath. There was no way she could evade his notice now—but it didn't mean she had to return his gaze.

'I shall await you and your men's company in the hall, Jarl Knud,' Earl Ingrid said before walking away.

Wren felt the Jarl's eyes burning into her and she ducked her chin in an attempt to further cover up her slave collar under the neckline of her tunic. For some reason, she didn't want this man to see her as weak. And she certainly didn't want his pity.

'Ah, the wild woman from last night. So you do live here. I wondered if we'd meet again.' His head was tilted slightly to the side to study her intently. Out of the corner of her eye, she could see his smile was slowly building.

'I'm sorry, Jarl Knud, you must be mistaken. I don't remember us having met. I'm sure I would have remembered a man such as yourself,' she said curtly, trying to focus on a vague spot just above his left shoulder.

His grin seemed to grow wider still at her lie and she noted his face had lit up with an inner glow of mischief. 'I have to admit I'm offended. Women usually say I'm unforgettable.'

'I'm sure they do,' she said flatly, trying to feign un-interest.

He motioned to his men to follow him, with the mere tilt of his handsome head, and she turned on her heel, beginning to walk out across the square, glad to escape the assessment in his dark, penetrating gaze. 'It's this way.'

He began to pull his horse behind him, somehow still managing to catch up to her with his long, powerful strides. 'It's amazing I recognised you in your clothes.'

'Helvete!' she cursed, stopping abruptly, rounding on him unwillingly. For a moment, she cast her eyes upwards, to gather her thoughts—and her strength—while she felt a flush burn in her cheeks. And then she forced herself to turn towards him without meeting his gaze. 'Forgive me, I should not have been out there in the pool alone,' she said, lowering her voice. 'And I would appreciate it if we could keep...our encounter last night...to ourselves.'

She felt his eyes narrow on her and, after a moment, he bowed his head slightly in acknowledgement. 'Earl Ingrid does not know you have a penchant for late-night bathing?' The smile still playing at the corner of his lips was distracting. Infuriating. But then he didn't realise what was at stake here. He didn't know who he was talking to, or what punishment would be bestowed upon her if he revealed her whereabouts yesterday evening. 'I take it you don't think she'd like it if she knew you were out there?'

She tipped her chin up. 'Do you plan to tell her?'

He studied her face and she hoped he didn't see the look of consternation beneath her proud demeanour. 'No, I don't think that will be necessary.'

She let out a little breath of relief.

'After all, who am I to get in the way of a woman's cleaning habits?' He was really enjoying mocking her, laughing at her. Like he'd laughed at the thought of using a woman as breeding stock or a concubine last night...

How could she have made a fool out of herself already, in front of this important, hateful man? she berated herself and continued to stride out towards the stables. As she finally stepped through the doorway, her anger had her biting back. 'Keeping secrets from Earl Ingrid already?' she tutted. 'That won't do.'

He joined her in the doorway and she crossed her arms over her chest, trying to create a barrier between them.

'I can tell you think it would displease her, hearing of your late-night whereabouts, so why would I want to make her unhappy?'

Wren refused to move, yet she was excruciatingly aware of his proximity, his chest almost brushing against her folded arms. Her breathing was momentarily halted. 'Since when do you care about her happiness? You don't even know her. And you made it quite clear last night you don't care for any woman's feelings—only your own.' She was so close, she could smell his spicy, leathery scent. It was annoyingly captivating.

He inclined his chin, lowering his voice. 'I would not have said such things if I knew I had an audience. But what you heard... I only spoke the truth. An alliance between Boer and our stronghold will strengthen Earl Ingrid's seat of power, not just mine. Yes, Nedergaard needs a bigger force of men, but a union between us will also help Earl Ingrid to secure a major trade route between England, Nedergaard and Boer. This marriage makes a lot of sense for both of us.'

She didn't know why he was explaining himself to her. Had he not yet spotted the metal cuff around her neck? 'It sounds like you have it all worked out already.'

'I do. And I admit I couldn't resist taunting you, especially when I realised you did not know who I was.'

She opened her mouth to chastise him some more, but when she stole a look at him, his molten brown eyes were resting on her lips and it had her biting her tongue for once.

'I feel as if we've got off to a bad start... Wren, is that your name?'

She nodded.

'Then, Wren,' he said, stepping even closer towards her, forcing her to drop her folded arms, 'please let us put last night behind us and be friends.'

She scoffed. She had never known a chieftain to be friends with a thrall, let alone talk to one. This whole conversation was absurd. She was sure, indeed she hoped, that he would forget her the moment he walked through the longhouse door. 'You really don't need to trouble yourself,' she said in the most scathing tone she could muster. 'We do not need to be friends, or even allies, Jarl Knud. After all, it's not me you need to impress, is it? I trust you can all find your own way to the hall?'

Chapter Two

Looking around the longhouse, everyone sitting on benches at the tables, Jarl Knud realised the people of Boer weren't all that dissimilar from his own in Nedergaard. The ample-sized hall was decorated with various hunting trophies, a central hearth was keeping them all warm and the ale was freely flowing. He enjoyed the merriment of the crowd, the group camaraderie and the banter of the table, but although he put on a good show, piling on the charm for the people, he was always on alert, never dropping his guard, not even for a second.

He knew from experience how quickly a feast could turn into a massacre—an enemy shrewdly choosing a moment when a village had let down their guard to attack. And he could never forget that his people were the very reason why he was here. This union was vital—it would bolster his settlement against the tribes in the south and help keep his people safe.

Seated opposite Earl Ingrid, he took the opportunity to assess his prospective bride-to-be. She was attractive, as he'd known she would be, and dressed in exotic silk clothes, her long, braided dark hair woven with gold thread. She was no doubt a strong leader, as Boer was prospering, and yet he felt nothing for her—not a pique of interest, or a flicker of desire. But that was a good thing, wasn't it? That was what he'd hoped for.

His first experience of marriage, when he was a younger man, had left him ashamed—and he had determined he would never wed again. But things had changed. These were perilous times. The Earl of Forsa's forces in the south were drawing closer every day and the happiness of his people meant more to him than his own. But this time, if he had to marry, things would be different. He would never again be weakened by love, or even lust.

His gaze travelled to the woman standing behind Earl Ingrid, trying to blend into the wall behind her and failing miserably. Wren. She had short, dark, cropped hair to her shoulders, half of it pulled back and tied in a knot at the top of her head. It was practical, plain, as were her clothes—and yet her face, bronzed from the sun, was incomparable in beauty. Her eyes were a unique shade of grey and she had such delicate features—was she really a defender of Boer? If so, where was her weapon from last night? Yet she was certainly fierce with her words and attitude—it all had him taking notice.

His gaze was repeatedly drawn to her—after all, he had been given a glimpse of what she looked like without clothes and it was a sight that would not be easy to forget. He clenched his fist on the table. What was wrong with him? It was not as if he hadn't seen a mostly naked woman before. He'd seen far too many, by most people's standards.

Yet, when she had risen out of the water, like the Norse goddess Ran, confounding him, pinning him in place with a challenging stare and then her knife, his mouth had dried, his throat had constricted. A sudden dart of desire—something he hadn't felt in a very long time—had taken him by surprise and his heart had begun to pound in his chest.

It was ridiculous and most inconvenient. He had travelled here to meet his new bride—to agree to the terms to their arrangement—and now he couldn't take his eyes off this other girl. A young woman—who must have been born at least six or seven winters later than him—who already thought the worst of him after hearing the careless words he'd spoken about women and marriage last night. Had she been eavesdropping in the hope of hearing something to use against him? She was clearly on her ruler's side, looking out for her, and it had him wondering why, as one of Earl Ingrid's most trusted warriors, was Wren not sat at her leader's table? His right-hand man, Rædan, was always at his side.

'Wren, these men want more ale!' Earl Ingrid commanded over her shoulder. And Wren immediately stepped forward and began refilling the tankards.

'Shield maiden by day, serving girl by night?' Jarl Knud asked her, surprised.

Wren looked at him in shock before abruptly turning away, but not before another ripple of awareness washed over him as their eyes clashed. Her chin tipped up again in that haughty way that amused him. He knew some people found him to be formidable, but was he that intimidating that she couldn't even look him in the eye?

Wren stretched over one of his men to reach his cup and the man, Ivar, leaned back, seemingly to allow her access to the table. But all of a sudden, he gripped her arm, tugging her on to his lap. 'Want to show me what else you can do, pretty one?'

Due to the abrupt movement, her clothes were pulled to the side and the collar around her neck came into view, on show for all to see, and Jarl Knud's whole body contracted in shock. The flash of anger in Wren's grey depths matched his. His outrage at his man's behaviour was instant and he launched himself from the bench to intervene, but her reactions were quicker— she didn't hesitate. She tugged back her arm, picked up a knife and brought it down on Ivar's other hand, the blade entering the wood between his splayed-out fingers on the table—and a hush descended among the group. Ivar pulled back his still-intact fist in disbelief, allowing Wren the chance to escape his hold and get to her feet.

Jarl Knud bit back a smile of admiration, despite his disturbance at seeing her bonds and his fury at the actions of his man. She could certainly handle herself— she had given Ivar a shock. But he would still make sure his warrior was reprimanded. He was furious! How dare he lay his hands on her? Ivar should know better than to act that way towards women and especially when they were guests here. Letting out a long, slow breath, Jarl Knud lowered himself back down into his seat.

'Wren! You will apologise to this man at once!' Earl Ingrid demanded.

Wren was back against the wall, standing tall, her nostrils flaring. She shook her head slightly.

'Now!'

'Do not worry, Earl Ingrid. It is no more than my man deserved,' Jarl Knud said quickly, trying to appease her. 'Tell me…are they not free women, your shield maidens?'

'Wren is not a shield maiden, Jarl Knud, she's a *bryti*, of sorts,' Earl Ingrid said, raising a cup to her lips and taking a long sip of ale.

'What's that?'

'She was given to me as a gift by my father. She is my bond servant…'

Jarl Knud saw Rædan's head snap up and the two of them shared a look across the table.

'I see.' So he could add cruel to the list of his wife-to-be's attributes. Since he had ruled in Nedergaard, Jarl Knud had made it his mission to make it a place free of thralls. He knew more than most what a devastating impact slavery had on lives…

'But as I have known Wren for so long, and she can *usually* be trusted, she has more responsibility than most.'

Vulnerable yet spirited, Wren now wholeheartedly captivated his attention, reminding him of ghosts from his past. He knew many men would see the collar around her neck and deem it acceptable to treat her however they wanted—she was at their mercy—and yet his instinct was to protect her. But he also knew from the dart of burning jealously at seeing Wren fall into Ivar's lap that he didn't want his man to touch her because there was a part of him that wanted to claim her for himself.

He put down his own knife, suddenly not hungry. He was appalled at the direction of his thoughts. What the hell was the matter with him? What did that make him? He was no better than Ivar. He didn't want to feel this way about any woman. But for a man of his standing, to bed a thrall would all but ruin his carefully crafted reputation.

His eyes strayed to Wren's once more, but she continued to stare stonily straight ahead, absently fiddling with the now exposed metal around her neck. Being a thrall would certainly explain her hostility, her closed-off stance, her avoidance of his gaze. Her status would also explain her desire to keep her late-night outing a secret and now he was glad he'd kept quiet about it—he didn't want her to get into trouble because of him.

'Do you own many thralls, Earl Ingrid?' he asked, leaning back in his seat, his smile forced.

'About thirty or so. Most have belonged to me since they were children—they know no different,' she said. 'I treat them well. Therefore they are content and serve me loyally.'

Since they were children? His heart clenched.

'But...to have a slave in such an honoured position?' he said, carefully weighing up his words before speaking. He was aware Wren could hear every single one. 'To give them weapons...'

'They are not allowed to carry weapons, Jarl Knud.'

Then had he imagined being held up at knifepoint by a wild, naked woman last night? It had been one of the most erotic moments of his life. His eyes travelled to Wren's again and he saw a muscle flicker in her jaw. She was slim—a little too slim, perhaps—and it only made the pert swells of her breasts seem more prominent beneath her tunic. He closed his eyes briefly, remembering yet again what she looked like when she rose from the water. But when he opened them, he was determined to keep them on her face.

Now he realised why his thoughtless words to Rædan at the marsh pool would have made her his enemy. She wouldn't have understood his wry comment about keeping a woman as a concubine. Rædan knew he of all men hated slavery and would never do that. Damn, he felt like such a fool.

'I did allow Wren to train with my warriors, but she has to double up on her duties. And she knows any servant who misbehaves will be violently subdued. But as you can see,' she said, motioning to Ivar, 'she is useful to have around while my army has been sent to fight. You must know Forsa's forces keep advancing, growing ever nearer, so I have sent my most able men to the border.'

'Which we are grateful for,' he said flatly. 'But your thralls—would they not better serve you as free people?' he said, unable to let the matter lie.

He was aware of Wren turning to glance at him

again, but he tried to block her out, focusing on Earl Ingrid. He needed to comprehend her motives, to better understand her reasons for this barbarity.

'If they were to be freed, they would not survive long outside these walls. They own nothing, know nothing other than this life. They *need* me,' Earl Ingrid said. She put down her cup, a deep crease forming in her forehead. 'I do not tell you how to run your settlement, Jarl Knud, so I don't expect you to tell me how to run mine. I can see we have much to agree on before we progress with this alliance of ours.'

They certainly did…

Grudgingly, he inclined his head. She was right—whether Earl Ingrid kept slaves or not wasn't anything to do with him. *Yet.* Not until he was ruler here. And as Wren had told him so last night, she was not his concern.

'What do you think, Wren? Is he handsome?' Earl Ingrid asked her as they watched Jarl Knud pick up a weapon and take his next turn in the axe-throwing contest, already dominating the game. The village square was packed with people watching the tournament, cheering loudly when a few of the axes hit the target.

'If you like a man who grooms himself far too often and wears more jewellery than a woman.' Wren shrugged. And Earl Ingrid laughed.

Jarl Knud was currently showing off, enjoying being the centre of attention, entertaining the crowd.

'I think he is very fine. He is everything a tribe

leader should be and more. Strong, attractive, wise…
if a little opinionated.'

Arrogant, overbearing, with dubious morality…
Wren added to the list. Mainly all she saw when she
looked at him was danger. But his brutish reputation
was very much at odds with his perfect appearance,
she thought. Waiting on him and his men in the hall,
her contempt for him had burned inside her gut—
especially when he had questioned Earl Ingrid's motives for giving her authority and allowing her to carry
a weapon!

Helvete! Had he been about to tell Earl Ingrid about
their meeting at the marsh pool last night? After he'd
given her his word that he wouldn't? But she would
rather feel anger towards him than the flicker of interest he'd already ignited. Interest she wanted to stamp
out as quickly as possible.

Sitting on the bench in the longhouse, which had
seemed far too small for his huge frame, his penetrating brown gaze assessing the hall, he'd seemed so at
ease and in control—and she'd felt sure his eyes had
repeatedly sought out hers while he was talking. Had
she imagined it—his mocking gaze burning into her?
She had found it difficult to stay on task, her hands
trembling as she'd poured the ale. And then his man
had manhandled her! Were all males the same? Could
none of them be trusted? Her heart had exploded in
panic and she'd reacted with force.

Now Jarl Knud was grinning at Earl Ingrid—that
wide, wicked smile—as he celebrated hitting the
wooden target on the opposite side of the square again.

'Well, there you have it. It seems I am the winner,' he said, swaggering towards them, gloating, as the crowd went wild.

'Of course you are!' Earl Ingrid enthused and Wren tried not to roll her eyes.

She didn't want this man to barge into Boer and change things. She didn't want him around at all. She would never be able to breathe easy with him in charge. She shuddered, thinking back to when Earl Ingrid's father, and then her brother, had been in power and all she had suffered at the hands of those men. Would Jarl Knud be just as evil once he took control?

She tried to keep her focus on the present, but the scene before her was equally repellent. Seeing Earl Ingrid and Jarl Knud together caused a strange sensation to smoulder in her stomach. It just seemed wrong. They didn't go well together at all. It also sought to remind her that she could never have what they had—she would never marry. Even if Earl Ingrid allowed it, she wouldn't want to be bound to someone else, or even have a family of her own. She could never bring a child into her life of thralldom—it would be too cruel.

'How can you be the best if not everyone has had a turn?' Wren muttered under her breath.

'Wren!' Earl Ingrid snapped in shock.

She knew she was playing with fire—Earl Ingrid had already chastised her for her surly behaviour in the hall, warning her she would be punished if she couldn't fall into line.

Over the winters that had passed, she had come to realise that while she had to do her best to be seen to be obeying in the way she behaved, she did not have to comply in thought. Her opinions would always be her own. It was just that, sometimes, she struggled to keep them to herself.

Jarl Knud grinned. 'It's all right, Earl Ingrid. I don't mind people speaking their thoughts.' Then he turned his attention to Wren. 'I take it you think you can beat me? By all means,' he said, spreading his arms wide. 'Take a turn and let's see.'

'Oh, no,' Ingrid said, quickly stepping in. 'I don't let the thralls take part in such games.'

'I'm sure we could make a special allowance on this occasion.' He picked up another axe out of the basket and flipped it over in his hand, then he held the blade as he passed the handle to Wren. 'So...what do you say?'

He was so cocky and confident and she felt anything but. Yet she stepped forward anyway, looking between him and Earl Ingrid, still not meeting his gaze, and with the reluctant nod of approval from her ruler, she took the weapon from his hand, accepting the challenge. Silence descended on the crowd, the people no doubt shocked to see Earl Ingrid's thrall being allowed to take a turn in the contest. Wren's pulse began to pound. Her feet shifting from side to side, she found a good stance and focused on her aim.

Slowly, the villagers who stood watching began stamping their feet, encouraging her on, and she desperately wanted to show off her capability to them. And to Ingrid. But mainly to the man who sought to be leader of this stronghold. Perhaps he'd respect her as a warrior, if nothing else. She was irritated that she even cared in the slightest what he thought.

When she was ready, she lifted the weapon above her shoulder, taking a deep breath in and out to steady herself. Putting in all her strength, drawing on her anger at him and Earl Ingrid and her whole life, she released the weapon and threw it forward. It arced through the air, rotating once before the blade split the handle of Jarl Knud's axe, piercing the target dead centre.

He let out a low whistle as the crowd erupted in glee. 'Impressive,' he said. 'Perhaps she should be out on the battlefield after all, Earl Ingrid. Her talents are clearly wasted here.'

Ignoring his compliment, for she couldn't be sure if he was mocking or praising her, Wren tipped up her chin and strode forward, heading to retrieve the axe, wanting to get away from his scrutiny. But she couldn't evade the trickle of delight his words had caused. It was worth the punishment Earl Ingrid would surely bestow on her later.

To her surprise, Jarl Knud followed her to claim back his own broken weapon. The farther away from the crowd they got, the more on edge she became, his arm brushing against hers.

'You have a good aim, Wren, but I'm still surprised Earl Ingrid has allowed you to train as a warrior.'

She was shocked he was engaging with her again, now he knew her rank as a thrall. And she wished he wouldn't. Did he just mean to insult her? He made her feel uneasy, an unwanted awareness of him rippling through her, and she stepped aside to put some distance between them, trying to evade his touch. Although she knew he wasn't the barbaric chief who had stolen her away from her family, she was certain it was something most warlords were capable of. Yet there was no way she would give him the satisfaction of knowing he unnerved her. She didn't want him to know that he had any effect on her whatsoever.

'Why? Because it makes me stronger in a world where you all ensure I have no power? Don't tell me you're worried what I might do with a weapon in my hand?' she added harshly, wanting to lash out at him.

'Only because I've been on the receiving end of your blade,' he said. 'Twice now.' His easy smile returned as he struggled to release the split-in-two handle of his axe from the plank of wood. 'I was merely surprised that Earl Ingrid allows you to learn how to fight as surely she's equipping you with the skills you need to escape—and if I were you, I'd certainly try...' He winked.

'What?' Her eyes lanced him, before remembering herself and looking away. Was he actually suggesting that she did?

'Is the axe your weapon of choice in battle?' he asked.

'I've never fought in one.'

'You see, I can't understand why the axe would be used,' he continued. 'You're effectively giving away your weapon as soon as you throw it. And then you have the trouble of retrieving it amid the fighting, leaving you vulnerable to attack… By the way, where did you disappear to so quickly after the feast?'

He liked to talk a lot, she realised. And she was struggling to keep up with the conversation. After the feast? She'd been livid. As soon as the meal was over and the bowls had been cleared away, Wren had seized her moment to escape the cloying, confined space in the longhouse. There were too many bodies crammed inside, more than usual with their guests from Nedergaard.

She'd retrieved her bowl of pottage and, pushing her way through the men and women, had taken it outside to enjoy alone. She hadn't eaten since first light and she'd been starving, the sights and smells from the meats and trimmings of the meal that had been made for the warriors of Nedergaard making her stomach rumble. The sea breeze on her skin had felt good, helping to cool her anger.

She couldn't believe they had all talked about her as if she didn't exist, as if she wasn't a real person with thoughts and feelings, while she'd been standing right there! But what did she expect? No one thought she had a right to those things, did they? And Earl Ingrid had spoken the truth—even if she could leave, she had nowhere else to go. Ingrid had raised her, been good to her, *needed* her, as she'd told her many times. But if Wren were ever given the chance to be free, she knew she would take it immediately.

As if someone was trying to remind her of her status here, her slave collar felt as though it was choking her today. She fingered the metal around her neck.

'I'm sure I wasn't missed.'

'Actually, I was looking for you.'

Her stomach flipped, and she busied herself by crouching down and filling a basket with the axes which were strewn over the ground, but not before noticing him running a hand around the back of his neck uncomfortably.

'I wanted to apologise about the way my man treated you at the table.'

She halted what she was doing for a moment. Glancing up, she wanted to know if he was mocking her again, but his gaze lacked any humour. Did he not know offering a thrall an apology was unheard of in these lands?

'My man had drunk far too much ale. He was excited by a new place, pretty faces. But that's no excuse for touching you.'

Pretty?

'No, it's not,' she said. When his man had put his hands on her, Wren had reacted. It was a natural response. She had been manhandled like that before and thoughts of it still made her skin crawl. It had taken every ounce of strength to bite her tongue when Earl Ingrid had scolded her, and she'd been amazed Jarl Knud had come to her defence, chastising the man named Ivar in return. 'But I'm used to people thinking I exist merely to benefit them.'

She picked up the heavy basket and he went to take it from her, his fingers crushing hers. 'Let me help you.'

'I can do it,' she insisted. And then she stopped, stock still. 'Shh!' she said, straining to hear.

'Did you just hush me?' he asked, incredulous, his eyes wide.

Maybe that was going one step too far, hushing the Chief of Nedergaard. But her skin had erupted in goose pimples and she couldn't decide if it was a reaction to his touch or if something was wrong. Possibly both. She glanced up at the bridge.

'What is it?' he asked.

'I don't know. I thought I heard something.'

All of a sudden, an arrow came whistling through the air towards them. There was a scream of pain and one of the villagers gasped as an arrow struck her chest before her body slumped to the ground.

It took a moment for everyone to comprehend it—to understand what was happening. Then they realised— they were under attack. Instantly, the women and children descended into panic, leaving the contest, running for the safety of their farmsteads, and the men looked to their leaders for instructions.

'Very observant,' Jarl Knud muttered, staring down at her. He reached for his sword and ran across the square to the steps and Wren, grabbing an axe out of the basket, was right behind him, closely followed by Rædan and Earl Ingrid. They all charged up to the bridge, taking the stairs two at a time.

Wren peered over the ramparts at the top, her breath hitching. There, on the other side of the fortress walls, was an army of what must have been a hundred men. How had they not heard them approach? Why had they not been warned? But quickly looking around, she realised all of the soldiers on the lookout posts were dead, each killed with a single arrow to the throat.

Wren picked up the warning horn from around one of the lifeless guard's necks and blew into it, sounding the alarm, just as a flurry of fire arrows came hurtling over the walls, making them all duck. Beneath them on the other side of the walls, a group of painted warriors charged at the gate with a battering ram, a strange rallying cry coming from their lips.

'It must be Forsa's forces,' Jarl Knud said. 'They've got here faster than I thought.'

'What are they chanting?' Wren asked.

'They're calling for Tyr—the god of war,' Knud said. 'How many of your men were sent to the border?' he asked, turning to speak to Earl Ingrid.

'All of them.'

'Helvete!' he cursed. 'My guess is Forsa saw your army moving south and realised the fortress had been left vulnerable to attack. Rather than fighting your men, he avoided them and came straight here.'

Keeping low, they raced back down the steps to warn the villagers left in the square what they already knew—their enemy was at their gates.

'If you are able to fight, ready your weapons. If you can't, get as far away from here as possible. Get the women and children to safety,' Jarl Knud ordered.

They immediately saw the impact of his calm leadership and his deep authoritative voice. The men and women who could fight took up arms, lining up in a shield wall in the square, while the rest of the villagers ran about like the cattle Wren had once seen stampede during a lightning strike. Buildings were already burning and with every pummelling of the battering ram that came against the gate, the enemy was getting closer to breaking into the fortress.

Wren's heart was in her mouth and she tried to brace herself for what was about to happen. And then the gates gave way, shattering into pieces, shards of wood splintering everywhere, and another barrage of arrows came hurtling over the walls. She watched in horror as Forsa's men flooded the main square, like a swarm of locusts, turning Boer into a bloody battleground.

For a moment, she was rendered useless. The last time she had been in a situation like this, she had been just five winters old and was brutally taken from her family. Her world had changed beyond recognition, and the hideous flashbacks of her past made her falter.

'Wren, look out!'

Jarl Knud's words forced her out of her dark reverie and she realised she had to move or she'd die. The enemy was upon them, showing no mercy, killing everything in their sights. Driven by a deep anger—that what had happened to her could now happen to the children of Boer, children she cared about—she gripped the axe in one hand and withdrew her knife from the inside of her boot with the other, and threw herself into the fray, a rush of fear and excitement thrumming through her.

Right beside her, Jarl Knud and his men met the painted warriors directly, disarming one man, then another. She had thought the Chief of Nedergaard's jovial, conceited manner was at odds with his reputation as a

ruthless warrior—she just hadn't been able to marry
the two images together—but now she saw the change
in him. Lethal, instinctive—an expert in combat—he
was suddenly a different man to the one she had seen
only moments ago, gloating over his win in the contest. Had it all been a front? He certainly didn't need
to prove himself in a game—he must know he had no
equal. He charged into the enemy as if he didn't fear
death, as if he didn't care whether he lived or died. It
was incredible—almost frightening to watch.

'You should take shelter. Hide. If they find you...'
he shouted between ferocious tussles, nodding to her
neck collar.

Humiliation burned. 'What? You think I'm an easy
target just because of this?' she spat in disgust. 'No
more than any other woman would be in this situation.'

It was an odd thing to consume his thoughts at a
time like this. But there was no way she would abandon the people of Boer and hide. She hadn't done that
when she was five and she wouldn't do it now. And she
couldn't deny a part of her was enjoying the power of
having a weapon in her hand, allowing her to release
some of the pent-up anger at the world. But even though
they were fighting, knowing the fortress depended on
it, it was already clear there wouldn't be enough of
them to deal with the onslaught.

Earl Ingrid was fighting fiercely beside her, trying
to defend her stronghold, and had cut down several
men before a particularly large beast bore down on her,
slicing his blade through her armour above her right
hip, and Wren looked on in horror as she watched her

leader crumple to the ground. She picked up Earl Ingrid's sword and swiftly dealt with the man who sought to send her the same way, before racing to her fallen ruler, slumped in a heap in the middle of the square.

Wren put a finger to her neck to check for a pulse. Earl Ingrid was still breathing, but she was quickly losing a lot of blood, the crimson liquid seeping into the earth. A man charged at Wren, but he was stopped just before he reached her by Jarl Knud, who had picked up an axe from the basket and thrown it. Her eyes wide, she nodded at him in thanks. Maybe the axe had a place in battle after all.

He came down beside her, his brow furrowed with concern. 'How bad is it? Is it mortal?'

'I'm not sure. I need to remove her chainmail—check how deep it is. But I can't do it here.'

'We're being overrun. We need to retreat. We must leave now.' He turned to call to his man who seemed equally as skilled at warding off the enemy. 'Rædan. You, Ivar and the rest—get to the horses.'

'We can't move her,' Wren said, shaking her head in dismay. 'It'll surely kill her. I need time to stop the bleeding.'

'I know, but we have to get her out of sight before it's too late. There's no telling what they'll do to the leader of Boer if they get their hands on her.'

Wren went to protest, but Jarl Knud had already turned to speak to Rædan again.

'We can't hold them back. Get as many of Boer's people to safety as you can. Head to Nedergaard. Keep to the undergrowth. We'll meet you there.'

Her head shot up. Did he intend to stay and help her?

Rædan nodded and then was gone, disappearing back into the fray, obeying his leader's orders.

'You're not leaving?' she asked, shocked.

'No, I'll stay with you and help Earl Ingrid. But we have to move. Now.' All at once she was both grateful and disturbed. She was glad she didn't have to do this by herself, but she also didn't want to be left here alone with this man—she was determined to hate him. But it seemed they were doing this. There was no time to think.

'There is a place we can hide…' she said, her thoughts whirring.

'Come, then. Show me. We'll have to move fast, before it's too late.' Lifting Earl Ingrid together, Jarl Knud slung his arm around the chieftain's back and under her shoulders, and Wren anchored hers around Ingrid's waist. Working together as a team, their arms rubbing against each other's, they ducked into the shadows and Wren wondered how she could be so aware of his nearness at a time like this. Why was her skin burning? And why were thoughts of his inked naked chest and the large muscles in his arms flooding her mind? *Helvete!* Why did *he* have to be the one to stay and help? Why couldn't it have been anyone but him?

'This way,' Wren said, squeezing between the now-abandoned burning farmsteads, belongings scattered about where villagers had left in a hurry. Wren took a quick glance back over her shoulder at the scene they were leaving behind. Bodies lay strewn around the square and the farm animals were running wild. It was hard to believe just moments ago there had been an atmosphere of merriment in the air as they'd competed with the axes. Now those very weapons were coated in blood, discarded on the ground.

'She's heavy. Can you manage?'

'Quite well,' she gritted out. She wasn't about to admit she was struggling. Not to him.

They made it through the fields unhindered, pushing through the towering rye to the outskirts of the settlement where they came upon the old, neglected farm building with weeds growing all around it. The broken door was banging open in the breeze and rusting tools still hung on the walls inside.

'What is this place?' he asked as they squeezed through the doorway.

'An abandoned crop store. I come here sometimes to be alone.' Having spent so much of her life in this stronghold, she often wanted to be somewhere no one could find her and she had come to know all the secret places. She doubted Forsa's men would bother to look here. Not for a while anyway.

They laid Earl Ingrid down on the hut floor and Wren tried to focus on checking her wound, while Jarl Knud furtively scouted out the place for entrances and weapons. He finally came down next to her.

'Will she live?'

'I can't see too well in this light. The wound doesn't appear to be too deep, but she's lost a lot of blood.'

He stood and paced. *'Helvete!'* he said, running his hand through his hair. 'How the hell did this happen?' And then he seemed to notice her again... Attempting to calm himself by loosening his shoulders, he came down on his haunches once more. He snatched up Wren's hand, making her gasp. 'Are *you* bleeding? Are you hurt?' he said, nodding to the blood coating her fingers.

She shook her head, shocked. 'No, not me—it's Earl Ingrid's blood.'

She pulled back her hand, her skin tingling from his touch, while he let out a long, steadying breath.

'But you are trembling.'

'Are you surprised?'

She thought she might be in shock and his nearness wasn't helping. Everything had happened so fast. They'd lost the fortress. Earl Ingrid had been hurt. Now she was hiding in this small hut where the enemy could find them at any moment. And to top it all off she was stuck with him! 'I told you, I've never fought in a battle before.'

'And I told you not to fight!'

'As if I could just stand by and watch! Besides, you're not my master. Not yet anyway. You don't get to tell me what to do.'

'I'm amazed you didn't see it as a chance to escape. Instead, you choose to defend the very people who hold you hostage. Here, let me do that,' he said, taking the bunched-up material from her hand that she was using to try to stem the flow of blood. 'Get your breath back. You're safe for now. What can we do?' he said, motioning to Earl Ingrid, who was neither awake nor responding to them, the colour seeping from her face.

'I'll need to clean the wound, but we need water for

that. There's not much I can do right now apart from wrap it up.'

He stood, roughly ripping a strip of material off the bottom of his tunic. 'Will this work?' he asked, holding it up to her.

She nodded. 'Yes, thanks. Help me?' she said, pulling off Earl Ingrid's leather vest and struggling to pass the material underneath her ruler's back to wrap the bandage around her waist. Jarl Knud helped her lift and roll Earl Ingrid from side to side, their fingers brushing as she passed the material to him.

'You had good instincts out there,' he said, and she could feel the whisper of his warm breath on her face. 'You knew something was about to happen, that we were about to be attacked.'

She shrugged. She wasn't used to receiving compliments. 'I guess I'm conditioned to being alert to danger. It was good of you to stay behind and help,' she conceded. Admirable, even. Perhaps she'd misjudged him? Perhaps he really did care for his future bride.

'I could say the same about you,' he said, bringing the material around over the top of Earl Ingrid's stomach once more, passing it back to Wren again. Earl Ingrid groaned for the first time, and Wren placed a hand on her forehead to check the heat of her skin.

She felt his eyes on her while she fastened the material into a knot, then she sat back, trying to come to terms with what had just happened. Trying to get her breathing under control, her arms crossed over her chest, she wasn't sure she would ever understand the barbarity. They could still hear the sounds of the bloodbath going on in the distance, and Jarl Knud stood and strode to the door.

'I want to go back. I might be able to help…'

She knew men like him yearned for the fight and the glory—and she had heard he was never one to give in, that he never surrendered. He seemed to enjoy being at the heart of danger. Thinking back to him fighting those men, he was like a fallow deer in their rutting season, antlers locked, fighting for supremacy. It must have taken a lot for him to decide to leave the battle-field. He must have done it for Earl Ingrid. But despite their defeat on this occasion, he still looked like the leader of the herd to her.

Wren shook her head, slowly standing and joining him. 'You saw it. There's nothing else we could have done. There were too many of them.' She took a last look as smoke swirled up into the sky over Boer and distant wails echoed across the fields. She imagined Forsa's forces charging into the longhouse, taking control of the heart of the stronghold. She just hoped if there were any survivors, the enemy would be merciful. Perhaps most of the villagers had made it out. Maybe they were safe. 'Do you think many of our people and your men escaped?' she whispered.

'I think we held off Forsa's men long enough to give them a chance. And my man, Rædan, is the best warrior I know. If anyone could get the rest of them to safety, it's him. He certainly wouldn't have gone down without a fight.' He grimaced. 'Neither would I usually.'

Wren shook her head. 'It was a total ambush. There was no warning.'

'They must have known your army had gone to the border. And I wonder if they knew you had visitors from Nedergaard and your people would be distracted.'

'Perhaps…'

'And if they knew I was here, after they've enjoyed the spoils of Boer and gathered their strength, they'll be heading for Nedergaard next… They'll want to strike while my settlement is at its weakest, without me there. I must get back before that happens. I can't leave my people alone to fend for themselves. I'll need to assemble our forces. We'll need to be more prepared than yours were.'

She reeled, hurt by the criticism, his tone of accusation. 'Are you saying it was our fault?' she cried.

'I'm saying Earl Ingrid should never have sent her entire army away, leaving her fortress completely undefended. It was very foolish of her.'

'Perhaps you being here *put* us in danger?' she snapped back, seeking to hurt him with a low blow. 'Perhaps they were looking for *you*.' Then she slumped down against the wall, holding her knees to her chest. She knew there was no point in throwing insults and blame at one another—it was done now.

He seemed to think about her words for a moment and dragged his hand over his face. Silence reigned, neither of them knowing what to say. The situation was less than ideal, the three of them stuck here in this cramped, uncomfortable space, total strangers, one too hurt to move, with the enemy surrounding them. Wren was certain Jarl Knud must wish he was anywhere but here. She knew she did.

As if he was reading her mind, he said: 'We can't stay here, they will find us eventually. And we'll need food. Water. Plus I need to get back to Nedergaard as soon as possible. We'll need to summon Earl Ingrid's army there, too. Only then can we think of trying to launch a counter-attack to get Boer back. There will be a reckoning for this.'

'What do you suggest? In case you hadn't noticed, Earl Ingrid was pretty heavy to carry. And she won't be able to walk any time soon.' Yet she knew he was right, they couldn't stay here indefinitely. She didn't know why she was being so difficult.

'How did you get to the marsh pool the other night? I take it you crept out unnoticed.'

She blushed in the darkness at being reminded of their intimate meeting, images of his incredible body filling her mind again, but she instantly picked up on the direction of his thoughts. 'There's a little gap in the palisade walls. On the far side of the fortress,' she said, pointing in the direction.

'Can we get there unseen—and can we carry Earl Ingrid through it?' She was astonished he was asking her for her opinion, involving her in his plans.

She nodded. 'Yes. But then what? The flatlands stretch out before the fortress—as far as the eye can see. They'll see us if we try to cross them, especially as we'll be slowed down by carrying her.'

'It might be our only chance. If we stay here, we're too vulnerable to attack.'

She nodded. 'I agree with you—on that if nothing else.'

'When the tide goes out, the mudflats will be exposed and with it the tidal creeks. Is it possible we can walk them and go unseen, perhaps make it to the *longphort* of Hafranes? It's a trade settlement—I have friends there. We might be able to get Earl Ingrid some herbs at their market. By then we should be out of Forsa's reach.'

'But if the tide comes back in while we're crossing?' she asked. 'It's incredibly dangerous. You can sink in the mud. We lost an entire herd to the mud one winter. People usually avoid that area. Like you said last night, it's no man's land.'

'And yet you still dared go out there alone.'

Her eyes narrowed on him. 'I'm just saying it's a bad idea.'

'Do you have a better one?'

She looked away, chewing her bottom lip. And then a thought struck her. 'I know how to plait willow and twigs for basket making. If we could find some, I could possibly make something to carry Earl Ingrid on?'

He nodded. 'Very resourceful, Wren. I like your thinking. How long would it take?'

'I could make a start now, do it through the night. Maybe it will be done by morning.' Was she really agreeing to spend the night out here cooped up with him? Could she trust him? If he tried anything, she'd be no match for his strength. Images ripped through her of being pinned down by a man once before. But what choice did she have now? She would have to take her chances...

He nodded. 'All right, then. I'll go and see what I can find. Let's give Earl Ingrid a night to rest, see if we can stop the bleeding.' He was firm, decisive. 'Then we will leave under the cover of darkness, before sunrise. We can do this, Wren—together.'

Chapter Three

Jarl Knud sat down opposite her in the small hut, leaning back against the other wall, stretching out his long legs as Wren set to work plaiting the various scraps of wood and branches he'd foraged from outside. Her sight and hearing were heightened in the darkness and she thought she could just make out the glint of his sword in the moonlight as he placed the weapon across his large thighs, ready to use if he needed to.

'Where are you from, Wren?'

His question stunned her. No one had ever asked her that before.

'What? Would you rather sit here in awkward silence all night? We may as well talk—it might help the dark hours pass quicker. Were you born here?' he added.

'Do you really want to know?' It was absurd, an important Danish chief asking a thrall about her life, wasn't it?

'Yes, I want to know. I wouldn't have asked if I didn't.'

'Well,' she said, her brow furrowing, 'I was freeborn.'

'Then how did you come to be here, like this?'

She shrugged, before realising he couldn't see her in the dim light of the hut. 'I was a prize of plunder. But I'm sure you don't want to hear about all that,' she said, unsure. Was she being disloyal to Earl Ingrid?

'Actually, I do, if you don't mind telling me. I want to better understand the situation.' His voice sounded deep and velvety—almost soothing—in the darkness.

'Why?'

'If I am to lead the people of these lands, I'm interested to know what goes on here. To know all the people—thralls, karls and jarls. I also feel strange sitting here with you and not knowing anything about you… Don't you? So won't you tell me what happened?'

Wren felt sure Earl Ingrid would not want her discussing this with him. But then, why shouldn't she? And she did want to tell someone, if only to hear how the truth sounded on her tongue. To see how he'd react. Perhaps even to feel a little vindicated. She swallowed before beginning.

'I was five when I was taken. I was kidnapped in the midst of a brutal battle.'

'A battle?'

'A tribe attacked our village, storming our settlement—a bit like today. To me, a young girl, they looked like giants on horseback, wearing animal furs and with painted faces, wielding their swords, bringing fire to the roofs of our farmsteads. I was so frightened. We'd lived in peace before that.'

'Is that why you froze when you saw those men enter the gates today? I imagine it brought back some awful memories for you.'

She was stunned that he'd noticed that, amid everything else that was going on.

'So what happened?'

'It was my fault.'

'I very much doubt that.'

'My mother was trying to get me to hide, but I wouldn't. I remember clinging on to her, protesting, wailing, not wanting to let her go, so she gave up and began running with me, trying to get me to safety...' Her voice wavered.

'Go on,' he said.

'We were nearing the frozen forest that surrounded our settlement when there was the sound of heavy horses' hooves behind us and suddenly my mother was knocked to the ground. I cried out for her, but I was torn from her arms, hoisted up on to a man's side and carried away,' she said. 'I often wonder what would have happened if I'd just done as I was told and hidden beneath the floorboards, as she'd wanted me to. Perhaps I wouldn't have been taken. Perhaps she would have been safe. I don't even know if she survived...'

'I'm so sorry, Wren. It must have been terrifying for a small child. You were only five, you said?' She thought she could see him shaking his handsome head at her misfortune. But she didn't want his pity.

'Yes. The man who took me turned out to be the Chief of Boer and, when he returned home, he gifted me to his daughter,' she said simply.

There was a long pause and she wondered what he was thinking. Perhaps he thought nothing of it. Perhaps he had done the same thing many times over. Although, by the tone of his responses, she didn't think so. He seemed genuinely appalled, which warmed her a little. 'What was life like for you here? How were you treated?' he asked.

'What do you think?' she said bitterly. 'I went from being a person, a beloved child, to being someone's property overnight. It was devastating. I mainly did chores—long hours of grinding, milking, washing—and I didn't have much food. But I suppose it wasn't all terrible. Ingrid and I played together, becoming firm companions. But whenever she misbehaved, they made me take the punishment for whatever she'd done wrong, hoping to make her feel guilty.'

'And did she?' he asked.

She bit her lip, her silence speaking for all she could not say.

He cursed beneath his breath, seeming to be angry for her, on her side—confounding her again. 'You must have missed your home. Do you remember what your settlement was called?'

'No,' she said, shaking her head, aware he was listening without judgement, still surprised he was even interested at all. 'Certain memories filter back, like the curve of my mother's smile, her gentle touch, the smell of her spicy stews… The name Orm often resounds in my head, but I don't know what it means. Do you know if there is a place called that?'

'I haven't heard of one.'

'I tried to cling on to as much as I could, but the other memories have faded over time.'

'Your parents must have been distraught. They must have searched for you…if they survived.'

Perhaps. But she'd realised quite quickly that there was no point pining for her mother and father—or her home. It just made the terrible ache worse. Survival became her priority and she was clever enough to know, even at such a young age, that Ingrid was the key to that. She'd even found herself feeling grateful for having her, perhaps had grown to care for her… Not that she still didn't long to be given her freedom.

'I always despised Ingrid's father. He robbed me of my life, my family and my home. But then there's always the fear that you'll be given to someone worse.'

He crossed his long legs, putting one over the other. 'I'm guessing you see me, the potential future ruler of Boer, as a threat—as someone who could be worse?'

He was very astute. She shrugged. 'From my experience, most male leaders are the same.' Ruthless and cruel…

'Did that have something to do with your hatred of me at first sight?'

'Your words caused that response, when you spoke so callously about women. You lived up to my very low expectations.'

'Ah, hell,' he said with a groan. 'It was just a careless remark. I really didn't mean it, what I said about making Earl Ingrid my concubine. I was jesting. It was something only my man Rædan would understand. In hindsight, it wasn't funny at all, I realise that. But it was never meant for your ears. In truth, Earl Ingrid and I— It's a good match.'

'You said that already,' she said, trying to peer at him, to seek out his brown eyes under cover of the darkness. 'Are you trying to convince me or yourself of that?'

'Most leaders marry for political gain.'

'Is that why you're here now? To make sure she recovers because you're intent on the marriage and all it would bring you?' she said, openly expressing her distrust of him.

'I'm here because I wanted to help...'

She made a gentle tutting sound with her tongue. 'Well, it doesn't really matter what I think, does it?'

He thought about that for a moment. Why did it matter? The truth was, he wanted Wren to like him, just as he'd admired her from the moment he had first laid eyes on her. He couldn't explain it, he just knew he wanted her approval.

She'd impressed him again tonight, with her bravery during the battle, her quick thinking and her kindness towards her ruler, and he wanted to know more about her. He knew how slavery could break people—he'd seen it, experienced it first-hand. So how was it that her spirit was unbroken, despite the harrowing past she had suffered? She was a much stronger person than he. It fascinated him.

He wondered at how the loss of her family at such an early age had impacted her. He knew the feeling of grief all too well. It was all consuming. But he had suffered the terrible loss of his wife as an adult, whereas she had been just a child when she'd had to come to terms with losing her whole family… He felt a dart of sympathy for that little girl, with no mother or father to love her, just hours of endless chores and punishments. It made him feel sick. No wonder she was tough. No wonder she struggled to trust anyone.

For a long time, after he'd returned from England and had discovered he'd let down his settlement—and his wife—he had struggled to trust people, too. He was almost glad his parents had both died when he was a younger man, so that they hadn't been around to witness his failures.

He would never forget the horrific scenes he'd encountered when his longship had sailed back into Nedergaard after all those moon cycles of being away raiding. Many farmsteads were burnt to the ground, with only the skeleton of the longhouse left standing. He had jumped ashore and raced to find Annegrete, just as his crew had scrambled about looking for their loved ones. The wailing in the square had been deafening, but it hadn't been able to drown out the pounding of his own heart when he'd discovered his wife had been taken.

'Maybe you're hoping I'll say *positive* things about you to Earl Ingrid when she wakes?' Wren continued, abruptly bringing him back to the present.

'Perhaps…' he said, resting his head back against the wall, sighing. But the truth was, although he was concerned about Earl Ingrid's wounds, he'd stayed behind to help Wren. It was her he hadn't been able to leave in Boer without his protection. Not that he was about to tell her that. He couldn't. He knew how ridiculous it was. Deep down, he'd wanted to show Wren he was not the shallow man she thought he was—to make amends for his cold words at the marsh pool. But had he gone mad? He barely knew the woman!

He wondered if Wren was right and he was to blame for the total ambush tonight, just as he blamed himself for the attack on Nedergaard all those winters before. Hadn't he even thought something like this could happen when he'd been feasting in the hall earlier? But then he'd got distracted. He'd been showing off in the axe-throwing contest, trying to get Wren's attention. He'd been so focused on her he had missed the signs of the enemy approaching. But she hadn't…

His fierce need to protect her had made him fight as he hadn't fought in a long time, throwing himself into the fray like the berserker he had once been. He didn't want to look too closely at his behaviour. He didn't like himself very much right now.

'You fought well tonight,' he said, thinking back to how she'd handled herself in the square amid the conflict. She'd taken down a few of Forsa's warriors by herself. 'Considering it was your first battle.'

He had been so determined not to let anything bad happen to her, he'd even put his desire for honour and glory to one side, leaving the battlefield before the end of the fight. But he was a fool! He already had a whole settlement of people depending on him, he did not need to protect another person on top of his other responsibilities. He hoped Rædan and his men and the people of Boer had made it out. If they hadn't, he shouldn't have, either.

'I spent a lot of time learning how to fight as I grew up, putting all my energy into that. I knew if I didn't toughen up, I wouldn't make it. I was lucky Earl Ingrid allowed it. And I never minded the hard labour—it helped me sleep at night.'

He understood that. Often he would go out swimming in the fjord before he went to bed back at home in Nedergaard to tire himself out, otherwise he'd lie awake all night, possessed by terrible memories from the past. 'Speaking of which…you should try to get some rest, if only for a short while. I will keep watch.'

'No, I should keep going with this,' she said, nodding to the plank of plaited wood. It was slowly taking shape.

He clenched his jaw. 'Do you have to argue with everything I say?'

'Why should I just accept your opinion to be correct? Is that the way you plan to rule here?' As she hurled the words at him, he saw the defiant flash of her stormy grey eyes.

He rubbed his brow with his fingers. Damn, it was going to be a long night. The pounded earth of the floor wasn't comfortable, and he would have to stay awake, on guard, to check none of Forsa's men came out here to take him unawares. But being this close to her…

He could just make out her small frame in the darkness—the curve of her shoulders and the glint of her slave collar in the moonlight. Her head was bent, intent on the task of winding the wood, and her legs were neatly tucked beneath her. Why was he so aware of her? he wondered.

'I'm just saying you should get some sleep, although I admit this ground isn't very comfortable,' he said heavily.

'I bet you've never had to sleep rough before, have you?'

He knew by the tone of her voice she was smirking at him, that she saw his position as privileged, and he could see why. Others had it so much worse, but he did strive to make their lives better. He'd also had to work hard to become Chief of Nedergaard—it had never been just a given. He'd had to prove his worth, time and time again... He still did. And he'd suffered greatly for all his achievements.

He'd come to realise there would always be someone who had their eye on the prize—and he'd have to defend his position at every turn. It seemed his latest foe was the Earl of Forsa, who seemed to be fearlessly committed to attacking every settlement in the land. But despite what she might think, more important to him than keeping his seat of power was keeping his people safe.

He could tell Wren was on edge, jumping at every creak or rustle. And he didn't like the thought of her not having a bed, not having enough food, or someone to care for her. Was that how his wife had felt when she'd been taken captive? Was that part of the reason why he wanted to make things better for Wren now?

He shifted uncomfortably on the floor and realised there was something small he could do for her tonight.

He heaved his big body off the ground and carefully stepped over Earl Ingrid's body towards Wren.

'What do you think you're doing?' she snapped.

As he moved into the sliver of light he saw her quickly swipe her knife from her boot. 'Don't come any closer.'

He reeled, stopping still. 'I'm merely offering you this,' he said, shrugging off his cloak. 'You don't need to draw your blade on me, I'm on your side!'

'What is it?'

'My cloak. To sit on.'

'Why?'

'Has no one ever offered you something to keep warm before?'

'No,' she said simply, trying to shun him. 'And I don't need it.'

'You should take it,' he said. 'To help you get comfortable.'

She shook her head fiercely.

'If you take it, I'll go and sit back down.'

There was a long silence before she took the cloak from him, snatching her hand back when their fingers touched, and he retreated to his place on the other side of the hut, as promised, unsure what she was thinking.

'Why do you believe I'm your enemy? I'm not. I won't hurt you, Wren. If I wanted to, I would have done it already.' It was true. He knew she kept her weapon in her boot now and he could easily overpower her if he wanted to, but he was not that kind of man.

'Well, how should I know what you're like? As you

suggested in the square earlier—most men see the collar around my neck and think I'm fair game.'

'Do you suspect all strangers of bearing such ill will towards you?'

'Yes. I have learned the hard way that the world is full of evil people.'

She seemed to particularly hate his kind after what had happened to her and he could understand why. She could certainly never like him. So why, he wondered, was he trying so hard to win her over? Surely it was futile? And yet, even as they were talking, she was sliding her blade back into her boot.

'I know more than most that in battle all rules get abandoned,' he said grimly. 'But normally, in your everyday life, isn't there some kind of code of honour about not touching an earl's property? Rules that protect you?'

He heard her suck in a breath and he instantly knew he'd said the wrong thing, calling her Earl Ingrid's property.

'There are, but some don't seem to care about that,' she spat.

'Well, I'm not one to break a rule, Wren,' he said. 'You can trust me.'

'If I wasn't safe in my own home, why would you expect me to feel safe anywhere else?'

He heard her shift about, trying to get comfortable. 'What…what fur is this anyway?' she asked, her voice strained. 'It's very soft.'

'Marmot.'

'A *mammut*? Did you kill one?' she gasped.

He let out a deep chuckle, unable to help himself, and it eased his tension a little. 'No, a *marmot*. Like a squirrel? Not quite as impressive as a *mammut*. I don't think they still exist, do they?'

'Oh,' she said and then let out a tiny giggle at her mistake—a delightful throaty sound that sent tingles through his body—and he allowed himself to laugh again, too. He was suddenly annoyed that it was dark, as he should have liked to see her smile.

When he sobered, he drew his hands down his face. Something was becoming quite clear very quickly… If they survived this night, and managed to escape Boer unseen…if this marriage were to go ahead, between him and Earl Ingrid, Wren would have to leave. He would have to eradicate this desire for her as he would his enemy. And to do so, he would have to send her away, set her free, because keeping her around would be too dangerous—she would be far too much of a temptation.

By the time the sky began to turn a glorious pink hue in the morning, Wren's hands were sore, but the trundle was almost ready. She could tell Jarl Knud was restless, that he wanted to be on the move. He had wanted to leave while they were under cover of darkness and, with every passing moment, she knew they were opening themselves up to being seen. He stood solidly by the door, a crease in his brow, constantly checking for signs of any of Forsa's men. His large hand on the hilt of his sword, he looked ready to face any danger directly and it gave her hope—maybe she and Earl Ingrid could escape from here with him on their side.

She was amazed they had survived the night without being found—and without storming out on each other! Instead, he had remained awake with her, staying alert, passing her pieces of wood from time to time, asking her about her life in Boer, and at some point she had found herself beginning to relax a little, almost believing he wasn't going to hurt her. Perhaps he wasn't the same as Earl Ingrid's father, or her brother, after all.

When she was finally finished with the wood, she held up the trundle for inspection. 'Do you think it will take her weight?'

He gave it a shake, testing its strength. 'It's really good, Wren. It should see us through. Do you do this a lot?'

'What, make trundles to carry wounded earls past the eye of the enemy? No,' she said, shaking her head.

'I meant winding wood,' he said, rolling his eyes. 'You have a talent for it.'

'Well, Earl Ingrid allows me to make and sell baskets, so…'

His eyebrows rose. 'What do you do with the coin you make? Are you allowed to spend it, or keep it?'

She shrugged. 'At first I thought maybe I could get enough ingots to purchase my release,' she said, her cheeks burning under her admission of her foolish hope. 'But after many winters of trying, I realised no matter how much I earned, Earl Ingrid would never let me go.'

When she spoke, she continued to look past him rather than at him, focusing on that point just above his left shoulder. She still felt winded that he'd called her a piece of property last night, that he'd reduced her to an object. But she didn't know why she cared so much about his opinion—after all, she had been made to feel like that her whole life.

'Before we go any further, can we get one thing straight?' he said, his voice suddenly stern.

'What?' she said, instantly defensive.

'Why don't you look at me when you talk to me?'

Her brow furrowed. 'Thralls aren't allowed to look people in the eye, you know that.'

He took her chin between his thumb and forefinger, and she stiffened, shocked at the sudden contact, and the combined strength and tenderness of his touch.

'And I say it's a terrible rule. It's polite to look at someone when you speak to them. It's as if you're ignoring me. It's maddening.'

Maddening?

'You're allowed to look at me, Wren. I'm giving you permission.'

She recoiled from his touch and lifted her chin out of his grasp.

'Why would I want to do that?' And then she realised her argument was pointless, so she sighed deeply. 'I suppose someone will need to tell you if you have a hair out of place, Jarl Knud,' she said in acceptance.

His mouth widened into a smile. 'Are you jesting?' he asked. 'You're funny!'

She braced herself with a deep breath before turning to look at him directly. She knew the reaction their eyes meeting would cause in her stomach. And there it was—looking up into his molten brown gaze caused an instant swarm of butterflies. She felt the inrush of breath, the tremble in her legs. He had beautiful eyes. You could get lost in them.

'That's better.' He smiled. 'And while I think of it, drop the Jarl. Just call me Knud.'

'Is that normal?' she protested.

'It is where I come from.'

And then his gaze travelled downwards. 'There's just one more thing we need to do before we go—sort your clothing.'

'What?'

'You're going to need some armour on out there. Here,' he said, deftly removing his chainmail and handing it to her. 'Put this on.'

'No, it's yours,' she said, shaking her head, suddenly aware that strands of her hair had come loose from her braids throughout the night. She brushed them aside angrily. 'It's far too big for me.'

'You need to wear something,' he said, his large body looming over her, crowding her, as he placed the chainmail over her head. 'I'm not taking you out there without you putting this on.'

'It's not necessary!' she protested.

Ignoring her, he tugged it into place, down over her chest, and began to tighten and fasten the straps. She stopped breathing, heat blazing in her stomach and her cheeks, and threw her hands up in a gesture of surrender, if only to get this over with as quickly as possible and put a stop to his fingers brushing against her skin, moving over her, causing her body to erupt in goose pimples.

She couldn't believe he cared so much about her safety. Why would a man of his status concern himself about the life of a thrall? Surely she was seen as sacrificial goods to someone like him? Was it because he couldn't carry Earl Ingrid by himself—that he needed her?

'What about you?' she gritted out, as he continued to firmly handle the armour. Now he only had a leather vest over his tunic to protect him.

'I'll be fine.'

Then he took a step back, admiring his work and giving a satisfactory nod. 'That'll do.'

'It's so heavy!' she said, pouting. 'Don't you find it restrictive?'

'Better that than take an arrow to your chest. Now come on, show me where we're going.'

She was still tingling all over from where he'd touched her, but she forced herself to focus on the task at hand. They placed his cloak on the trundle as a blanket and gently lifted Earl Ingrid up and on to it. Then, taking an end each, trying to keep it balanced, Wren led the way out of the hut, keeping down amid the fields of rye. Her heart was in her mouth.

As they crept round the abandoned farmsteads to the hole in the palisade walls, all was quiet. Had Forsa's forces worn themselves out in battle? Had they spent the night enjoying their spoils and drinking Boer's ale? If so, she fervently hoped they were now sleeping it off.

They struggled to get through the gap, Knud prising open the wooden stakes and holding them apart while also juggling the trundle, which couldn't have been easy, but they finally made it through. Yet it was on the other side, out in the open, where Wren knew they were most at risk. They would have to keep low within the brushy edge so as not to draw any attention to themselves. But if they were seen by the guards on the ramparts, they were done for.

'Which way from here?' Knud whispered. She couldn't help feeling shocked he was even asking, allowing her to lead rather than follow.

'This way,' she said, nodding with her head in the direction of the tidal pool.

But the instant they stepped out on to the flatlands, they were spotted, and her heart began to pound. Forsa's men were more alert than she'd thought. A warning cry from one of the enemy sounded from up above on the battlements before a barrage of arrows came tumbling down on them.

'Wren, run!'

They charged across the bare, flat land as fast as they could manage with the trundle, with terrifying sounds of the fortress coming to life above them.

'They'll be after us soon. Hurry.'

'I am!'

Wren couldn't bring herself to look back. It took all her focus to maintain a grip on the trundle as she tried to match Knud's long, fast strides over the uneven ground. It was tricky to keep the trundle level. 'If we get through this, we'll need to strap her down,' Wren called, worried that Earl Ingrid was rolling about too much from side to side, terrified she'd fall.

Arrows landed all around them, narrowly missing

their bodies, the whooshing sound rushing past their ears. One even got stuck in the edge of the trundle, but finally they neared the rocky outcrop, out of the enemy's reach, without being struck.

Gasping for breath, Wren was momentarily relieved when they arrived at the marsh pool, but it held no solace for her now. 'What do we do?' she asked. 'We're an easy target out here. They saw where we were heading and we can't outrun them.'

'You're right. They'll be here within moments. We'll have to hide her.' He glanced all about them, and then motioned to set her down. 'Here,' he said.

They moved Earl Ingrid into a deep, winding ravine, chucking mud, weeds and vegetation on top of her to disguise her. If she was awake to see this, she'd be appalled, Wren thought, but it might just keep her alive. In the distance, they could see some of Forsa's men leaving the fortress on horseback and her fingers began to tremble.

'Now you, climb in there.'

Wren looked at where Knud was pointing halfway down the bank to a rocky crevice. 'No.'

He grabbed her arm and tugged her with him, shoving her forward.

'Wren, this is no time to argue with me. Get in.'

She heard the charging of horses' hooves, the thrum of her heart pounding, and relented, doing as she was told. She threw herself into the crevice, just big enough to lie down in, and then he followed, tucking himself in behind her, curving his body around her back. Her whole body stiffened.

She lay on her side, facing into the darkness of the rocks, and closed her eyes tight, trying to focus on her breathing. She could hear him pulling a branch and loose rocks across the opening, his body moving against hers as he shoved the camouflage into place, blocking out the daylight, plunging them into blackness.

It was damp and smelt of seaweed and she could just make out the heavy patter of horses at full gallop drawing closer, but it was all drowned out by the sound of Knud's soft breathing in her ear.

She shoved him with her elbow, angry at his nearness. 'Do you really need to be this close to me?' His chest was as solid as it looked, but warm as he crushed himself against her.

'I'm sorry, but there's no room… Sshh, they're coming.'

She went very still.

Her mind raced, excruciatingly aware of the sound of men calling to one another above them on the rocks, but also Knud's body heat against her back at odds with the cold ground. His enticing yet now familiar scent of leather and spice began to wrap around her once again in the confined space. But mainly she was aware of his large hand resting on her hip, steadying himself so he didn't roll backwards.

Why did he have to touch her? Every time he did, her body went up in flames. It was most strange. Surely she should find it repulsive and unpleasant? But she had to stop herself from leaning back against him, seeking his comfort and protection.

His voice dropped to a whisper. 'Are you all right?' His beard tickled the skin on her shoulder.

She nodded, not trusting her voice.

'I thought you'd stopped breathing then for a moment.'

She had!

'Just relax,' he said, but how could she possibly do that? Her bottom was nestled against his groin, his hard upper thighs pressed against the back of hers.

'I'm worried about Earl Ingrid.' She swallowed. 'What if they find her?'

His fingers lightly grazed her hip in a soothing movement. 'They won't. We hid her pretty well…' he whispered, his calm voice helping to placate her.

They both lay there in the darkness, listening to the sounds of the men searching for them above. She could just picture them walking over the boulders, looking into the water she'd bathed in so often, and realised she would probably never be able to come back here again. Not now the fortress had been ransacked.

'Why do you care so much?' he asked.

'What?'

'When Earl Ingrid got hurt yesterday, why did you not seize your chance and run away? Or do you hope that by helping her now, she will finally decide to free you?'

Wren tried to shift her position, a rock digging into her side, but the movement made her brush against him once more and she froze, cringing. 'I help because that is who I am, not because of what it could get me. Unlike you.'

His fingers stalled. 'I didn't mean to offend you, Wren. I'm just trying to understand. I wonder why you care for her, when she keeps you captive—treats you this way? I've not known a...'

'What? Never known a thrall care for their master before?'

'Yes. How do you not harbour hatred towards her? It is very unusual...'

'It is not her fault her father gave me to her. She doesn't know any different. Besides, she needs me...'

The silence stretched and she sighed heavily.

'I did try to run away once,' she finally admitted, as talking to him seemed to help calm her fear and distract her from the strange ripples of excitement flowing through her.

'You did?' His strong, gentle fingers began to move over her hip again, encouraging her on.

'It was when Ingrid's brother came into power. I almost got as far as Hafranes but realised I didn't know where I was going, or how I'd live when I got there, especially with my collar still locked around my neck, so I swallowed my pride and came back, accepting that I'd be punished.'

'And were you?'

'Yes,' she said bluntly.

He repositioned himself, trying to get comfortable, and heat swept through her body again where his touched hers in so many places. She squeezed her eyes shut again, trying to stay as still as possible to stop the tingles of awareness rushing through her. 'Earl Ingrid's brother...did he mistreat you?'

Her body went rigid. 'That isn't your concern!' she snapped.

'You seem to think nothing about you is my concern, yet here we are, out in the middle of nowhere, and I'm the one saving your life.'

'You're saving my life? I think it's the other way round.'

'Sshh,' he hushed her. 'I merely wondered how you'd been treated, as you grew up in Boer. That's all. I know some thralls…'

'Live a life of sexual servitude? Because so many believe a slave's body is free for bedding?'

'Not everyone thinks that way.' He removed his hand from her hip and used the rock above them to steady himself instead. She should have been relieved, but she found herself strangely missing the contact. What was the matter with her? 'But, yes, I was wondering if you had been made to do things against your will,' he said, choosing his words carefully.

Earl Elias had tried to have his way with her many a time. He used to catch her on her own and put his hands on her and try to force himself upon her. He'd say she brought it on herself, that she encouraged it. He'd demanded her body for bedding from Earl Ingrid, as if she wasn't a person but an object, as he did with so many other women.

'No, he was never successful in making me his bed slave,' she said. 'But it wasn't for the want of trying.' She could hear the bitterness in her voice, at being devalued her whole life, and it felt good to let it out, to answer honestly, without holding back. She somehow felt safe to do so in the darkness. 'But it is the right of a Norseman chief, is it not? To sleep with whomever they desire?' she said icily.

'Surely a man only has the right if the lady is willing, no matter what their status.'

Did he really mean it?

'Well, each time he tried, Earl Ingrid prevented anything from happening and for that I am truly grateful. Perhaps that is why I feel indebted to her now...'

They both abruptly stopped talking as the footsteps grew louder above, the pressure on the rocks making the stone move slightly, water dripping down on to them, splashing their faces, making Wren jump.

His hand came down to rest against her hip again, perhaps to reassure her, and this time she didn't recoil. She was almost relieved he was here. Almost. 'I can understand that. And I know all about having a sister and how they have a way of keeping everyone in check,' he said, as the footsteps moved off again.

'You have a sister?'

She felt him nod against her hair. 'Her name's Brita.'

'And she does not allow you to have bed slaves back in Nedergaard?' she asked.

'We don't allow any thralls in Nedergaard at all.'

'What?' She tried to turn slightly to look at his face, her shoulder pressing into his chest, to see if he was telling the truth. It was almost unbelievable.

'I made Nedergaard a place free of slaves many winters ago, when I first came into power.'

She swallowed, allowing herself a moment to let that information sink in. 'Why?'

'Because I don't believe in it,' he said simply. 'Because I know what damage it can cause… My right-hand man, Rædan, was a former slave. He was taken from his father and lover and kept captive on a ship for six winters.'

'That's awful. How did he escape?'

'I found him at the market in Hafranes, half-dead, and paid a few silver ingots for him.'

Her breath hitched.

'To set him free, not to bind him to me,' he added quickly. 'Brita nursed him back to health and, when he was well enough, he went in search of his long-lost love and they're now together, happily married with two children, settled in Nedergaard.'

She could scarcely believe what he was telling her. Did such a place really exist, where people weren't bonded to others in cuffs? Everything she'd thought about him marrying Earl Ingrid, about him being a worse master, was now challenged. If he were to marry Earl Ingrid, their union could change her world for the better. And yet, for some reason she still didn't like the thought of them together.

Had he really forged such a strong relationship with a former slave? A man of his stature? It would explain a lot about the way he had treated her so far. 'Why are you telling me this?'

'So you don't think quite so badly of me,' he said. 'When I saw your collar at the feast yesterday, I was appalled. Not all Danish warlords are the same, Wren. In Nedergaard, we don't believe in keeping people as chattel.'

'But at the table in Boer, you didn't agree with Earl Ingrid training me. You seemed to see it as a threat…'

'You misunderstood me. I'm all for people…like you…carrying weapons, especially if it means you can protect yourself. I was just surprised Earl Ingrid didn't think you would use your skills to fight your way to freedom.'

Her brow creased. Was he advocating that she should? She was so confused. Had she got him all wrong? Was it possible he wasn't like all the other men she'd encountered in her life?

'And the words I spoke when we were out here the other night, about keeping Earl Ingrid as some kind of concubine, I was jesting, I promise. It was in very poor taste, I know. But Rædan knew it was something I would never do…'

She bit her lip. Had her opinion of him truly been overturned in just a matter of moments? And in the dark, with his huge body pressed against her? She fought to regain some of the anger she'd felt towards him, as that was better than the other, more unsettling feelings currently tearing through her. She really didn't want to like him—Earl Ingrid's future husband. It would be so vexing.

'It's gone quiet now. Do you think they've gone?' she whispered.

'I'm not sure. What are those good instincts of yours telling you?' His breath tickled her ear, his beard brushing against her skin.

'That I'm ready to get out of here.'

He nodded. 'I'll go. You stay here while I check it out.'

'There you go, ordering me about again.'

'I may not own thralls, Wren, but I'm still the leader here. And I'm trying to keep you alive—remember that.'

Chapter Four

Knud carefully shifted the bracken, branches and rocks he'd placed over the opening and unfurled himself from the crevice, surprised they hadn't been discovered. He had taken a chance, but it had paid off. Standing up in the ravine, he scoured the barren terrain and saw the retreating backs of Forsa's men returning to the stronghold. Perhaps they didn't think just two of Boer's people were worth searching the flatlands for.

He took in a deep breath, assessing their situation. He needed a moment to gather himself before calling for Wren to join him. Being so close to her in that small dark space had been pure torture, her back crushed against his chest, her bottom nestled against his groin. He had hardened the minute he'd pressed against her and had struggled to get his desire in check. He still was! She had felt so soft and warm and he'd been shocked by the strength of the lust heating his blood, despite the danger they were in.

And then he'd started to reveal facts about himself—something he never did and never to women he'd just met. But he'd found himself telling her he'd bought slaves and set them free, all because he'd wanted her to know she was safe with him, to reassure her that he wasn't a bad person. But surely now he'd revealed so much, it would open up questions about his past he didn't want to answer. Surely she'd want to know why he'd behaved the way he had? And he cursed himself for being so open.

He didn't want to think about it any further. He had no intention of telling her he saved lives because of a mistake he'd made many winters ago, changing his life for ever—and that he would never, ever stop trying to make amends for it. He struggled to explain that to anyone. After returning home to Nedergaard and finding his settlement destroyed, he'd set out for the neighbouring settlements, determined to find his wife.

It had taken many moon cycles, but he'd eventually tracked her down and been devastated to discover she'd been taken to service the needs of other men. It was why he'd needed to know if Wren had suffered the same fate. If she had, it would have been more than he could bear. When she'd told him about Earl Elias, he had felt his old anger at the world resurface and he'd wanted to seek revenge all over again—for himself, for Annegrete and for Wren. But he didn't want to be that bloodthirsty barbarian again.

'Have they gone?' Wren said, startling him as she uncoiled herself out of the cave.

'I thought I told you to stay back.' He sighed. At least the tightness in his trousers had eased.

'I wondered what was taking you so long.' She came to stand beside him and he checked her over. Her tunic was slightly damp on one side and her raven-coloured cropped hair dishevelled, but she was unharmed. Safe for now.

'They've retreated. And it looks like they didn't discover Earl Ingrid, either,' he said, nodding to the mound of earth she was still hidden beneath.

'Thank goodness.' Wren raced over to check on her, pulling the weeds and undergrowth from her, and he saw the concern on her beautiful face fade away when she discovered her ruler was all right. Well, not all right, exactly. They needed to find a healer and fast. But at least she hadn't been captured by Forsa's men. He wondered again at Wren's feelings towards her ruler. Did all thralls feel some kind of affection for their masters? Surely not.

'So, if you were to marry Earl Ingrid, what would you do with her thralls?' she asked him, returning to their conversation moments before.

'I will do all I can to help you, Wren,' he said. 'I promise.' He would fight to free them all. 'But if there is to be any kind of union between us, first we need to get her out of here and get her well again.'

His thoughts flew back to what Rædan had said to him the other night—about Earl Ingrid helping to patch up the cracks in this land, and possibly his heart, but he knew she could never do that—the wound was too deep.

'Have you been married before?' Wren asked, as if following his line of thought.

His jaw hardened before he gave a single nod in response. 'Yes. A long time ago. She died.' The less Wren knew about his past the better. He didn't want to talk about it with anyone. It didn't make him look good. In fact, what he'd done in leaving his people to go raiding elsewhere was unforgivable.

'I'm sorry.'

He bent down and helped her swipe the last of the mud off Earl Ingrid's clothes. He removed his belt from around his waist and used it to secure the ruler to the trestle, pushing the ends through the gaps in the wood.

'You'll have no clothes left at this rate,' Wren said and he laughed.

'I'd better stop then, for your sake.'

Her cheeks turned a pretty shade of pink. 'Is that why you don't want to marry again?' she said, flustered.

So she had been eavesdropping out here the other night and she'd heard more than he thought.

'Because I'll have no clothes left of my own?' he quipped, trying to delay having to answer her. He raked a hand through his hair. If it was down to him, he would never marry again. He had thought being on his own was for the best. He had vowed never to take another bride or have a family of his own. He had enough people to care for, enough orphans to raise after the devastation he'd brought upon his settlement.

He knew how fortunate he was that his people had forgiven him for letting them down in the past. So many of his men had lost loved ones that day and he carried their grief around with him every day. He owed them his gratitude for sticking by him despite it all.

But being the leader of so many people, the caretaker of their lives, it seemed being on his own for the rest of his life was impossible. He had a duty to secure his people's safety. And when it had become clear he could use his position to better their lives, he knew that he must go against the vow he'd made to himself and take a new bride to safeguard his fortress. It was why he had resigned himself to marrying a woman he didn't particularly like, because by gaining an ally and an army he could ensure everyone in Nedergaard remained unharmed.

But this time he had determined to take a bride he felt nothing for. He never wanted to feel the pain he'd experienced before at losing Annegrete. He wouldn't ever allow himself to care for someone like that again. He didn't want to love or be loved again, knowing what suffering it caused.

He was drawn back to Wren's face. She was looking at him expectantly, waiting for an answer. She looked exhausted from being up all night. The tension in her face at the danger they were in was evident in the lines around her stormy grey eyes and in her clenched jaw, the taut line of her lips, and yet she was still the most beautiful woman he'd ever seen.

'It is true I have never had the desire to marry again until now.'

'And Earl Ingrid has managed to change your mind?' she asked. 'Or perhaps her army...'

He smiled. So she understood why he was doing this. He supposed he'd made that pretty clear when he was speaking to Rædan the other evening. 'How about you? Does Earl Ingrid allow her thralls to marry?'

'Yes, it has been known to happen.' She gave a half-shrug. 'But I don't need another master, therefore I shall never take a husband.'

He nodded, thinking back to what she'd told him in the dark—about Earl Ingrid's brother wanting her to be his bed slave. The very idea of it sent a shaft of pure anger through his blood—the thought of anyone hurting her, forcing her, using her. He was glad Earl Ingrid hadn't allowed it. Perhaps his bride-to-be had some redeeming qualities after all. But if Earl Elias had tried, it would explain why Wren was so standoffish in his company, why she was wary of men—and flinched beneath his touch. She had suffered greatly at the hands of men all her life.

'I can understand that.'

'How could you?' she accused. 'You know nothing of my pain. Of grief and loss.'

His eyes narrowed on her. He knew more than most. He knew it felt like having your heart ripped out of your chest. He knew it felt so bad, it made life not worth living. But he wasn't about to share that with her, because he preferred to bury his feelings, not share them. Telling her would also mean sharing the terrible thing that he'd done when his grief had eventually transmuted into rage and he couldn't do that. She would see the blood on his hands. She wouldn't understand or forgive.

Instead, he rose to his feet. 'We'd better keep moving,' he said.

'How far is it?'

'Not far on horseback, but walking and carrying Earl Ingrid like this, perhaps a day? Maybe more if we have to keep wading through this thick mud,' he said.

They'd been heading towards Hafranes all morning, keeping the *longphort* in their sights in the distance. But the sinking terrain was hard going under foot and the further they meandered from dry land, the more blustery the bracing sea winds became, slowing them down. They'd taken a few breaks, but they were aware the tide was against them. It was imperative they kept moving and crossed the shimmering mudflats before it came back in. If they had to go round the long way through the hinterland, they might be seen.

Instead, they would pick a ravine and follow it as far as they could, until they came to a dead end and had to scale the bank into the next one. They had to work together as a team to keep the trundle flat, to stop Earl Ingrid from toppling out. Knud was tiring himself, so he was worried about how Wren was faring, yet each time he glanced at her, he was taken by how at home she seemed in the outdoors, climbing on rocks, trudging through mud. Despite their strenuous task, she made little fuss and he was impressed with her endurance and determination.

She was stronger than she looked with her slender frame and delicate features—it was only her rank that sought to make her weak. Right now, she had no power in this world, bound to the rules of others, yet out here, where no one but he was around, perhaps she felt able to shake off some of those chains. And if they made it to Nedergaard, Knud determined he would ensure that her freedom became a permanent thing.

'I think I could live out here for ever,' she said.

He smiled. 'I told you that you were wild.'

And he was sure the corners of her lips curled up a little, her eyes glittering in the sun.

'Have you ever travelled far from Boer?' he asked.

She shook her head. 'Apart from that time I ran away...no. Those wooden walls have kept me prisoner for fifteen long winters. I must admit it feels good to be outside them for a change, to taste a little freedom. But I feel bad saying that given the circumstances. Now if only I could do something about the company...'

He grinned.

Since he'd told her he didn't keep thralls, it had been as he had hoped. She seemed to have relaxed a little around him, dropping her guard slightly. And he was pleased. She even appeared to be good-humoured.

When the midday sun began to burn down on them, Knud checked Boer's forces were still nowhere to be seen before finding them a sheltered spot in one of the trenches.

'I'm going to see if I can find us something to eat,' he said, after they'd set the trundle down. 'I'm starving, aren't you?'

She shrugged. 'I'm not too bad. I'm probably used to surviving on a lot less food than you.'

He swore underneath his breath before taking off again over the mounds of earth. He didn't like the thought of her ever being hungry. At the top of the bank, he glanced back. 'Stay here.'

She gave him an exaggerated eye-roll before leaning over to check on the heat of Earl Ingrid's forehead.

'Any change?'

'She's pretty hot.'

He grimaced. 'I'll be back shortly.' He scaled a few banks before he came to shallow water. They couldn't linger long. The tide would be upon them and Earl Ingrid seemed to be deteriorating. She needed some healing herbs, fast.

He glanced back and could just see the top of Wren's head in the trench, before she ducked and disappeared from view, and he set to finding them some food. He loved how she'd been curious about the little crabs scurrying between their feet, wanting to follow them, and how she'd pointed to various shells or plants on their journey this morning, asking him questions, wanting to know what they were. He liked seeing the world through her interested eyes—it made it seem larger than just his problems.

The sun was beating down and he was so thirsty, but he knew from his seafaring days they mustn't drink the saltwater. He'd seen how it had sent some of his men mad. When he'd gathered as many clam shells as he could carry, he headed back to where he'd left Wren. When he reached the trench, Earl Ingrid's limp body was still there on the trundle, but there was no sign of his companion. Panic flooded him. He dropped the shells in a pile on the ground and strode back up the bank.

'Wren?' he called. But he couldn't see her anywhere. Bringing up his hand, he shielded his gaze from the sun and frantically glanced all around. There was no sign of Forsa's men, so had she wandered off? Run off? 'Wren?' he shouted again.

And then he saw her head pop up amid a ravine farther back. 'I'm here,' she called and he blew out a breath in relief.

He jumped down into the next trench, and up again, before tearing down the next rivulet towards her. Reaching her, he gripped her shoulders, livid. He gave her a little shake. 'Why the hell did you wander off? I told you to stay put! I was worried. Do you have no regard for your safety?'

'I was just looking around.'

'At what exactly? More mud? How can I keep you safe if I don't know where you are?'

'You don't need to know where I am at *all* times, watch my every move. For once can't I just explore by myself without worrying about being reprimanded?'

She slumped down, the heat and the tiredness suddenly becoming too much, and his anger gave way to concern.

'Wren?'

She closed her eyes. 'I think I must have drifted off for a moment, as the next thing I knew I heard you calling my name. I'm so thirsty,' she said, licking her parched lips.

'I know, I am, as well,' he said, relenting now. 'Come on, I've found us something to eat. You'll feel better with some food in your stomach,' he said, his hand circling her upper arm. He helped her up, placing his other hand around her waist, steering her back in the direction of their food. It was a wrench to let go, but casting her back down on to the floor in the trench next to Earl Ingrid, he motioned for her to hold out her hand.

'They're clams. You can eat what's inside,' he said, tumbling a few into her open palm.

She turned her nose up at the little slimy morsels.

'They're slightly salty, but you get used to it.'

She watched him eat one, before she warily copied him, tentatively sucking the flesh out of the shell. She licked her lips and then, as if deciding she liked them, she set to scooping out the rest of the clams with her fingers, shoving them into her mouth as fast as she could, seeming ravenous.

He laughed. 'Someone *was* hungry.'

She halted, slowly sucking her fingers clean, her face heating, suddenly aware of her actions, and he felt bad he'd teased her.

'We ate all kinds of things when we used to be out at sea. Anything to keep us going,' he said to take the scrutiny off her.

She nodded. 'We were told stories of your raids to the lands west of the ocean. What was it like, heading off in search of new places?' she asked.

He shrugged. 'I was much younger then. It was back when I felt I could conquer the world. I wanted to go on journeys of exploration, find new places and make a name for myself.'

He had always been a restless creature, even as a child. He'd often wander off when he was supposed to be helping his father, longing to make new discoveries. He had been raised to become the next leader of his father's stronghold, but it had never been enough to simply inherit his title. He'd wanted to prove his worth, show people what he was capable of.

As he grew into a man and built up a fleet of ships, he'd spend the winters gathering his strength, enjoying the season with his wife, but he'd always yearned for summer when the seas were calmer and it was safe to take to the ocean again and go in search of new places. The men he took with him dreamed of expanding their riches, adding to their lands, inspired by his vision, but for Knud it was all about the glory.

When they'd returned from that first raid with their ships laden with riches, and stories of all that they had seen, they had been treated like gods. But it hadn't been enough, that was just the beginning. It had been like an addiction, one he couldn't satisfy.

'It seems you were successful. What were the places like that you saw?'

'Beautiful. England…it was full of monasteries and riches, people with unmarked skin and silk clothing… The land was a lot greener than it is here. Good for farming. On our third visit, we overwintered there and some of my men decided to stay.'

'Did you ever think to do so yourself and tend to the land there?'

'My home was always here.' His duty was here. And he had put everything at risk for his obsession with his raids and his reputation.

'Where will your next journey be to, I wonder?'

He lifted his head, surprised by her question. 'I no longer desire to plunder the lands in the west. I gave it up a long time ago.'

'Why?'

Because now he had no desire to go anywhere. Because he had experienced the atrocities he had once thought nothing of unleashing on others. He had received his retribution for his actions. 'I didn't think of the consequences, the dangers.' He still carried a great deal of guilt for all that had come to pass. 'I must think about my people and keeping them safe now. I can't do that if I'm not here.'

Wren picked up her last shell and resorted to tipping the clam into her mouth and swallowing the flesh whole.

'What kind of name is Wren, anyway? As of right now, you're reminding me of a little bird.' He grinned, changing the subject to a lighter topic.

She pulled a face at him. 'Earl Ingrid gave me my name.' Wren shrugged. 'She said something about it meaning rebirth—and because I looked small and fragile, like a little wren, when I was given to her.'

Knud looked over at Earl Ingrid, lying motionless on the trundle. 'Does she not know a wren can fly higher than most other birds? They're also known for their intelligence, and often out-think their foes,' he said, winking, turning back to her.

And she smiled. It was the first time she'd smiled properly at him and his stomach soared. It was a glorious sight, lighting up her whole face, her unusual crystal-clear grey eyes sparkling. A wren about to fledge, he thought. She really was absolutely stunning—she took his breath away and suddenly he felt more than a little shaken.

'What were you called before that—before you came to Boer? Do you remember?'

'Yes. Genevieve, although my parents often called me Neva.'

Interesting. He knew the name meant leader of the tribe, as his sister's eldest daughter was called the same. He'd helped Brita choose the name because of its meaning. Perhaps Wren was of importance, wherever she had come from. When he returned to Nedergaard, he would be sure to ask around about the name Orm—and a missing child named Neva.

'Do you long to see them again—your family?'

'Of course.' She frowned. 'I'd like to know what happened to them. Whether they survived that day. But I worry there isn't anything to return home to. That I'll never know my heritage and who I was before I came here. It is my dream to discover who I truly am. My one mission in life. I envy you, that all your life it was foretold that you would be a chieftain and you have fulfilled that destiny. I wonder what destiny had in store for me, before I was taken, or if this is all I was always meant to be.'

'No one in this life is meant to be a thrall, Wren. Do you remember anything about where your settlement was? Can you remember what it looked like, picture it and describe it?'

'Not really,' she said sadly, shaking her head. 'I was so young. I remember it was near the sea, not far inland, backed by a large pine forest, and I recall a little stone bridge. I wonder if I would know it if I saw it, though, if one day I happened to chance upon it.'

He nodded. 'You never know… If you've never strayed this far from Boer before, who knows what you'll find on our journey,' he said, rising to his feet once more. 'Speaking of which, let's talk and walk. The sea is coming back in, so we'd better get moving, get to higher ground. We don't want to be cut off by the tide.'

As they set off at a steady pace once more, Knud regaled her with tales of the people he'd met and the places he'd seen on his travels, holding her interest and making her laugh. He often used his humour as his armour, she thought. He always attempted to lighten the mood with a playful wink or a funny quip and he never seemed to delve too deep beneath the surface.

She realised he had two sides to him—the jovial, confident, larger-than-life Jarl Knud, who he wanted to portray to his people, and the subdued, brooding version she had seen in quieter moments, who rarely shared anything too serious about his past or his life. She wondered what secrets he was trying to keep hidden.

When he had found her in the trench and chastised her, she had felt his anger and concern—and it had shocked her. Seeing the reproof in his eyes, his large hands on her shoulders, she should have been scared of him. And yet she wasn't.

She was only frightened at the feelings that rushed through her body whenever he touched her, a bolt of unexpected heat striking low in her belly, her heart beating erratically. She had never experienced anything like it. No one had ever made her feel these things before. And she couldn't deny it felt good to have someone look after her, taking care of her for once. But did he really care about her? She still found that absurd.

She stole a glance at him and he immediately smiled back at her, and she felt slightly annoyed. She had never been this far from home before and she wanted to enjoy the scenery, take it all in, but her eyes kept being drawn back to him. The vast ocean and the enormous skies were sights to behold, yet instead this imposing man was somehow even more fascinating to her, commanding her attention, and it was infuriating. What was the matter with her?

As they began to wind their way back towards higher ground, the tremors coming from under her feet had her head snapping up. Surveying the foreground, with a sinking heart she saw them—Forsa's men patrolling the hinterland on horseback. The same ones they'd seen leaving Boer fortress and heading towards the tidal pool this morning. Every muscle in her body tensed and her blood chilled. She stalled abruptly and Knud pushed the trundle into her by accident, not realising she'd halted.

She put her finger to her mouth and nodded towards the backwater, and he followed her line of sight. Were Forsa's men searching for them, knowing they'd come this way, or was it a coincidence?

Get down, he mouthed and they gently placed the trundle on the ground, crouching beside it. If they'd carried on just a few more steps, they might have been spotted. And counting the riders, she realised they were greatly outnumbered.

'If I was on my own, I'd take up my sword and fight them,' he said quietly. 'But I can't risk it—not with Earl Ingrid out of action and with you to protect.'

'I'm not completely unskilled,' she muttered back.

'I know that. But, no. We're not fighting them unless it's absolutely necessary. Unless we have no choice.'

She could sense his frustration, his desire to do battle rippling off him. But he must know what was at stake… If Forsa's men got their hands on the Chief of Nedergaard and the Earl of Boer at the same time, the Earl of Forsa's land-grabbing ambitions would soon become a reality. Their people would perish. She shuddered at the thought.

'We can't continue on to Hafranes while they're out there looking for us,' she whispered. 'So what do we do?'

'We will have to wait—hope that they will soon give up the search, or we could return to the mudflats and try to go round the coast a bit farther, but we'll be knee-deep in water at best. What do you want to do?'

She was still shocked that he was asking for her advice and input. But then the decision seemed to be taken out of their hands as the enemy began to move off the hinterland. She let out a long breath, relieved beyond measure to see the back of them.

'That was close.' She sighed. She drew her hands over her face, sitting back on her bottom in the mud.

He nodded. 'It's been quite a day.'

She watched as he dipped his finger in the mud and, as if needing to do something to alleviate the uncertainty of their situation, he smeared it down her cheek, grinning.

She narrowed her eyes at him.

'What? You need it, it's for camouflage,' he said innocently. 'A bit of war paint.'

'Is that so?' She bit back a smile. She turned and scooped up a big handful of thick, gloopy mud, then spun round and threw it at him. It smashed against him, covering his leather vest. For a moment, he looked down at his coated garments, dripping in wet silt, and she held her breath, wondering if she'd gone too far. She'd just thrown mud at the Chief of Nedergaard!

Then he broke out into laughter and she did, too.

'I'll get you for that,' he warned.

At the look on his face promising swift retribution, she squealed, launching herself to her feet and starting to run.

But he was too fast for her, catching up to her and tugging her arm back, and she gave a little yelp, knowing she was done for. He held her body to him as he placed a handful of mud on her head. She gasped, he let her go and she fell back into the mud on her back, laughing again unrestrainedly.

He fell down beside her, chuckling, too, as they lay there shoulder to shoulder. She knew it was a release from the stress of running for their lives and she was suddenly glad he was here. She had never had fun with another person quite like this. There was something about Knud that made her want to behave like a child again, to not be quite so serious all the time. She loved that he allowed it. And she thought the people of Nedergaard must really cherish him being their leader.

She turned to look at him, lying in the mud—he was like a different person to the impeccable chieftain who'd headed up the convoy and trotted into Boer yesterday. But with his unkempt hair and his muddy, rumpled clothes, he was still devastatingly handsome. Possibly more so, seeming at one with the elements. And she wondered how he'd managed to crush all the opinions she'd formed about him before she'd even met him in the space of only one day.

Since the raid of Boer, memories of the attack on her settlement when she was little—and her capture—had returned with force. She had always tried to bury her pain, but now the images kept rising to the surface.

As they'd walked the ravines this morning, she'd wondered if her parents were still alive and how they would have felt, knowing she'd been taken from them. She imagined it would have broken their hearts to see her as someone's thrall. And what would they think of her now, traversing across the barren landscape with an important jarl? She still couldn't quite believe it herself. He had a strange effect on her…but she felt her courage increasing with every step they took together, every conversation they had, every touch…

She turned her head to look up at the clouds drifting above them. 'Do you ever see Odin or Freya when you gaze up at the sky?' she asked. 'Sometimes I imagine I can make out their faces in the clouds and see them looking down on me. Perhaps the sliver of sunlight shining through is Heimdall's golden smile, mocking me, for isn't it said he created the three ranks of man?'

Knud sat up in the mud, looking down on her in surprise. 'You believe in the Norse gods, like us?'

'The people of my settlement were practitioners of

the Norse religion, as is Earl Ingrid and the whole of Boer.'

He studied her face, as if taking that new information in. 'I thought perhaps, where you'd come from, you'd been converted to the new religion.' He seemed heartened by her revelation—but what did it matter? It didn't make them the same. Their stations in life couldn't be more different.

'I always feel as if the gods are watching, laughing or weeping along with us.' He dusted himself off before standing up. He held out his hand to help her up and, tentatively, she took it, putting her fingers in his, finally willing to trust him. But the sparks that tingled in her fingers unnerved her and, as soon as she got to her feet, she pulled back out of his grip. She was struggling to work out the conflicting feelings inside her. They were terrifying, so she just wanted to crush them, ignore them. Ignore him.

'We should go and wash this mud off,' she said, hating the tremors in her voice. 'Before we head into Hafranes.'

He nodded. 'I know just the place.'

Knud's hand was still smarting from where Wren had carefully placed her fingers in his, accepting his help at last, before just as quickly disentangling herself, as if she was irritated at his touch. He wondered exactly what Earl Ingrid's brother had done to make her flinch whenever he came near her. And just how much of a fight must Wren have had to put up each time, before Earl Ingrid came to her rescue? He had the strong desire to wipe those memories from her mind, to show her his touch could be gentle, pleasurable, but he knew he mustn't. There were so many reasons why he couldn't. He was meant to be marrying another, for one. And Wren belonged to that very woman—for now.

There were laws about these things and touching another person's property. And a thrall who went to bed with a chieftain was seen as a bed wench—it would be a smear on her reputation, as well as his own. No, he couldn't do that to her. Not that she'd let him either, he thought ruefully. Besides, he had told her she could trust him and he felt she was slowly beginning to. He didn't want to ruin the progress he'd made with her now.

On the outskirts of the settlement of Hafranes, there was a little freshwater stream marking the border of the town. When they reached it, they both drank greedily, scooping up handfuls of clear, crisp water until they'd quenched their thirst.

'Feeling better?' he asked.

'I will when I've got this off me.' She grimaced, picking off a few pieces of dried mud from her arms.

He reached out and touched her hair, pulling some of the mud from it, feeling a bit guilty for covering her in the stuff. Her eyes widened and he felt her breath hitch, so he instantly dropped his hand.

She struggled with the chainmail, trying to work it off her, until she gave up. 'Will you help me take this off?' she asked shyly, pulling at the heavy armour, her cheeks burning.

He tugged at the straps, loosening them. Had it only

been half a day since he'd fastened them this morning? It felt like so much had happened in that time. They'd come a long way in terms of the distance they'd travelled and their companionship. To think last night in the hut she wouldn't even look at him and had barely talked to him, but now...

She lifted her arms and he tugged the armour off her, casting it down on the ground, and she didn't hesitate. She shucked off her boots and began to wade into the water, but he halted her.

'You should take that off,' he said, motioning to her tunic. 'Otherwise you'll be walking around in wet clothes for the rest of the day.'

She scowled at him, obviously not liking his suggestion, the mistrust clouding over her eyes again.

'It's not as if I haven't seen it all before,' he teased.

She splashed some water at him and he raised his arms in defence, laughing. But then he did the right thing and turned around, despite finding it an effort. 'I promise I'll keep my back to you.'

'Just like last time?' she muttered.

But she must have realised she couldn't go into Hafranes soaking wet, so she had no choice. He heard her pull off her tunic and saw her throw it on the bank before wading in. 'Don't look,' she warned him.

He followed her in, keeping his back to her, and discarded his own tunic before scrubbing off the restrictive, dried mud that was cracking on his body, and he did it in silence. It felt good to get clean and wash off the strain of the day. When he was done, he felt rejuvenated. They were nearly at Hafranes. They could get

Earl Ingrid the help she needed. And they were half-way to Nedergaard.

It took all his strength not to turn around and look at her in the water. It was the second time she was practically naked just an arm's reach away from him and it wasn't helping with the constant, throbbing ache in his groin. He was relieved when she finally got out and had pulled her clothes back on, telling him she was decent again. He sent his silent thanks up to the gods.

But then he turned and saw her tugging her hair from its band and shaking it out, combing the wet strands through with her fingers, the water dripping on to her chest, soaking her tunic anyway. His eyes dipped to her breasts where her dark, hardened nipples were showing through the damp material and his cock stiffened again in immediate response. What was it about her that stole his breath away? He was immensely relieved they hadn't been seen out there on the hinterland, for the Earl of Forsa's men would have quite the prize if they caught her.

He sat down on the bank, topless, letting the sun dry his skin, and he watched a male and female bird dart about on the surface of the water, becoming intimately acquainted. He caught Wren's eye and he smiled, holding her gaze for an overlong moment.

Wrapping her arms over her chest, she came and joined him on the bank.

'What are all those marks on your chest—and your back?' she asked, blushing fiercely.

Had she been studying him when his back was turned? So it was clearly one rule for one... 'The scars or the ink?'

'Both,' she said, biting her lip.

'The scars are from all the battles I've fought in. They're either marks of glory or lucky escapes, I don't know which.'

'The wounds must have hurt at the time.'

'Some were deeper than others. The ink is to represent my character. My *fylgjur*—my totem animal—is a bear.'

'Why a bear?'

'I'd often wear the skin of a bear into battle when I was younger. I was part of the berserkers. I'd wear bear skin and no armour. I'd fight without fear...' He sometimes wondered if he'd been punished ever since for the way he'd behaved so brutally, so recklessly, back then.

'But now you wear a *mammut*? Sorry, marmot...'

He grinned. 'No, that just happened to be the animal skin on that particular cloak.'

He picked up a stone and skimmed it across the water. 'Do you have any ink? I know some thralls...'

'No, Earl Ingrid never branded me, if that's what you're asking. But I do have this.' She tugged the neckline of her tunic down a little to expose the pale curve of her shoulder. At the top of her back was a black circle of ink and inside was a little knotted triangular shape.

Lifting his hand, he smoothed his thumb over the mark and she shivered.

'What is it?'

'I don't know. I've had it since I was little. I'm unsure what it means… I wondered if you might know?'

'In our lands, that symbol means family. Perhaps it means the same where you come from?' But this peculiar symbol, the way it was done, with its intricate knotwork, triggered a memory. He was certain he'd seen it somewhere before, but he couldn't recall it at this moment.

He had been shocked when she had said she practised the Norse religion earlier. He had assumed she had been taken from one of the tribes down south, who had converted to the Christian faith. But perhaps her home wasn't as far away as he'd thought.

She ran her hand along the metal cuff around her neck. He noticed she often did it when she was nervous. Was he making her feel that way? His fingers were still on her soft skin and he didn't want to remove them.

'Does that bother you?' he asked, nodding to the collar, suddenly feeling his stomach simmer with anger. 'You say Ingrid didn't brand you, but she still makes you wear that. I don't know which is worse.'

'You get used to it.'

'I could try to take it off for you if you'd like,' he said, his fingers curving over her shoulder.

She shrugged off his hand from her skin. 'I don't think Earl Ingrid would like that.'

'Earl Ingrid's not awake to notice. She might not even make it.'

She frowned. 'Don't say that.'

At the mention of her ruler's name, Wren moved

away from him and set to finally cleaning Earl Ingrid's wound, now they had clean water. He came with her to help, kneeling beside her to the side of the trundle and helping to unwrap the makeshift bandages.

'Well, as I'm destined to serve her for ever, even in the afterlife, let's hope she does survive—I'm not ready to be her grave goods just yet.'

He scowled, ripping another piece of material from his already tattered tunic. 'Don't talk like that, Wren.'

'Why not? It's true,' she said, taking the material from his hand and leaving him momentarily to go and submerge it in the stream before coming back and beginning to clean the wound. 'Earl Ingrid has told me many times she means to take me with her when she goes, have me buried alongside her, saying she would need me in the next world. I've seen it happen before. Earl Elias had three of his slaves buried alongside him. They were all pleading for their lives, but no one listened.'

The thought turned him ice cold. He would never allow that to happen to Wren.

Thoughts of the afterlife plagued him often and he looked up at the sky. When Wren had mentioned seeing the faces of the gods earlier, it had resonated with him. He had often wondered if Annegrete was with the gods, looking down on him. It was his wish, as of all warriors, that when he died it would be in battle and he would be chosen by Odin to go to the Great Hall of Valhalla.

But it tortured him, not knowing where his late wife

was now. What if she was with the giantess, Ran—for it was known she harboured people who died at sea? But wasn't it also said that those who died of other causes went to Hel? If he and Annegrete were sent to different places, then he would never see her again… and he would never be able to ask for her forgiveness.

'And anyway, I could say the same to you,' Wren said, bringing his focus back to her. 'This is your future bride you're speaking about. How can you discuss her in such a cold way?' she scolded him, finishing up. 'How can you marry her? You clearly do not feel any love for her.'

He ripped yet another strip of material from his clothes to use as a fresh bandage and handed it to her. 'As you no doubt heard me say to Rædan at the pool, it is a legacy I need, not love. Every great leader wants their name to live on. To be remembered. I have a whole settlement of people who are counting on me, depending on me, who will share stories of me when I'm gone. That is what's important to me.'

'And you think Earl Ingrid can provide all that for you?'

'There was a big battle in Nedergaard recently and we lost a lot of men. We still have small bands of skilled warriors, but no great army. Earl Ingrid does. And perhaps our union could do some good for you and those like you, too. Maybe when I'm in charge she can adopt our ways. Perhaps I can convince her to free you in return for your long service.'

Wren shook her head. 'Unlikely.'

'Or will she not allow you to be bought?'

Her eyes swung to look at him, her jaw clenched. 'You want to buy me like cattle? I am not a piece of meat.'

'I mean to free you, Wren, nothing more.' His arms went wide in explanation, sitting back. 'Believe it or not, I am not one of those men who buys thralls to use for their own pleasure. I wouldn't lower myself.'

Her lips parted on an affronted gasp and he raised his eyes to the skies again. 'I mean I wouldn't lower myself to emulate their behaviour, not lower myself to sleep with someone of your status… Good grief, woman! I meant no offence.'

He pulled her into his shoulder, giving her no choice, trying to placate her. And for the first time, she didn't fight him, she almost sagged against him instead, giving in to the comfort he was offering.

'What about those rules about touching someone else's property? Isn't it forbidden for you to do this?' she whispered.

'We're all alone, so the rules don't apply out here. They're ridiculous anyway.' And they just sat there together, watching the birds on the water some more.

'What do you think my totem animal would be?' she asked him quietly. 'A bird? A wren?'

'No, it would have to be an eagle—a symbol of freedom and strength.'

'I like that.'

After a while, she pulled away, sitting up straight, and he tugged on the remains of his tunic. When he

stood and she looked up at him, she realised the bottom
half of it was completely missing now, his taut stomach
showing, and she couldn't help but giggle. 'What are
they going to think of you in Hafranes?' She laughed,
shaking her head.

Chapter Five

The sights and sounds of the market enthralled Wren as they passed through the bustling square of Hafranes, stall-holders shouting about their wares to attract buyers, their tables laden with goods, various vendors stepping out in front of her, trying to get her to feel the softness of their silk or to taste the spiciness of their food.

It was so much busier than the Sunday market in Boer—and much noisier. Steam rose from the various meats being cooked over open fires, hissing and spitting, making her mouth water and her stomach grumble, and she kept falling behind Knud, fascinated and distracted by all the delicious sights and smells.

Before they'd come here, they'd stopped at a small farmstead. Knud had told her to stay at the gate and she had watched as he'd spoken in hushed tones to a man, motioning to her and Earl Ingrid as he did so. Then he'd called her forward and introduced her to his friend, Petar, who he said he'd known for many winters.

The kindly-looking man had agreed to let them hide Earl Ingrid in the little boathouse on the water's edge while they went to the market in search of healing herbs. Wren had been reluctant to leave her ruler, but Knud had assured her the shipbuilder and his wife would keep watch for any of Forsa's men until they returned.

'Wren, keep up,' Knud called to her, exasperated, stopping to wait for the third time. 'I'm worried I'll lose you. Stay with me.'

But when he started walking again, they immediately got separated by a woman who halted her, wanting Wren to smell her wild flowers. Knud gripped Wren's arm, pulling her aside. He tugged at her tunic, pulling up the collar slightly to try to hide her metal cuff. 'Keep it covered,' he said. Then he trailed his fingers down over her arm, over the bare skin of her wrist, to take her hand in his. 'Stay with me.'

Her mind returned to their earlier words at the stream and how she'd said he shouldn't touch her. She'd felt ridiculously deflated when she'd thought he was referring to her as if she were an animal he could bargain over. It had hurt her more than it should. Was it because, up until then, he'd been the first person to actually treat her as an equal?

She had started to think it wouldn't be so bad, him being her master—the new ruler of Boer. But then his words had reminded her of her low rank again. He'd said he'd never been inclined to be with a thrall…but that was a good thing, wasn't it? She didn't want him to be the type of man who would take a slave to bed.

She certainly didn't want him to be interested in her in that way. Did she?

And he clearly wasn't. Yes, he had made some protective gestures—giving her his cloak and his armour, feeding her and looking out for her, but it didn't mean anything. Perhaps he was just a good person after all. And yet, right now, as his fingers entwined with hers, gripping her tight as he guided them through the crowds, she felt alive. For a man who ran his own settlement, he certainly didn't mind breaking a few rules.

Finally, they found the stall he was looking for, the one he'd described to her as having lots of colourful tinctures. And when they saw the healer look between them, he released her from his grasp. She instantly missed his touch, but tried to focus on all the little potions and powders instead, wondering if there was one here that might be able to help Earl Ingrid, to heal her wound and bring her back to them. She would get well and be able to marry, but suddenly the thought of Knud taking Earl Ingrid's hand in his, wrapping his strong, warm fingers around hers, made her feel queasy.

Knud explained to the healer—a peculiar-looking woman with straggly, long grey hair, black eyes and a string of animal bones around her neck—that they had a friend who'd been hurt and described the wound in detail. In response, the woman began explaining what the suitable options were.

'We'll take them all,' Knud said, removing two of his silver armbands and handing them over in return for the medicine.

Wren's heart went out to him. It was wonderful of

him to exchange his silver to help them. To save his future bride. She swallowed down the lump in her throat.

They listened intently as the healer explained how they must deliver the various herbs for them to work, before they went to leave. They were just turning to go when the woman caught Wren's hand with her claw-like nails and Wren gasped. The woman's black eyes bored into her.

'Beware a triangle of enemies. Your blood flows thick like a river in the middle.'

Her heart froze in terror. What could she mean?

Knud prised Wren's hand from the tight grip of the healer, muttering his words of thanks to the older woman, before putting his arm around Wren's shoulder and ushering her away.

'What was that?' she whispered, shuddering.

'She is a *vølve*—a seer. She can see visions of the future, foretold by the gods.'

'What do you think she meant?'

'I wouldn't think too much about it,' he said, trying to reassure her. 'It probably meant nothing.'

And then she felt him tense. She looked up to follow his gaze and caught sight of a couple of Forsa's men working their way through the crowd, heading straight for them. They were the same men they'd seen on horseback earlier today. Her chest exploded in panic and she and Knud gave each other a grim, knowing look.

He took her by the hand again, guiding her in the opposite direction of the men, through the unruly hordes of people, as fast as they could push their way through.

At the end of the row of stalls, they glanced back. There was no sign of the enemy. Had they lost them?

She wasn't sure she liked this place—she felt very unsettled. She just wanted to get back to the boathouse, to be alone with Knud, away from all these strangers. How odd that last night she had been afraid to be alone with him in that rundown little hut, but now, in the space of a single day, she felt safer with him than anyone else.

'How much do you want for her?' a man said, stepping out in front of Knud, taking them both by surprise. He had gnarled teeth and wayward eyes.

'What?' Knud barked, glancing over his shoulder, still checking for any sign of Forsa's men.

Wren glanced down and noticed that in the hurry of trying to evade their enemy, the neck of her tunic had come loose under the chainmail Knud had insisted on putting back on her, revealing her thrall collar.

'For the woman,' he sneered. 'Have you brought her to auction? I've got quite the collection already,' he said, nodding to a group of dirty, scrawny women huddled together like pigs in a pen, shackled and whimpering. 'But there's room for one more. Those men over there were admiring my stock, but they can't decide…and this might just sway them. Have you had your fill of her and want to exchange her for another? I'll need to check her over first, see if she's fit for purpose.'

Wren glanced at the men he'd mentioned, their greedy, eager eyes roaming over her, and she reeled. She felt sick for those other women and the cold grip of fear for herself. And then a thought lanced her. Was this the market where Knud had found his right-hand man, Rædan, and rescued him?

Knud tugged her into his side, keeping her behind him, and she curled her fingers around his solid upper arm, seeking his strength. She noticed he'd placed his hand on the hilt of his sword for all to see, asserting his control. 'She's not for sale.'

'Everyone has a price. How much did you pay for her? She really is a beauty, this one. Let me give her a closer look,' the trader said, grabbing her by the chin.

Wren gasped in horror. She didn't want him anywhere near her, his grubby hands on her skin. But Knud's reactions were lightning quick, his hand coming up to grip around the man's throat.

'Take your hands off her. Now.'

And it was in that moment, she saw the other side of him again—the ruthless warrior with a complete lack of regard for his own safety, as if he didn't care whether he lived or died.

The man dropped his hands from Wren's skin, his face turning puce in Knud's iron grasp, and she squeezed his arm. 'Knud, let him go,' she said gently.

A muscle flickered in his jaw before he released his hold on the man's throat, and the trader bent over, choking.

It wasn't a good idea to cause a scene. Not when they knew Forsa's soldiers were here, among the crowd. But it seemed it was already too late. The other men who had been watching them, hoping to barter for the women, for her, began to gather around them, blocking their way out. Their interest had been stirred and they obviously liked their chances, three against one. Anger and disgust rippled through her.

She noticed Knud's knuckles turning white as he gripped his sword tighter, removing it from his belt. 'Stay behind me,' he commanded her.

'I do not wish to fight you,' he announced to the men. 'But there are laws about a man's property and this girl belongs to me,' he said.

'We're simply wondering if we can convince you to change your mind,' the largest one snickered, moving in closer, crowding them. 'We can be very persuasive.'

Wren gripped Knud's arm tighter, her other hand coming up to rest on his broad back.

'Sorry to disappoint you. I will not be moved on the matter.'

'Even at the risk of losing your life?'

Wren glanced over at the other women, who were watching the exchange take place. Should she offer herself up to be thrown among them, in order to save Knud?

'No. I'm afraid that this time you have picked the wrong man. For I do not care for my own life, only hers.'

Wren's breath halted. Surely he couldn't mean it? And then she thought back to how he had thrown himself into the fight back in Boer, and what he'd told her about being a berserker—a man who fought in fury and didn't fear death. Did he really want to go to Valhalla that much? Did he not want to live?

She knew she had at times behaved recklessly in the past, hoping that perhaps someone would end her life, putting her out of her misery. But he couldn't feel like that, could he? And if he did, why? Did it have something to do with him losing his wife? Did he truly know the pain of grief and loss just as much as she did?

'A man in love with his slave. How touching,' the burly one with missing front teeth sneered and the others all laughed. 'If you do not care to live, that makes killing you all the easier, then,' he said, coming towards him, drawing his own sword. 'Because your woman will be mine.'

Suddenly another of the men threw themselves into Knud's body, knocking him backwards, and Wren gasped, springing out of the way just in time. But Knud was quick to get back on his feet and he was taking them on, three against one, while the slave trader saw his chance and grabbed her, trying to haul her away towards his horde.

'Knud!' she screamed. But there was nothing he could do—not right now while he was trying to deflect three men's blades, sidestepping each slash and stab, each swipe of metal slicing through the air causing her to wince.

She struggled against the man's hold, knowing she could fight him if she could just release herself from his grip and reach her weapon, but he smacked her around the face, causing her to fall to the floor. Her knife tumbled out of her boot to the ground, out of her reach. He grabbed her by the hair and began dragging her, and the pain was unbearable, but so was watching those men trying to wound Knud. Still, she tried to prise the man's greasy fingers from her scalp.

This was bad. If Knud was to die, she would become the property of this sick, twisted man, or one of the others. They would do what they liked with her… there would be no Earl Ingrid to save her this time. And Ingrid…what would happen to her? She would be lost to them and her people.

How had it come to this? Just yesterday morning she'd been worried about Earl Ingrid marrying this Danish chieftain, but now she would gladly return to that moment, to wish them both well if it meant they would all be safe. Now everything was wrong. They'd lost the fortress of Boer. Earl Ingrid was hurt. And Knud was fighting for his life…in just one day he had managed to change her opinion of him—she now believed that not all men were evil. He had stood up for her over and again and now he was trying to save her from the hands of these brutes.

Dragging her into the pen, the trader roughly bound her to the other women. 'You're a monster,' she screamed, bile rising in her throat, and he spat on her in response.

But she didn't care about herself, her attention was drawn back to the man still fighting. He was her only chance. She needed him to stay alive. She *wanted* him to stay alive—because she cared about him—and the thought brought her up short. It was true, he had become her hope. She'd been right when she'd first seen him come through the gates at Boer—he was larger than life itself. In just one day he had become her whole world.

He'd managed to dispose of one of the men and another lay injured and groaning on the floor. It was now one on one, but they'd both seemingly lost their weapons, and the big burly one threw Knud to the ground and they began wrestling, their skirmish bloody and violent. She didn't think she'd ever seen such a vicious, bare-knuckled fight and she shut her eyes, not wanting to watch as the man straddled Knud's body and pummelled his handsome, bearded face.

But she realised she also couldn't not watch what was happening, as she needed to know he was all right. She was willing him to get up, to fight back. She looked on in fear as the huge man managed to reach his lost blade and he brought it down, slicing through Knud's shoulder, and Wren gasped at seeing his blood. She wished she hadn't agreed to wear his armour again because right now, he needed it much more than she did.

But Knud barely flinched at the injury, instead fighting even more ferociously, kicking his strong legs and knocking the man backwards. All the women looked on in awe and Wren noticed a crowd was gathering around them, enjoying the entertainment. She glanced about, fearful of seeing Forsa's men in the throng. That was all they needed.

In a last burst of anger, Knud felt around on the ground, trying to reach something—was that her knife?—and then he delivered the final, deadly blow to his assailant, the man slumping down lifeless on top of him. The girls beside her whimpered and the slave trader looked on in horror, realising it was all over and that this mighty warrior would be coming for him next. When he quickly took off down the row of stalls, Wren almost wilted in relief.

She couldn't believe it. Knud had done it. He'd saved them.

Despite his injury, he wasted no time in coming over to them. He unlocked the pen and then he released the chains that were binding the women together.

'Free yourselves. Get away from here,' he barked and the women leapt to their dirty feet, muttering their grateful thanks before fleeing.

Knud gripped Wren by the elbow and hauled her up. She'd thought he was about to embrace her, tug her to him, even hoped he would, but instead he launched her forward, out of the pen and down the square, steering her back to the boathouse, as fast as their legs would allow. His eyes were wild, his breathing ragged. He was like something possessed, as if wanting to get out of this place as fast as possible, his rage practically shimmering off him.

'How badly are you hurt?' she tried to ask him.

But he didn't answer and she was unsure what he was thinking.

When they finally neared the boathouse, away from the crowds, where there was nothing but the sound of the water and the leaves rustling in the trees, he suddenly stopped and spun her around, so her back was facing him, and he swept her hair out of the way.

'We need to get this off you. Now!'

He struggled with the lock of her collar, tugging it this way and that.

'Knud, stop!' she said, the metal grazing the skin of her neck.

When it wouldn't budge, he instead started trying to prise the metal apart with his fingers. But it was too strong. *'Helvete!'* he cursed, slamming a hand into the side of the hut, making her jump.

She turned around to face him, resting her back against the wall, her eyes wide.

'It's all right,' she said, trying to calm him.

'It's not all right!' he exploded, raking his hands through his hair, which had come loose during the fight. 'The things they said about you, the way they treated you… None of it is all right. If I could just take it off…' His fingers came up to curve over the metal at her throat again.

She placed her hand on his chest, shocked at the waves of anger rippling through him on her behalf. He really was a good man. Earl Ingrid was a lucky woman…

'*You* saved me. And those other women. We're here, we're alive,' she said. 'They're gone now. They can't hurt me any more. It's over…'

Her hand moved up from his chest to hold his bruised face, her thumb moving over the gash on his right cheekbone. And he stared down at her, the wrath seeming to drain from his veins, and he nodded, as if finally hearing what she was saying. He took a step towards her, so their bodies were nearly touching, and he gently rested his forehead against hers. He was so close she stopped breathing.

'I thought I'd lost you,' he said raggedly.

'You didn't. You haven't.'

His fingers strayed down from her collar and his palm flattened over the top of her chest, over her racing heartbeat.

'I should never have taken you there in the first place. It was foolish of me. Forgive me. When those men circled us...' He shook his head. 'I didn't care what happened to me. But the thought of those men laying even a finger on you...' He stared down into her eyes and she knew all the hideous, appalling things he was thinking. 'They had no right to do that.'

'I know. But they didn't. I'm back here, with you. Safe.'

'Did he hurt you?' he said, his voice raw with emotion.

'Just a few bruises, but I'll survive.'

Her heart began to pound faster as his hand came up to cup her cheek, inspecting her face where he saw the trader had hit her. And when he tenderly stroked her hair, her eyes drifted shut, letting him comfort her. She had never wanted a man to touch her before, but his touch was different to all others she had experienced. It was firm but gentle. Careful.

She realised this was what desire must feel like—to want a man to put his hands on you, to want to press up against him and create more of the spine-tingling feelings he was causing. But why did she have to feel this way about him—a Danish chieftain? The man who was meant to be marrying her ruler?

'What about you? Are you badly hurt?' she said, her eyelids fluttering open. She knew he'd been injured, but to what extent?

'A few more scars to add to the collection.' He grimaced. 'But it was worth it.'

He looked down at her. She felt sure he was about

to lean in and press his lips against hers—and she panicked, her heart leaping wildly, so she flattened her hand against his chest, pushing him gently away.

'I should take a look at them for you.'

He pulled himself up, shaking his head, stepping away from her. She was both disappointed and glad he hadn't tried to kiss her, all at the same time. 'No, I can do it. You check on Earl Ingrid, give her the herbs, then you'll need to leave.'

'Leave?' she asked, her brow furrowing.

'Yes, Petar has a horse and small cart he said he can carry you and Earl Ingrid on. He agreed to take us the final part of the way to Nedergaard tonight, but I won't fit on the cart and I fear I cannot walk it now. I will only slow you down. But I want you and Earl Ingrid to go with him. I trust him, I know he will keep you safe. I shall stay here tonight and rest, tend my wounds and catch up with you all on the morrow.'

'No,' she said, shaking her head fiercely. 'I'm not leaving you here alone and injured.'

'You must. We need to get Earl Ingrid back for treatment—you said yourself she's burning up. We've got the herbs, we've done all we can, but Forsa's men are still right upon us. We can't waste another moment.'

'Well, you can let your man take Earl Ingrid, but I'm not leaving. I'm not going anywhere if you're hurt.'

'Wren,' he said, his voice stern, a muscle flickering in his cheek.

'You can't patch up your wounds yourself. You need me.'

He raised his eyes to the skies, as if trying to gather

his strength. But he must have been weakened by the fight, as for once, he relented. 'All right…you can stay. Now help me with Earl Ingrid. Petar is waiting.'

They went inside the hut to give Earl Ingrid the herbs, as directed by the healer, and then they carried the trundle across the fields of the farmstead to where Petar and his wife were waiting with the horse and cart.

Knud was struggling with his share of the weight of the trundle now, so she knew he must be suffering with his wounds, and she was keen to take a look at them, to see how bad they were and how she could help, but she knew he would insist upon dealing with Earl Ingrid first. Petar's wife passed them some bread and water, and they muttered their grateful thanks.

After they slid the trundle on to the cart and covered up Earl Ingrid's body with furs and blankets, Knud nodded to his friend, and they set off immediately to make the most of the last of the day's light. Wren prayed they would have a safe journey and that they would be reunited soon.

Back in the hut, Knud shucked off his tattered tunic and inspected the sword wound to his shoulder. 'I've had worse.' He grimaced.

It looked pretty bad to her, blood dripping down his arm and on to his trousers. He ripped off another strip of material from his discarded tunic, using his teeth, and dipped it in the bowl of water.

'There'll be nothing left of that soon!' she said.

He smiled, but it didn't quite reach his eyes. He must be in considerable pain, she thought. He went to mop up the blood, but she rushed forward.

'Let me do it,' she said, taking the material from him.

She had never touched a man's naked body willingly before, but this was the least she could do after he'd saved her life. And he was a beautiful man, all muscle and smooth skin, despite the scars that crisscrossed over his chest.

She studied the inked figure of an enormous black bear that reared up along one side of his body. It fascinated her and she wanted to trace her fingers over it, but she knew she had to focus on the task at hand. She could see why he would have that as his totem animal. When he fought, he was intimidating just like that bear and he dominated all others. Yet she knew he had a soft, tender, caring side, too.

He was so close, she could feel his warm breath on her cheek, the radiating heat of his body. She could see and feel the rise and fall of his chest and she drew her palm across his skin, holding him in place as she cleaned up his shoulder. Her fingers were trembling at being so close to him and she bit her lip nervously.

She momentarily had to force herself to step away and rummage around for one of the tinctures the healer had given them, before coming back to place some of the ointment on his wound. He sucked in a sharp breath.

'Have you met that woman before? The seer? Was that how you knew she had the herbs to help Earl Ingrid.'

'Yes, I've met her before.'

'She scared me. I keep going over her words in my head, wondering what she meant.'

'Like I said, I wouldn't dwell on it too much.'

'Has she foretold your future before?'

'Once. A long time ago.'

'And did it come to pass?'

'Wren, I really shouldn't worry about it.'

'It did, didn't it?'

He sighed. 'It is hard to say. She talks in riddles.'

'What did she see? What did she say?'

'It doesn't matter what she said… Let us not talk any more about it now, it is in the past.'

'Did you mean what *you* said—about not caring if you live or die when you fight like that?' she asked.

He shrugged. 'It's useful to feel that way. If you do, you aren't really afraid of anything for yourself, only for others. I honestly don't care if I die, but I want you to be safe, Wren. And my people,' he said, reaching out and tucking a strand of hair behind her ear.

'And Earl Ingrid?'

'Of course.'

'But a lot of people would be upset if something happened to you. A lot of people are depending on you,' she said, stopping what she was doing. 'Why do you care so little about yourself?'

'I know they need me. It's why I came to Boer, why I'm here. I guess I just fell out of love with life a long time ago.'

She frowned.

'It amazes me that you haven't, after all you've been through… I'm in awe of your strength. Are you telling me *you'd* be upset if something happened to me?' he said, his smile slowly building.

'Knud!' she said, gently chiding him, a blush rising in her cheeks.

'Would you?' he pressed.

She tutted. 'You know I would be.'

'And I you… I felt compelled to rescue you from the moment I saw you in the hall in Boer that night. Maybe even before that…'

She swallowed. Did he?

'And who's going to rescue you?' she whispered, finishing up with his wounds.

She thought back to what Rædan had said at the tidal pool, about Earl Ingrid healing the cracks in his heart. Was he still grieving for his late wife? And if so, would marrying Earl Ingrid make it all better?

'I think you just did,' he said, looking down at his patched-up skin.

And she smiled. She felt as if today, being with him, had broadened her view of the world. And even though they had faced their fair share of danger together already, she would do it all again if it meant she'd end up here with him.

He reached out and took her chin between his thumb and forefinger and tilted her face so she was looking up at him. 'Thank you, Wren,' he said. And he dipped his head and placed the sweetest, softest kiss on her lips.

'I don't know about you, but I've had just about enough excitement for one day. Shall we get some sleep? If we can make an early start, leave at dawn, we might make it back to Nedergaard by mid-morning.'

He wasn't sure what she'd say after he'd just kissed

her. What the hell had he been thinking? But he was reaching the edge of his restraint. He was finding he wanted to touch her, be near to her all of the time. He wanted to make her smile and hear her laugh. Instead, he'd taken her to a dangerous market and had almost got them both killed. Damn it.

He'd been so livid with those men—for speaking of her in such a way. For wanting to make her their own. Well, they'd got their retribution and he wasn't sorry. He might have failed when it came to saving Annegrete, but he'd die before he let anything bad happen to Wren. Yet he had to wonder what he was doing, kissing her after the ordeal she'd just been through, and a wave of guilt washed over him.

He was a chief—she was a thrall. His bride-to-be's thrall, no less. He should know better. And yet, despite all this, he couldn't seem to help himself. If only she knew the truth—that deep down, he wasn't a man she could rely on, perhaps she would have gone ahead on that cart to Nedergaard with Earl Ingrid. But unbelievably, she'd wanted to stay with him, knowing they'd be alone. He was starting to believe he'd earned her trust and he mustn't ruin such a fragile bond now.

She gave a hesitant nod. 'All right.'

His past had haunted him for many, many winters— he'd struggled to get over it and had never been able to forgive himself. And he'd meant what he'd said. After Annegrete died, he had no longer cared for life—he'd longed for death to come in battle, throwing himself into the fray, hoping this was his time. But since he'd met Wren, something had changed...

He'd watched her earlier as she'd tended to Earl Ingrid's wound, then his own, applying the various powders and tinctures carefully and meticulously. She was too kind. Too beautiful. It hurt his chest just to look at her.

'I keep thinking it should have been me, not Earl Ingrid who got hurt,' Wren said.

He frowned. 'Don't say things like that.'

She shrugged. 'Earl Ingrid has people depending on her, a wedding to plan… Me, I'm not important at all.'

'That's not true…' he shook his head fiercely '…you are important.' To him at least. 'You mustn't blame yourself for any of this, Wren. I know it's hard. I keep thinking if I hadn't come to Boer, maybe the attack on the fortress wouldn't have happened. And maybe I should have stayed there and fought them off, instead of helping you with Earl Ingrid…'

'I'm glad you didn't,' she said, reaching over and touching his arm.

He smiled.

She went to sit down on the straw-covered floor and winced.

'Wren?' he asked, sinking down to his knees next to her. 'Are you hurt?'

'I'm all right, it's just a bruise,' she said.

'Are you sure?' he asked, his brow furrowed. 'Where is it? Maybe I should take a look.'

She shook her head. 'That's not necessary.'

'Wren… I let you patch up my wounds.' He knew he was asking too much—he was asking for permission to see her bare skin and it was not appropriate. She was rooted to the spot, pursing her lips, unsure whether to let him. But she was clearly in pain and he wanted to see if any serious damage had been done, yet he also didn't want to make her feel uncomfortable in any way.

'I'm honestly all right. I just fell hard on my hip and he dragged me a little way on the ground, grazing my skin,' she said, her voice wavering. 'It's just a bit sore.'

'Show me,' he demanded.

'No,' she said.

'Yes.'

'Oh, all right,' she said, flustered, trying to tug off the heavy chainmail. She struggled again, and he moved closer to help, but as he pulled the material off her body, she flinched at the pain. He watched as she took her arms out of the sleeves of her tunic and twisted it round, so the lace-up opening was at the back. 'There, can you see anything?' she asked, turning round and offering her back to him.

He came closer, loosening the ties and pushing aside the material so he could see the expanse of her back, and when his fingers trailed over her skin, she shivered. His eyebrows drew together and he pulled in a deep breath. Her back was covered in deep scratches and a large bruise was steadily appearing along her right side. But that wasn't what shocked him. It was the silvery lines of old wounds hashed across her back that disturbed him more.

'Well?' she asked. 'How bad is it?'

'You have lots of little cuts—more like burns from being dragged along the ground. The armour probably saved your skin a little—they should heal soon enough.

But what are these?' he said, running his fingers along her spine, over some of the raised bumps and lines.

'Souvenirs from Earl Elias.' She grimaced.

'What?' he exclaimed in horror.

She pulled her tunic back round the right way, hiding her scars from him, pushing her arms through the sleeves again and fastening up the ties.

'It was my punishment for not succumbing to his desires,' she said matter-of-factly.

He cursed under his breath, a sudden spurt of rage shafting through his body. 'Is there no end to this barbarity? And Earl Ingrid allowed this to happen, did she? This punishment?'

'She felt it was the lesser evil. She had already saved me from his bed, she could not save me from his whip, too.'

He took her hand, bringing her with him as he sat down on the floor, leaning his back against the wall. He wondered how she'd got through the grief of being separated from her home and her parents, and then dealing with this brutality, as well. He knew she was strong, but this... He bristled. It explained a lot about the way she behaved, the way she baulked when he touched her, the way she shunned him coming near her, but it only made him want to protect her, look after her, even more.

'Will you tell me about it?' he asked, clearing his throat, his thumb stroking over her fingers.

'There's not much to tell,' she said simply.

'Explain it to me, so I know what you've been through,' he insisted.

She shrugged. 'He used to pull me aside in the long-house and put his hands on me, and I'd try to fight him off, to get away…sometimes he got further than others, until he got frustrated with me struggling against his hold and he hit me, or Earl Ingrid caught him and stopped him. But he'd always make sure I was punished for my disobedience later.'

'I'm so sorry, Wren,' he said, squeezing her hand.

'I used to think all men were like that,' she said. 'Until I met you…'

He pulled her into his side, holding her close, stroking her arm, wanting her to know she was safe with him, and she turned her face into his uninjured shoulder.

He listened as her breathing gently slowed and grew heavier and was pleased she was relaxed enough in his company to finally drift off. She must have been exhausted after their long day. And he was glad she'd decided to stay with him. That was why he hadn't fought it. He wouldn't have got any sleep if they'd been parted—he would have just spent the whole night worrying whether they'd reached Nedergaard, whether she was safe without him.

Looking around the little boathouse, he knew they'd be undiscovered here for the night, but he feared sleep would continue to elude him. The actions of those men still had rage coursing through his blood, and the words the seer had spoken to Wren had unsettled him, too, for what she had once told him had ended up coming true.

Most of all, he was restless because it was sheer torture holding her next to him, tucked into his body, knowing he couldn't act on his desires. But she'd just told him she believed him to be better than most men— and he really didn't want her to find out she was wrong. He didn't want to let her down.

Wren woke in the early hours to find she had a pillow that was gently rising and falling. Lifting her head slightly, she noticed she was lying on the floor of the boathouse, snuggled into the shoulder of the Chief of Nedergaard—the bravest man she had ever known. A warrior who had saved her life more than once. Her body was curled into his and her hand was resting on his solid chest.

She should have been disturbed. She should have moved away as soon as she'd realised that she was nestled into him, but she didn't want to. He smelt and felt good and she liked the sensation of his protective arm around her, holding her to him, keeping her safe.

She was regretting pushing him away earlier, outside, when she'd thought he was going to cover her mouth with his. Because later, when he'd placed that soft, innocent kiss on her lips after she'd patched up his wounds, it had felt wonderful, but all too brief.

Now, lying here, she wanted more. Just thinking about it made her pulse race, but she knew nothing of what she should do. She had no experience in these matters. Not good ones anyway. Courageously, she pressed her body closer towards him, her leg curling over his, to test the sensations rushing through her.

Knowing he was sound asleep, she felt brave enough to allow her palm to roam upwards to reach the opening of his tunic and steal underneath, to feel the heat and silkiness of his smooth, warm skin. She ran her fingers over the lines of his ink, tracing the shape of the ferocious bear with the tender heart, and she thought how quickly she had cast off her shackles out here, in the wild, feeling safe to share her secrets with him.

His large hand came up to cover hers and she gasped. Had she woken him?

'Wren?' he asked.

And in that moment, her name became a million questions. Her heart pounded, her body trembled, but she knew she couldn't ignore him. She wasn't even sure she wanted to.

She turned and raised her head, coming up on her elbow, looking down at him. His deep brown eyes were focused on her in the darkness. Words stalled on her tongue, so she answered him by lowering her head and placing a soft kiss on his mouth, like the one he'd given her earlier, before pulling back abruptly, all of a sudden feeling foolish. Heat filled her face. She had no idea what she was doing. Was it obvious?

'Wren?' he said again, his hand leaving hers on his chest and coming up to hold her face. He lifted his head off the ground as he brought hers down towards him and, this time, he covered her lips with his, taking control.

It was like nothing she'd ever felt before. His lips were firm, gently moving against hers, slowly opening them up for him to taste her, his tongue gliding inside her mouth so tenderly, so fully, making her shiver. His other hand came up to stroke her back carefully, aware of her injuries, but still holding her to him, wanting to deepen the kiss.

Her hand moved up from his chest to cup his bearded jaw, then her fingers stole into his glorious mane of hair and she realised she'd wanted to do this since she'd first seen him that night at the tidal pool, but he'd been so out of reach. Now, he was right here with her. Holding his head in place beneath her, she bravely pushed her tongue deeper, fully possessing his mouth, testing his careful control—and he groaned.

His arms came down around her waist and he tugged her on top of his body and when she felt the hard ridge of him beneath her, pressing into her hip, she gasped in surprise, heat blooming low in her belly. If it had been anyone else, she might have been frightened, but instead, she felt strangely excited. Was she causing that reaction in him? And in an experimental little move, she writhed against him, wanting to torture him some more.

He groaned again and his hand came back up to delve into her hair, his fingers against her scalp sending tingles right through her. Then his hot mouth left hers to trail down to her chin and nipped at her jaw and she lifted her head, encouraging him to explore further. He ducked lower, his lips kissing along the top of her tunic, his beard tickling her skin, down her open neckline.

As she hovered above him, his hands came up to cup her swollen breasts and his thumbs moved over her nipples, teasing them into hard peaks beneath the material. It felt so good. And when his tongue trailed the length of her cleavage, she gasped, tipping her head back to give him better access. She squirmed on top of him and one of his hands came up to gently grasp her bottom, tugging her closer into his body, moulding her into his groin.

She wanted to surrender to all the exquisite sensations rushing through her. She didn't want him to stop. She wanted him to strip away her clothes. She wanted to give him permission to put his hands and his lips on her—everywhere. She wanted him to make her his, she wanted to belong to him and the very thought brought her up short.

She pulled back slightly, staring down at him where his face lay between her breasts. And in an instant, she was up, standing on trembling legs, tugging her tunic back together, wondering what the hell she was doing.

What about Earl Ingrid? This was her ruler's husband-to-be she was writhing against, pushing her tongue into his mouth, exposing her breasts to—and wanting more. Things she'd never desired from a man before. She had wanted him to make her his by giving him her body, but he might own her for real if he became her future master...

Her hands flew to her mouth in shock, still feeling his lips on hers, the taste of him on her tongue, and she felt giddy and hot. She moved her fingers to her hair, to smooth it back into a band.

Knud sat up carefully, bringing his arms around his knees. 'Are you all right?'

'Yes. No,' she said tremulously, shaking her head. 'That should not have happened.'

He nodded slowly, taking in what she was saying. He blew out a long breath. 'You're probably right.'

'Only probably?'

He shrugged. 'I've wanted to kiss you from the moment I first saw you in that tidal pool,' he said. 'So I'd say it was inevitable.'

She gasped. Had he really? She could scarcely believe it. And yet he didn't sound shocked about what had just happened between them—he sounded more resigned. 'That doesn't mean it's right. Earl Ingrid—'

'I know,' he groaned. 'I'm sorry, Wren. I shouldn't have done it. I should have known better. Will you forgive me?'

She frowned. She didn't really want him to be sorry. After all, she had been the one to start it. If anyone was to blame it was she and her wandering hands. She and her inquisitive tongue, and her untutored body writhing against him. If truth be told, she wanted to lie straight back down and pick up where they'd left off. But they couldn't. She didn't know what was going to happen when they reached Nedergaard. He was meant to be getting married—to her ruler. And what would happen to her after that? The future was so uncertain.

She hoped Rædan and the rest of Knud's men had made it back, along with as many people from Boer as possible. And she hoped Earl Ingrid had arrived now, too, and her wounds were being tended to. She hoped Knud's settlement, including his sister and his friends, were safe. And she hoped she would be treated fairly there.

But no one knew for sure what was going to happen

when Earl Ingrid woke up—Wren might have to return to her duties as a thrall. Knud might not have a say in the matter and then what? She couldn't have him kissing her like that, putting his hands and his lips all over her body, without knowing any of this. He shouldn't be kissing her at all.

She nodded. 'Let's just forget it ever happened,' she said, her voice strained.

'I'll try.'

She wondered if he was thinking that would be impossible, like she was. Just as getting any sleep was going to be now. There was no way she could lie down next to him again, not with her heart beating so erratically, and her fingers itching to touch him again. Perhaps it wasn't he who couldn't be trusted—it was she!

Chapter Six

They'd been walking all morning and Wren was starting to think they'd never reach Knud's settlement. The Danish chief had been less talkative today, and she wondered if it was because his wounds were hurting him, or if he, too, kept thinking about the illicit kiss they'd shared in the night. Because she was struggling to think about anything else.

They had both been unable to sleep afterwards, sitting at opposite sides of the boathouse, making small talk to pass the night, and she had been relieved when dawn had arrived and they could finally leave, walking off their frustrations.

Knud finally stopped at a rocky summit, marked with a runestone, which overlooked the vast fjord below, and he pointed out the thriving settlement of Nedergaard beneath them. She cast her eyes over the view, taking it all in. It was more incredible than she could have imagined, far more beautiful than the barren landscape of Boer, but she could instantly see why they needed Earl

Ingrid's army—there were no fortress walls. The place was far too big, too sprawling. It wouldn't be very easy to defend.

'This is a wonderful outlook,' she said.

He nodded. 'Early summer, hundreds of daffodils bloom up here. I come up here sometimes...'

'To be alone?'

'With my thoughts. To be as close to the gods as I can get.'

'What does this say?' she said, motioning to the runes carved on the stone.

'Free in death, if not in life...' he said, his voice sounding strained.

She nodded, taking in the poignant words.

'As far as you can tell, does it look like anything untoward has happened while you've been gone?' she asked.

He shook his head. 'No, everything looks to be normal, thank goodness,' he said, his relief evident.

His arms came up to hold her and he tugged her into his body, just for a moment. 'We made it,' he said. 'You were amazing, Wren.'

She smiled back at him, letting him hold her, his large hands resting gently on her hips, for perhaps this would be the last time they would ever be alone together. Might this be the last time he'd ever take her in his arms? Was that why he seemed just as reluctant as she was to let go?

They hadn't discussed what had happened between them in the early hours of this morning and, while she was pleased they had safely reached their destination and that their long and difficult journey was almost over, she was also concerned about what would happen next. She knew arriving here, at his home, meant they could finally rest and regroup, but she wondered how she'd be treated by the people of Nedergaard. And if her people from Boer had made it back here, too, would things return to the way they were before?

Things would inevitably change between her and Knud when they walked through the doors of his longhouse—they would have to. Even if Nedergaard didn't have thralls, he would still have to act within the boundaries of his settlement's laws. He would have to act appropriately towards her. There could never be a repeat of last night. It wouldn't be just the two of them against the world any more—and she was reluctant to let him go. But she knew that she must.

It took a while to traverse down into the heart of the settlement and they both fell into silence. As they passed the outskirts of a forest and descended further to the soft golden sands of the shore, she wondered what Knud was thinking. Would he miss the camaraderie and connection between them, too? Or was he just quiet because he was desperate to get back to his people now that his home was within touching distance, wanting everything to return to normal?

He would no doubt have much work to do when they arrived and many people to speak to. She wondered who he might have missed and who he was most looking forward to seeing. Were there any women in his life? Surely a man such as he would not have spent his nights alone, despite the grief he'd suffered on his wife's death? Could she bear to see them fawn over him? And Earl Ingrid…if she was on the mend, he would now have to spend his days with her. Wren would have to assume a secondary position again and she shuddered at the thought.

When they reached what looked like the village square, there were bellows of excitement as one by one the people caught sight of them and realised that their chief had arrived home alive and well. Word quickly spread and more and more people began crowding round them, wanting to speak to their Jarl.

The doors to the longhouse were thrown open and more villagers rushed out to greet them. Wren stepped aside as men and women wrapped Knud up in a group embrace and he was grinning, hugging each of them back, including the children who were gripping his legs and he ruffled their hair in turn, telling each one how much they'd grown in his absence. And Wren, delighted for him, stood and watched the happy scene. They were really here. They'd made it.

Seeing she was getting pushed away, waiting awkwardly on the fringes of the group watching on, Knud stepped in. 'My friends of Nedergaard, I am glad to be home, but it would not be the case if it wasn't for Wren,' he said, presenting her to the crowd. 'And tonight, we will feast in her honour.'

And with that the people clapped and cheered and lifted them both up on their shoulders, doing a lap of honour around the enormous square, whooping in joy. Wren felt her face break out into a smile, then laughter, to be a part of it, to have come so far and to be welcomed so wholeheartedly. She savoured the moment, basking in the feeling of achievement. She suddenly felt invincible, capable of anything.

And then she saw Rædan and groups of people from Boer running into the courtyard and she was overjoyed that they had all made it here, too. She knew what this would mean to Knud, that his right-hand man was safe. Knud clambered down and Rædan clapped him on the back, pulling him into a fierce hug. 'I knew you'd make it,' Rædan said with satisfaction.

'You, too.' Knud grinned. 'This calls for a celebration, and you must fill us in on everything that's happened.'

Next Knud embraced a woman and swung her round, and she wondered who she was, feeling uncertain, jealousy burning in her stomach. But then he turned and immediately introduced her. 'Wren, this is my sister, Brita.'

'Welcome, Wren.'

'Thank you. I have heard much about you.'

Brita matched her brother in height and colouring, her long blonde hair intricately braided. She was a very attractive woman. 'Knud tells me you are a healer, Brita? Would you be so kind as to tell me, did my... did Earl Ingrid make it here last night?'

'She did,' Brita reassured her with a smile. 'And she is doing well.'

Wren almost wilted in relief. 'Thank you for looking after her. Earl Ingrid hadn't awoken in a whole day and night and we were growing more and more uneasy for her health.'

'I'll take you to see her now and then we can get you cleaned up. Come with me.'

Wren glanced back at Knud, hoping he might follow, but he had been commandeered by his men, so she stuck with Brita as they walked up the steps into the hall—and she drew in a breath of astonishment. It was far grander than the hall in Boer. It was much bigger, with a huge open fire roaring in the centre, a soaring ceiling and long tables and benches stretching the length of the building. There was a large wooden single seat at the head of the hall and she could just picture Jarl Knud sitting there.

'I'm sure Knud will be along in a moment,' the woman said. 'But they have much to fill him in on.'

Had Brita said that because she'd noticed her crestfallen face? Wren wondered. She would have to do better at masking her feelings in the coming days.

Brita directed her to a small room at the back of the longhouse, where Earl Ingrid looked comfortable, sleeping on a mass of furs. She spotted the trundle next to the bed and Wren couldn't believe the thing had held out, that it had got her ruler here. Her fingers were still sore from winding the wood that first night and blisters were beginning to appear from carrying it, but it had worked and she felt gratified for her part in it.

'Did you carry her all this way?' Brita asked.

She nodded. 'Between us, yes.'

'That's very impressive, Wren. You must be exhausted.'

Wren filled Knud's sister in on what she'd applied

to Earl Ingrid's wounds, as told to do so by the healer at the market.

'You've done well. It looks clean and like it should heal nicely. Her skin isn't too hot. I will keep giving her water, but you and Knud have already done the hardest part. It wouldn't surprise me if she was awake within days.'

'That is so good to hear,' Wren said, genuinely pleased.

'Now I think you deserve to be rewarded with a bath and a good hearty stew. I can take you to the beach to bathe if you wish to and find you some clean clothes. But we'd better be quick before the children come looking for me.' She winked.

'Thank you,' Wren said, tears stinging her eyes. She had never known such compassion before, apart from that bestowed on her by this woman's brother.

'You can stay here, in this room, with Earl Ingrid if it's suitable?'

'You are very kind.'

Soaking in the crystal-clear waters of the fjord, with just Brita on the beach standing guard, Wren relished the feeling of lying back and washing her sore, weary body. As she did so, her mind kept going over all the events of the past few days and it was funny how she only seemed to focus on the good things that had happened, not the unpleasant ones. It was as if the journey hadn't been tough, but wonderful—life-changing. She felt bone-achingly tired, but satisfied that she had fulfilled her duty, and knowing Earl Ingrid was going to pull through simply enhanced it all.

She knew Forsa's men would also be heading this way—it was inevitable, but she tried to put the dark thoughts out of her head for now. They'd just have to trust in Knud's plans and make sure they were ready. And then what? If they survived, would Earl Ingrid try to reclaim Boer once she'd gathered her strength? Was there to be a wedding?

Jealousy smarted at the thought. Even though the marriage alliance would be beneficial to her, knowing Knud didn't keep thralls, she didn't want him to marry Earl Ingrid, she admitted to herself. He could do better. And yet he seemed so set on this wedding, as did her leader. The image of Knud kissing Ingrid filled her mind and had her lowering herself under the water, shaking her head, trying to rid herself of the disturbing thoughts. How could she bear to see them together? Could she stay here, thrall or not, and watch it happen?

Returning to the small room at the back of the longhouse, Brita kindly lent her some clothes and helped her into them—a pale grey tunic that matched her eyes and a deep purple pinafore, which they fastened with two simple brooches. Brita averted her gaze as she dressed—not mentioning her collar or her scars—and she took Wren by the arm as she led her out into the busy hall, finding her a seat and some food. She introduced Wren to her five children, who were tearing about the place, but made to stand still long enough just to say hello, and Wren laughed. So Knud was an uncle several times over...

Next she met Rædan's wife, Rebekah, and their two children, and she was starting to see why Knud might feel it was time for him to settle down and have a family of his own.

She felt an enormous sense of contentment. Everyone had been so welcoming. But she couldn't help glancing around, looking for the man who she had spent the past few days with. She hadn't seen him since they'd arrived and she was ridiculously missing seeing his handsome face, having him to talk to and make her laugh.

'He'll be here in a moment,' Brita whispered, patting her hand.

She flushed furiously. 'I was just wondering if he was all right after the journey. He's probably having a well-earned rest.'

'Drinking ale with his men, more likely.' Brita winked.

And Wren smiled.

As if his ears had been burning, the heavy doors to the hall were suddenly pushed open and Knud was there, walking into the hall with Rædan and the others. Her stomach flipped at the sight of him and when his eyes locked on hers, he smiled, heading straight for her.

He took her breath away, as he had that night she'd first seen him at the pool. Dressed in a fresh dark tunic with a gold edge, and dark trousers, with washed, damp hair, combed and pulled back into a band, and a neatly trimmed beard, he looked perfect, she thought wistfully.

He lifted his long legs over the bench to sit down

next to her and his men did the same, all finding a seat round the table. As they all piled in, he was pushed closer towards her and his thigh and arm pressed against hers. She felt the immediate, familiar response of heat flaring low in her belly and she knew she should move away, but she really didn't want to.

'That's a pretty dress,' he said. 'Rather less feral than before. You're glowing, Wren. All that fresh air and activity must have been good for you.'

He had been good for her, she thought.

'I missed being away from you for all of half an afternoon,' he whispered, leaning in, a huge grin on his face.

And she couldn't help but return it as she sipped on her ale.

She had never been allowed to sit as part of a group at a table before. She'd always served others, and it felt so good to be surrounded by Knud's family and friends. Everything he'd told her about this place seemed to be true—no one mentioned her bonds, not seeming to notice or perhaps feel it right to speak of them. Instead, everyone listened to her and their chief regale them with the story of their perilous journey across the mudflats.

Revisiting the obstacles they had overcome, she felt proud of herself, and him, for all they'd accomplished. He nudged her in a conspiratorial gesture from time to time, and she realised she didn't want this feeling to end. She felt alive when she was with him, as if she was really living for the first time. He made her feel as if she was important. And his people seemed to embrace her as one of their own, not caring about her rank, just accepting that she had helped, that she was a valued part of this. That they were all in this together.

They heard how Rædan and the rest of Knud's men, and many from Boer, had managed to escape, fighting their way to freedom before crawling along the hinterland in the dark, amid the brush and bracken, getting covered in mud and scratches, until they'd reached Hafranes. It was amazing that they hadn't bumped into any of them along the way, but she guessed she and Knud had likely been a whole night behind them.

And it was good to regroup with the people of Boer. They were grateful to Knud for his men's help. The trauma of losing their home but being rescued and welcomed into Nedergaard seemed to have brought them all closer somehow. Their newfound approval and appreciation for her for looking after Earl Ingrid was a little harder to get used to, creating a warm feeling in her chest. It felt wonderful to be recognised and acknowledged for once.

Yet even with this all going on, she couldn't deny she missed having Knud to herself. He had single-handedly renewed her faith in men. And feeling his thigh pressed against hers, his arm touching her skin as they both held their tankards on the table, neither of them seeming to want to break the connection, she felt a fool for having stopped their kissing last night. If she hadn't, would he have continued? Just how far would they have gone? She wondered what it would have been like if they'd met under different circumstances, if she hadn't been a thrall, if she was the woman who could give him what he needed…

After everyone had eaten the wild boar and vegetables that Brita and many other women had happily served up, all pulling together, and as the ale continued to flow, Knud reluctantly excused himself from her company and went to stand on the raised platform. He used the palm of his hand to bang on the nearest table to demand silence.

'Friends,' he said and all talk and movement around the room abruptly came to a stop, the people wanting to hear what their chief had to say. He stood tall, his wide stance conveying the confidence he felt in his position here, and she marvelled at what a beautiful man he was.

'It is good to be back here with you in Nedergaard.' In response to his words, the cheers and heckles from the people showed he was clearly loved and respected. 'I am so pleased that most of those who came with me to Boer have made it back safely. And to our new friends from Boer, you are most welcome here for as long as you'd like to stay. Let it be known that we will stand by you and help you regain your fortress as soon as we are able.'

The people of Boer began banging their tankards on the table in a sign of solidarity and appreciation.

'But first, we have much work to do,' he said, his face turning serious. 'Our enemy is just days behind us and we have seen what they are capable of. On the morrow, we must pull together and get ourselves ready for a fight. Every sword, shield and scythe will be required.

'But for one last night, let us put that out of our minds, for we must celebrate those who fell in battle and honour those who are the heroes in this fight—let's hope right now they are feasting in the Great Hall of Valhalla. But now I would like you all to raise your cups and make a toast to someone incredibly brave, without whom neither the leader of Boer nor of Nedergaard would be here right now. To Wren. *Skal.*'

All of the people in the hall raised their cups and repeated the toast. 'To Wren. *Skal.*'

Knud motioned to her with his cup, tipping the last of his ale down his throat, not breaking their gaze.

Wren felt her heart might burst with pride—and something else…

But then, out of nowhere, a stumbling, ghostly figure approached Knud where he stood at the top of the room, drawing Wren's eyes away from him. She gasped. It was…

'Earl Ingrid. You're awake!' Knud said, sounding just as shocked as Wren felt.

The hall fell silent. She looked frail, yet her face was stone-hard as her eyes swept all around the hall in disgust, taking in the happy scene before her, as if it was in extremely bad taste after she'd nearly been killed, after she'd lost her stronghold. 'I am indeed.'

As Ingrid scoured the room, her piercing gaze finally finding what she was looking for, Wren's skin prickled in anticipation as it always did when something bad was about to happen. Earl Ingrid glared at her, sat among Knud's men, very much part of the gathering, and being honoured with a toast no less, and her lips curled.

'Wren! What are you doing sitting at that table? Get away from there immediately.'

Wren blanched at her harsh words, immediately pulling her out of her happy state, and fumbled to stand, conditioned to obey.

'I invited her, Earl Ingrid,' Knud said.

'Well, you shouldn't have,' she replied, lancing him with a look. 'And where did you get that dress?' she said, turning back to her bond servant.

'It was given to me.'

'You will take it off at once,' she barked, as if disgusted by her thrall's blatant disobedience.

'Earl Ingrid, we are glad to see you up and about,' Knud interjected firmly. 'But you should know it was Wren who helped me bring you back here, putting her own life at risk to stay behind and help you, and then making the challenging journey. I couldn't have done it without her.'

But this only seemed to make Ingrid more angry. 'Who'd have thought you had it in you?' she sneered. 'Now take off the dress.'

Wren's toes curled up in shame, knowing everyone in the room could see and feel her discomfort. It was mortifying.

'I must insist she leaves it on, Earl Ingrid. This is my settlement and therefore my rules. Perhaps you are not feeling well…'

'I am quite well, Jarl Knud. And I won't have my slave running around in such attire. Take it off. Now.'

Wren clenched her jaw. It seemed Earl Ingrid had decided to refuse to recognise her contribution to saving her life and bringing her here, instead determined to put her back in her place. She had never felt so unappreciated. Anger simmered in her stomach, like hot water bubbling up under the surface of a geyser, and she used it to feed her strength, her defiance.

A few days ago, she would have taken this insult, swallowed down her hurt, but now? She could no longer bear it. Not now she'd had a taste of freedom. Not after she'd risked her life—and Knud's—for this woman's. What made her life any more valuable than theirs? And most of all, she knew she couldn't let Knud fight all her battles and witness her total and utter degradation.

Wanting to expose her ruler's foolishness, she drew herself up to full height and thrust her chin forward. 'I just saved your life, Earl Ingrid. Is this all the thanks I get?' she said, offering her a challenging stare.

'You will do as I say and remove yourself from that table and those clothes before I have you whipped.'

Gasps and dark mutterings rumbled around the hall.

'I am still the Earl of Boer and your owner and you shall obey my rules.' Ingrid added in an icy voice. 'You only continue to breathe because I say you can.'

Wren drew her fingers into fists, her eyes burning with unshed angry tears. 'You flatter yourself, Earl Ingrid. Your father took my life many winters ago and I have barely lived under your family's rule ever since.'

For once she was determined to have the last word. 'And perhaps I will strive to break your rules as I have no respect for the person who made them. I have clearly done something to offend you and I shall now take my leave. But if you wish to punish me, Earl Ingrid, then you shall have to come after me and drag me back here yourself.'

She had a strong desire to turn and flee, but instead she forced herself to walk slowly out of the hall, her head held high, aware of everyone's eyes on her. Aware she could get pulled back by one of Earl Ingrid's men from Boer and punished at any moment. Only when she reached the courtyard did she allow herself to break out into a run, her stomach heaving, her throat burning. And finally, when she reached the deserted moonlit beach, she allowed herself to sink into the sand and let her tears fall.

'I thought I'd find you here.'

Wren rubbed her eyes, knowing they must be red and puffy, her face streaked with tears, and she suddenly felt vulnerable and exposed. She prided herself on being tough—she had never let anyone see her cry before.

Knud came and knelt down before her and reached out to take her chin in his fingers. 'Are you all right?'

She shrugged. Her chin quivered with the effort of keeping in her tears and she nodded, sitting up on her hip, her legs curled out behind her. 'You'd think... you'd think she'd be at least a little grateful, for my—our—help.'

'She should be most grateful.'

'I saved her because I wanted to. Because it was the right thing to do. But you were right. I thought... I began to hope, somewhere deep down, the further we went on, that because I saved her life, she might save mine by setting me free. Instead, I'll probably be punished now for speaking out against her...'

'Not if I can help it. I'll talk to her.'

'Why would you do that?'

He took a strand of her hair in his fingers, tucking it behind her ear. 'We're a team, aren't we?'

She stared up into his eyes, seeking some of his strength. A team. She liked the sound of that.

'I feel like the last few days I was given a taste of freedom—only to be caught and imprisoned again. And now her harsh words seem so much worse than before. They really hurt me.'

'I understand.' He took her hand loosely in his. 'I think we were all shocked by the way Earl Ingrid behaved in there. But she's returned to bed now—Brita said she's asleep. Won't you come back to the longhouse?'

She shook her head.

'We were having fun back there, weren't we? With all my people. Everyone in that hall was on your side.'

She shrugged a slim shoulder. 'I suppose I hoped I could earn people's respect.'

'You have. Not many people would have stayed behind to help your ruler like you did, Wren. Not many people would have made that journey to try to save her, let alone survived it. Everyone is in awe of you.'

'*You* did. Perhaps you shouldn't have stayed behind to look after her after all,' she said bitterly.

'I didn't,' he admitted. 'You saved her—and I stayed behind in Boer for you.'

'What?' She shook her head a little, not understanding.

His thumb stroked over the top of her hand. 'On the battlefield. I knew I needed to help Earl Ingrid, but I wanted to stay for you.'

She swallowed. Her feelings were bubbling right beneath the surface tonight, like a hot spring ready to erupt. Perhaps she was tired from the long journey. Or perhaps it had everything to do with the man in front of her, making her feel things more deeply...

'Me? Why?'

'I told you,' he said, lowering his head, holding her gaze. 'I wanted to kiss you from the moment I first saw you. I felt this compulsion to rescue you. I still do.' And then he lifted her hand and bent his head to place the softest kiss on the inner crease of her arm, sending shivers across her skin.

On hearing his words, having his lips on her skin again and feeling reckless enough to cast her good judgement aside, she leaned forward and planted a reciprocal kiss on his lips. She didn't know what possessed her to be so brazen—she wasn't thinking, just acting on his words, her feelings. She'd been wanting to kiss him again since this morning, regretting pushing him away last night.

When she sat back, he cocked his head to one side, studying her. 'Was that to get back at Earl Ingrid or do you really like me?' he said, his smile building.

She shook her head, laughing. She loved how he always managed to break the tension. 'You do keep telling me to follow my instincts,' she said.

'They're good instincts,' he acknowledged with a grin. But then he sobered. 'I don't want to take advantage of you, Wren. I respect you too much. I still need an army to keep Nedergaard safe...'

She knew what he was saying. Still, she bravely leaned forward and rested her forehead against his. 'I understand,' she said. 'But just for one night, can we put the future out of our minds and forget about everyone else? I only need this one night. Can you give that to me?'

She had her answer when he pulled her closer towards him, wrapping her up in his strong arms, holding her against his chest. It felt so good to be held by him again. She thought she could stay like this for ever, protected in his arms, under the blanket of stars above. But then he was taking her face in his hands and taking her lips with his. Her eyelids fluttered shut. She didn't want to think any more, she just knew she wanted him to take control again, as he had in the middle of last night, making her feel all those exquisite sensations.

While his thumbs stroked her cheeks, his lips were firm, holding her mouth open as his tongue caressed hers, making her tremble in pleasure. Her hands came up to curl over his shoulders and clasp around his neck and he tugged her closer, into his lap, and she couldn't believe this was happening again. She couldn't believe he wanted her as badly as she wanted him.

Her confidence building, she pulled him down

with her as she lay back on the soft, cool sand, and he stopped kissing her for a moment, looking down at her.

'Are you sure about this?' he said.

And she nodded.

He bent his head and kissed her again, and she relished him taking ownership of her mouth, his tongue stroking hers, and she writhed beneath him, wanting him to put his hands on her skin and stroke her body as he'd begun to do last night. As if he could read her thoughts, his hand smoothed over her shoulder, down to skate over her chest and curve over her breast, and he gently squeezed.

She arched into him, wanting more, whimpering softly. His expert fingers flicked the clasp on one of the brooches, letting the strap of her pinafore fall, and he tugged the opening of her tunic, pushing aside the material so he could move his fingers over her heated skin. She gasped in anticipation of his touch.

Then his palm was moulding to her bare flesh, cupping her breast in his hand, teasing her nipples into taut, tight peaks between his fingers, and her head tipped back in pleasure. His lips pressed gentle kisses near her ear and down her throat to her chest, and she pulled his head down farther, wanting his hot mouth to join his fingers at her breast. But he stalled, smiling down at her.

'That night at the marsh pond, when you got out of the water—my eyes were drawn to you,' he whispered. 'I wanted to do this to you then.'

Then at last his mouth complied with her silent urging, following where his fingers had already blazed a trail, knowing where she wanted him, and she squirmed beneath him as he suckled her rosy bud between his lips, making heat and liquid excitement pool between her legs.

He lifted his head to kiss her on her mouth again and pressed his body harder down on hers, both of them needing more pressure, more friction.

'I want to touch you, see you everywhere,' he whispered, and his words matched her desire to strip away their clothes and get closer. 'Do you want that too, Wren?'

She nodded. She wanted this. She wanted him to take possession of her body. She wanted to belong to him. She wanted him to claim her—no one else.

He lifted himself away from her and tugged her up to a sitting position. 'But not here,' he said, glancing all around them on the moonlit beach, checking no one else was nearby. 'Come with me.'

She didn't think she could walk, let alone stand—her legs felt too weak, trembling with desire—but she was somehow putting one foot in front of the other as he took her hand and led her down the beach, past the dark water of the glittering fjord lapping at the shore and the longships quietly bobbing about to the side of the jetty. They walked a little way until they came to a hut and he pushed open the door. Inside, the floor was covered in straw and there was a horse in a pen up in the corner, gently chewing on hay.

'Do you mind if we have an audience?' he asked.

And she shook her head, smiling shyly. She didn't trust her voice to speak.

She stood, shaking, as he unclasped his cloak and spread it out on the floor. Then he came towards her, tilting her face up towards him before he unclasped the other brooch on her pinafore, the other strap coming loose, and the garment dropped to pool around her ankles on the floor, leaving her in just her tunic. He motioned with his hands for her to lower herself down and she was grateful to sit again, steadying her legs.

Kneeling in front of each other, he took her hands in his, looking into her eyes.

'Just tell me if you want to stop,' he said seriously before pulling her back towards him, slowly picking up where they'd left off on the beach. His kisses were deep and all-consuming as his hands smoothed over her back, still being careful of her wounds, and then round over her ribcage and up to her breasts again. And her fingers roamed up into his hair, caressing the back of his head. He gripped the material of her tunic between his fingers, skilfully working it over her hips, navigating it over her bottom before lifting it off her, her arms outstretched above, helping him.

'I've seen you in your undergarments twice now, but nothing compares to seeing you up close. Being able to touch you,' he said, leaning in to nibble her ears, reaching out to cup her breasts in his hands again, feeling the weight of her.

'Twice? I thought you promised not to look when I was bathing.'

He grinned. 'I peeked a little, I couldn't help it,' he admitted. 'Forgive me. You're too stunning not to be looked at.' And then he pushed her down so she was lying on her back and in an instant he'd whisked away her undergarments, rolling them down her legs and lifting them away so she lay naked beside him, his eyes raking over her.

She willed herself to keep her hands by her side, to try not to cover herself up, as this was what he was telling her he wanted. He wanted to look at her. And she hoped she pleased him. She writhed beneath his heated gaze, pressing her thighs together. What was happening to her? She felt nervous and yet lustful all at once, wanting more.

He sat back on his knees so he could study her, and his gaze heated. He pulled his own tunic off over his head before his body came down to stretch out beside hers, holding himself up on his elbow. 'You are the most beautiful woman I've ever seen,' he said, reaching his hand out to trail his fingers between her breasts and down over her flat stomach.

He kissed the sensitive spot beneath her ears, making her gasp, before kneading her breast again, enjoying seeing her creamy flesh beneath his fingers and watching her reactions to his touch. She noticed he moved his hands over her skin slowly, unhurriedly, building her trust—and her excitement. It reminded her of his slowly building smile.

The need to touch and explore him in return was too great and so she allowed her fingers to drift over the corners of his mouth, pushing a finger inside, and he kissed and sucked it, and then her moist fingertip trailed over his injured shoulder.

'How is it feeling?' she asked.

'All better now,' he lied, as if he was not thinking about his wound at all right now.

And so she continued her exploration down, over his muscular chest—traversing his scars and his ink, curious. He was magnificent. She marvelled at his solid exterior, even though she knew now he was tender underneath.

'Who did this for you?' she asked, her eyes roving over the large creature etched on his skin, feeling as if she could properly study it now.

'One of the women in Nedergaard.'

'So she's seen you naked? Should I be jealous?'

He chuckled. 'No. Absolutely not. She's old enough to be my mother!'

His large hand stroked over her stomach and roamed lower, while his knee came down between her thighs, parting her legs, and suddenly she felt feverish, knowing he was getting her ready for where he intended to touch her next, knowing he meant to satisfy the need building inside her, and her breath quickened. Heat tore through her as the tips of his fingers drove through the triangle of hair at the junction of her thighs, intimately curling into it.

'You've never been touched like this before?' he asked.

She shook her head. 'Only above clothes, unwanted.'

'I'll be gentle. I promise.'

And she knew he would be. His hand stole down to curve over her moist heat, and she gasped as pleasure rippled through her. His palm pressed against her tiny nub, before his knuckles slid down her crease, open-

ing her up to him. And then he pushed a finger inside
her and she moaned, holding his body to her, burying
her head in his shoulder.

But he lifted his face to stare down at her. 'Look at
me, Wren. How does it feel?' he asked.

She nodded, unable to speak, unable to put into
words the pleasure he was creating. She felt the hard-
ness of his cock nudging into her parted thigh, pressing
down on her leg to hold her open as he slid his finger
inside her more deeply, before slowly drawing it out
again, bringing with him a rush of moisture, before
delving back inside her again—and she never, ever
wanted this feeling to end.

His molten brown gaze stared down at her, and her
breathing became frantic. She was aware her head had
tipped back and, as he pushed her legs farther apart,
allowing him to stroke her even more intimately, pushing a second finger inside, she cried out as the pleasure reached its peak and she came apart, trembling
in ecstasy.

When she came to a few minutes later, he was above
her, kissing her temple, her earlobes, her mouth, and she
wrapped her legs tight around the back of his thighs,
not wanting to let him go.

He was still straining against his trousers, pressing
into her flesh, and she knew she needed to touch him
in return, to repay him for all the incredible things he'd
just done to her. But where should she begin? She had
no clue how to do this. She closed her eyes briefly as
she bravely reached her hand down between them and
tugged at the waistband of his trousers, trying to push

them down, not wanting any clothing barrier between them. And then he was right there, his silky hot skin against the moist heat of her most sensitive parts.

'Wren? Touch me.' It was a whispered direction, as he wrapped her hand around the base of his cock, showing her how to hold him. And he groaned, his forehead resting against hers.

His fingers still covering hers, he showed her how to move her hand up and down him, while guiding him to her entrance, replacing where his fingers had been moments ago. She wanted this so badly. She wanted him inside her, more than anything. She was ready.

And with a gentle thrust, he granted all her wishes. The tip of his shaft entered her body, making her gasp and writhe.

'Wren?' he whispered. 'Keep looking at me.'

She moved her ankles farther up his legs, opening her hips, wanting to hold him in place, wanting him deeper, wanting all of him, everything he could give. 'You feel good,' she said as she bucked beneath him, encouraging him on, trying to bring her body up to take him farther inside.

He grinned at her movements, as if knowing she was ready for more, knowing he was driving her crazy.

'Do you want more of me?' he asked.

'Yes,' she whispered. 'All of you.'

And as if it was all he had needed to hear, he thrust again, harder this time, his body sliding all the way inside her, and she cried out in pleasure. His one hand caught her wrists above her head and his other gripped her bottom, bringing her right up against him, as he impaled her body with his, filling her up, taking her so completely, so slowly, so intimately, that her climax came thick and fast, causing his speed to quicken, his excitement to tip over. As her muscles spasmed strongly around him, it had him roaring out his own intense, powerful release inside her.

They lay there like that for a long time, trying to catch their breath, until, after a while, he lifted his head to look down at her beneath him, her dark hair splayed out across the straw. 'I think we should let you follow your instincts more often,' he said with approval.

She smiled happily, her cheeks glowing pink with pleasure.

And then she realised his arms were trembling. A strong man such as he. 'Are you all right?' she asked. Had it been as intense for him as it had been for her?

'Shouldn't I be asking you that question?' He laughed, his voice gruff.

He eased himself out of her and the loss of heat, of connection, wasn't pleasant, making her whimper a little. He rolled off her gently, resting back on his cloak on the hay, tugging her into his still-intact shoulder, pulling her in for a hug, and she lay her head on his chest, feeling it steadily rise and fall. 'I'm fine. Are you all right?'

'Never better.'

He seemed so at ease in this situation, she thought, his one hand casually behind his head, his knee bent, his taut, muscular body on show for her to see it in all its glory. And yet his breathing still seemed decidedly shaky, as was hers.

She wasn't sure what to say or do, so she just lay quietly in his arms, tucking herself into him to hide some of her nakedness, enjoying his fingers grazing over the skin on her shoulder, then down to stroke her hip, like he'd done that day in the cave. She didn't think she could move—her limbs felt so heavy, her body sated.

She would endure anything—go through all the anguish of the past few days, even the past fifteen winters, if it all led her to this one moment, and being here with him. To what they'd just done together. Was this to be her reward for all her suffering?

'I feel different,' she whispered.

'I tend to have that effect,' he teased. 'You look different, too. You have a rosy glow.'

'I felt it before this,' she tutted. 'Before what we just did.'

'How do you mean?' he asked, his fingers now back on her shoulder, trailing over the small inked mark there, as if it fascinated him.

'Like my eyes have been opened to a whole new world. Like I'm awake for the first time in my life. That is, until I was reminded of my place earlier…beneath everyone.'

'Beneath me isn't so bad, though, is it?' he said with a wicked smile.

She gently punched him in the chest, laughing, but he caught her face and kissed her softly on the lips. And then his tongue swept inside her again, tasting her deeply, as if he couldn't get enough of her, just like she couldn't get enough of him. And then he rolled on to his side, pulling her against him, looking into her eyes, deepening the connection. He tugged her leg over his hip and she was aware his shaft was throbbing between her thighs again. She was glad she had the same effect on him as he did on her.

When he released her lips, she was breathless.

'Now I've come so far, I don't want to go back,' she said, looking up at him.

'I know. I will pay for you to purchase your freedom, Wren,' he said, suddenly serious. 'Whatever the cost.'

'Even if you try, I fear she won't allow it,' she said, shaking her head. 'And she'll wonder why… I think she got so angry before, in the hall, because she heard you praising me. You know even being here with me is a risk, don't you?' It was forbidden. He wasn't above punishment for bedding another earl's thrall without permission. There would be drastic consequences for them both if they were caught.

But as he thrust inside her again, taking her to the brink almost immediately once more, he whispered, 'It would have been worth it.'

Chapter Seven

'Where have you been?'

Rædan caught Knud re-entering the back of the long-house at first light, his clothes back on, but carrying his boots so as not to make a sound on the wooden floor.

'Nowhere.'

'Really?' his friend said sceptically, his eyebrows raised, leaning back in his seat by the fire. He propped up his legs and crossed them slowly. 'You know you can't lie to me. Your eyes betray how you really feel.'

'What are you talking about?' Knud said shortly, irritated.

'Wren. You couldn't keep your eyes off her when you first saw her in the square in Boer—and then at Earl Ingrid's feast. And you couldn't keep your eyes off her in the hall last night, either… I've never seen you like this before. Was she all right, after what happened?'

'Not really.' He shrugged, throwing his boots down in the corner.

'But you made it all better?' Rædan winked.

Usually, Knud would have laughed at his friend baiting him about a woman, knowing he meant no harm, but right now, he didn't feel like smiling. He didn't know how he felt. He raked a hand through his dishevelled hair. He was still angry about the way Earl Ingrid had behaved in his hall, in front of his people, and the way she'd treated Wren, and he couldn't help feeling he should have stepped in and done more.

But Rædan was right, he had helped put it out of Wren's mind afterwards. He had kissed away her tears and more. It had been an incredible night. She had the most beautiful body he'd ever seen…and her touch, it did things to him, stirred him in ways he'd never known, making his body tremble. He'd taken her body with his more than once, unable to get enough of her, unable to satiate his desire for her. Was that what he'd been hoping for? That he could bed her and rid himself of these unsettling feelings he had for her?

He'd wanted to make her his since the moment he'd first seen her and, now he had, he should be satisfied. His desire for her should be ebbing away. So why wasn't it? Holding her in his arms as she slept, after he'd stormed her body for the second time, he still hadn't wanted to leave her.

He'd taken her innocence—was it wrong of him? It hadn't felt wrong at the time, it had felt natural. So very right. So why was he feeling like a complete and utter bastard now? He scowled. Yet despite that, all he wanted to do was go back there, pull her close and claim her body all over again. He wanted to stare down into her wild grey eyes and get lost in them as she allowed him to lose himself inside her body.

But then the guilt came, thick and fast. Not just for Wren, but for Annegrete, too. The betrayal made him feel sick. He should not be having these feelings for another woman. He had vowed never to let this happen again. And yet, even while he was battling with himself, he struggled to bring Annegrete's face into his mind, only seeing Wren there instead.

'Are you still determined to go ahead with this ridiculous farce of a marriage to Earl Ingrid?' Rædan asked. Was he trying to wind him up, provoke him? Could his friend not see he wasn't in the mood for this? His wounds were smarting cruelly and he rubbed his hand over his chest to try to ease his pain.

'As I've already told you, this ridiculous farce of a marriage, as you call it, can enhance my power. It could keep you and your family safe, as well as the rest of our people,' Knud said sharply, pouring himself an ale. He downed a whole tankard in one go, before drawing the back of his hand across his mouth.

'Perhaps. But at what cost? Does your happiness not mean anything?'

'No, it doesn't.'

'Then you're a fool. You deserve to be content, just like the rest of us. We're big boys and girls, Knud, we can all take care of ourselves. Don't you think it's time you stopped trying to punish yourself for something that happened many winters ago?'

'I don't want to talk about it,' Knud said, pushing past him.

Rædan gripped his arm, holding him fast. 'No, you never do. But maybe you need to hear it, before it's too late, from someone who cares about you, who's looking out for you. You're letting your guilt about the past—and your fear about the future—affect your ability to open up to people, to love again.'

'You're wrong, I don't feel fear,' Knud denied, shrugging him off.

'No? So you're not afraid to tell Wren how you really feel. And not just show her the way you showed her last night—I mean really make it known?'

'You don't know how I feel. I don't even know how I feel!' he said, throwing his hands up in despair. But through his frustration, he knew what his friend was saying was right. He struggled to let anyone get close. Brita and Rædan were the only people he tended to share his thoughts with and even then he kept them to a minimum.

'Have you told her about your past? About Annegrete?'

Knud drew in a breath and released it slowly, trying to quell his anger. 'A little.'

Rædan raised his eyebrows.

'Not much,' he conceded. 'You know I never want to talk about it. Besides, my past has nothing to do with Wren. She doesn't need to know.' The truth was he didn't want Wren to know about his earlier failings, all the wrong choices he'd made. For then she wouldn't look up at him with the same admiration she had earlier, would she? She would be bound to see him differently.

Guilt, for all the death and devastation he'd brought upon his settlement and his wife with his selfish desire for glory, came rearing back up, hitting him full force. And then came the familiar feelings of loss and abandonment. If Annegrete had really loved him, she wouldn't have done what she'd done in the end, destroying him in return.

'Anyway I'm a jarl and Wren's a thrall...'

'Sounds like you and me once. Look how far we've come since then.'

Knud shook his head. 'And right now, you're making me regret it.' He grimaced.

Rædan sucked in a breath and Knud knew he'd gone too far. He dragged his hand across his face.

'I didn't mean that, you know I didn't. I'm sorry, my friend. I'm just saying she belongs to Earl Ingrid. Who would never allow it—anything—to happen between us.'

'Might be a little late for that,' Rædan said wryly. 'And since when have you let anyone get in the way of something you want?' he asked.

Knud sighed heavily.

Rædan stood and placed a hand on his shoulder. 'I know you're trying to right a past wrong—something everyone else has already forgiven you for, even if you can't forgive yourself. If you feel you need to look after everyone as their Jarl, then that's all right, but punishing yourself like this is taking it one step too far. Annegrete shouldn't stop you, either. She would want you to be happy, Knud. She made her choice a long time ago. Don't you think it's now time for you to make yours?'

Knud kept himself busy all morning, first sitting around one of the tables in the longhouse with a handful of his most trusted men, coming up with a plan to make the settlement more secure in light of Forsa's imminent attack, and then heading outside, commanding his people, deciding who to put on what tasks.

They were fortunate they were protected on two sides by the vast glittering waters of the fjord and he didn't think Forsa had the means to launch an attack from the sea. Instead, they concentrated on starting to build up the palisade walls, creating large embankments of earth and digging ditches on the inland approaches. He also asked a group of men and women to make more weapons. It was amazing what they could achieve when they all pulled together.

But despite the enormous undertaking, he was struggling to focus. He hadn't seen Wren all morning. He knew it was a good thing, because if he saw her, he'd want to pull her to one side and make her his again, and right now he had so much to do. Yet it didn't stop his mind drifting back to her constantly—the way she'd felt in his arms last night, the taste of her mouth on his and the feel of her breasts as he'd tweaked her pert nipples.

He'd slid inside her tight body so perfectly, as if she was made for him, and he'd come so hard and so fast the first time, blinded by the pleasure of being inside her, that the second time he'd been determined to make it last, thrusting slowly, torturing them both, teasing her, building up the pressure until she couldn't take it any more, until she'd thrashed beneath him, finally begging him to finish and give her that sweet release. And then, when dawn had arrived, he'd struggled to leave her warm embrace.

* * *

The things they'd done together kept interrupting his day, as did the words Rædan had spoken to him afterwards. *Did* he deserve to be happy? And could being with Wren make him so? His friend obviously thought so. After Annegrete, he didn't think he'd ever feel this way about a woman again. He had never wanted to, determined to be loyal to his wife. He owed her that.

Of course he had bedded women since, too many, to help ease his pain for a short while, or for a quick release—after all, he was a man, he had needs. But he had locked his heart away, promising himself he wouldn't ever care for another. But now Wren had come into his life, totally unexpectedly, making his pulse race like it never had before. Was Rædan right—was he afraid to let her get too close?

He tried to push his thoughts away as he concentrated on helping his men dig the trenches. The only thing he was certain of right now was that he had to try to fix Wren's situation. He couldn't allow another outburst from Earl Ingrid like the one everyone had witnessed last night. No, he had to make things right and he could start by attempting to break her slavery bonds. To do so, he would have to win the Earl of Boer around to his way of thinking.

He had begun to ask around his men last night if any of them had come across the name Orm, or Neva, but he'd been met with blank faces and many of them shaking their heads. It was frustrating. Someone must know something. He was fascinated by the mark on Wren's shoulder, too, and had found his fingers straying to stroke over its lines during the night. He was determined to find out what it meant.

His blood chilled when he heard the warning horn echoing across the settlement, and he and Rædan dropped their scythes and raced up to the top of the lookout tower. Surely the enemy weren't upon them already? But he was relieved to see it wasn't Forsa's men who were approaching, winding their way down the path from the forest, but another force entirely, who looked as if they hadn't yet seen any fighting. Were these Earl Ingrid's warriors? They must be. His heart lifted in hope.

After speaking to the leader of the army, who said they'd come as fast as they could after receiving word of what had happened in Boer, and that they hadn't encountered any of Forsa's men on their journey, Knud instructed his guards to welcome the soldiers through their newly constructed borders.

Then he went in search of Earl Ingrid, to tell her of the developments. If she wasn't in a better mood this morning, perhaps this might help. He certainly needed to get her on his side before bargaining for Wren's freedom.

Making his way to the back of the longhouse, he found the Earl sitting up in bed, where Brita was tending to her wound. It seemed to be healing rapidly.

'Excuse the interruption, Earl Ingrid. I am glad to see you are looking brighter today.'

'Well, your sister is a wonderful healer, Jarl Knud.'

'I know,' he said, resting his hand on Brita's shoulder and giving her a gentle squeeze. 'Thank you.'

'Should we be readying to fight? We heard the ox horn.'

'No, it is good news I bring you. Your army is just this moment making its way into Nedergaard.' And he told her all that the leader of her force had said.

'That is very good news, Jarl Knud.'

'And now you're back on your feet, I wanted to talk to you about our plans going forward...'

'I shall take my leave, so you two can speak alone,' Brita said, giving Knud a knowing look, and she left the room, pulling the door closed behind her.

'Earl Ingrid, I very much hope you will allow your army to join forces with my men, who are readying themselves for Forsa's warriors to arrive. And if your army helps us to defeat them, I will assure you we will repay the favour and assist you in reclaiming Boer.'

She nodded thoughtfully. 'That is very noble of you, Jarl Knud. Thank you. But what of the marriage alliance we were discussing before all of this happened?'

He coughed awkwardly, clearing his throat. 'I have given it a lot of thought over the past few days, Earl Ingrid, and I'm not sure that a marriage between us would succeed. Yes, a union between Boer and Nedergaard could benefit us both, but I feel we want very different things for our people and ourselves.' Images of Wren gasping out her pleasure beneath him entered his thoughts and he tried to push them aside, just for now. 'It must not have escaped your attention that our opinions differ rather drastically.'

'What things do we want to do differently?' she said, getting to her feet, her brow forming a straight line.

'Well, for a start, I do not tolerate slavery in these lands. Nedergaard has been a place free of serfs for some time. I have come to realise we have very conflicting views on that matter, especially after your outburst last night.'

'I see.' She studied him, before pacing away and coming back to him, putting her hands on her hips. 'Well, I admit I wasn't feeling myself when I awoke yesterday. I am much better today. And I have given the matter some thought. If we marry, I have decided I will release all my thralls from their bonds, if it will make you happy.'

His lips parted on a gasp, shocked. He had not been expecting that. '*All* of them?'

'All of them.'

'Including Wren?'

'She is very valuable to me.' Her lips twisted. 'But, yes, if I must.'

He had thought he would have a huge battle on his hands where Wren and her freedom were concerned, knowing how much Earl Ingrid seemed to rely on her.

'Just like that?'

'I am not saying it won't be an enormous loss of property to me,' Earl Ingrid said, her face pinched, her arms crossed tightly across her chest. 'But I imagine you shall more than make up for it as my husband.'

He swallowed, his skin suddenly feeling clammy.

'And, if we fail to take back Boer, I should think I could live contentedly here in Nedergaard. I am rather beginning to like this little place. Your people have looked after me well. So, on your immediate proposal,

I shall command that my army becomes your army, Jarl Knud, and they will loyally fight under your banner. I shall release my thralls in the correct manner under our laws and you will help me to reclaim my family's fortress. Do we have an agreement?'

He blew out a breath. Could he really agree to this? He might have achieved Wren's freedom, but by doing so he was tying himself to a woman he did not care for—who had been one of the causes of his new lover's hurt over the past fifteen winters.

But this had been the plan all along, to form an alliance with Boer, and it was still a good one. He would have a very good chance against Forsa's forces and perhaps be able to keep his people safe. In doing so, he could atone for his past failures. And he could also protect his heart... Because in marrying a woman he didn't like, let alone love, he would never again suffer the hurt and grief that had broken him once before.

'Very well,' he said slowly. 'If you release your slaves now, today, and bring your army under my rule, then I accept.'

Yet even as he spoke the words, he still wondered how he could do this. He could already feel the weight of his decision falling heavy on his shoulders—the noose tightening around his neck. How could he marry Earl Ingrid when all he could think about was Wren and the things they'd done together last night? His thoughts kept returning to the sound of her breathless gasps as he'd moved inside her, the feel of her legs wrapped around him, holding on to him so tightly, trusting him completely with her body. Would she ever forgive him for this?

But surely, when she was set free, that would mean more to her than anything—more to her than him. After all, she herself had told him she never wanted to marry. She had told him that she wouldn't want a husband ruling over her—that she wanted to make her own choices. And he had to make decisions that were right for him and his people, too. Yes, she would understand his reasons for going through with this. Eventually.

'It is settled, then,' Earl Ingrid said determinedly.

And he thought it must be the most unromantic marriage proposal ever.

She held out her forearm for him to shake and he took it, sealing the deal.

Wren was helping Rebekah and some of the other women in the hall, as the children ran around them playing. A mountain of potatoes sat piled up in front of her, ready for her to peel, for they had many more mouths to feed now Boer's army had arrived. But she didn't mind. She felt as if everything was finally coming together. Now Boer's warriors were here, Knud would be relieved. It was what he had hoped for and it gave them all the extra protection they needed.

She hadn't caught sight of Knud all day and she was eager to see him. She had been missing him from the moment he left her this morning. She had tried to get him to stay, tugging him back towards her as he'd dressed, and he'd laughed, saying he had to go before someone found them there, together.

As if to compensate for him not being around, her thoughts had kept returning to them, sweaty and naked, pressed against each other, their bodies a tangle of limbs, and his brown eyes glowing down at her as he thrust inside her over and again. It had been glorious. Better than she'd ever thought it could be. Who knew a man could give a woman so much pleasure?

'Wren?' Rebekah said, trying to catch her attention. 'You didn't hear a thing I just said, did you?' The other woman laughed. 'Can you tell me what you were thinking about?'

And she blushed. She had been absorbed in her own thoughts—thoughts about him. And then, as if she'd conjured him up just by thinking about him, he was there, striding into the hall. He was coming from the back of the longhouse, his brow furrowed as if he had a huge problem to wrestle with, yet he looked more handsome than she'd ever seen him, his sleeves rolled up, his hair pulled back neatly in a band. Her mouth dried.

'Ah, I think I have my answer.' Rebekah winked knowingly.

When Knud looked up and saw her across the hall, he stopped still and she raised her hand to give him a little wave, before he nodded in acknowledgement and then frowned harder, averting his gaze. He quickly exited the longhouse on the other side, as if he couldn't even bear to be in the same room as her.

She felt choked, pain, swift and brutal, rupturing her heart. That was not the greeting she'd been expecting, especially after what they'd done together last night. After the intimacy they'd shared. She had thought he might come over to say hello, or to check on her. It wasn't as if she expected him to make his feelings towards her known to everyone, but she had thought he would at least look at her and give her that slow smile, as if they shared a secret.

When he'd left her arms this morning, his eyes had been full of… She didn't know what exactly, but she had thought that he cared about her. She knew he had struggled to leave her, and she hadn't wanted him to go. But now? It had been as if it was a different man staring back at her. A stranger, cold and aloof. It was as if he couldn't get out of there quickly enough. It was as if he felt terrible about what they'd done.

Her mind scrambled to make excuses for him. Maybe he didn't want to make a scene in front of the other women? Or perhaps he was just trying to conceal what had happened between them. Yes, that could be it.

Rebekah, having seen the brief exchange, patted her hand. 'He's complicated, but a good man. The best, so my husband always tells me.'

Wren frowned. Complicated was right. He was a man of such contradictions. He was fierce yet tender, strong yet had a softer side, ruthless yet kind and caring… And she realised, she didn't know all that much about him. Not enough anyway. She knew about his raids when he was a younger man, the little he'd told her, and she knew he was a great warrior and a wonderful leader, a loyal brother and friend.

She also knew what he looked like without his clothes on, how his magnificent body felt beneath her fingers and that he was an expert lover. But he had never revealed too much of himself, his emotions, or his hopes and his fears, not like she had shared her history with him and her desires for the future. Suddenly, she wanted to know more, to better understand him. Didn't she deserve that?

'Did you know his late wife?' she asked Rebekah and her cheeks heated again, wondering if she was laying her feelings bare by asking. Was it traitorous of her to ask someone else about his past?

'I never met her, but I heard she was very beautiful. And fierce. A true shield maiden. She ran the settlement in Jarl Knud's stead for a while.'

Of course he would have married someone like that. Wren could just picture her now—beautiful and strong. 'How did she die?'

Rebekah came to sit down beside her, picking up a potato and helping her peel.

'She drowned—a tragic accident off the rocky cliff-top up there,' she said, motioning outside in the direction of the site Wren and Knud had stood the morning before, as they'd made their approach into Nedergaard.

'That's awful,' Wren said, letting the information sink in, wondering why he hadn't said anything about it, and her heart went out to him. Was that runestone there as a mark of where she'd died? Were the carved words about his wife? None of it made any sense.

'I believe he loved her very much and has struggled to move on since her death.'

Wren nodded. She must have left a huge hole in his life. He must feel her loss every day.

'I know he once told Rædan he would never wed

again, not wanting to tarnish her memory, not wanting to be disloyal, so we were surprised when he made the arrangements to visit Boer,' Rebekah added.

That would explain why he didn't relish the idea of marriage, Wren thought. But because he was a compassionate leader, he had been determined to seek a marriage alliance anyway for the sake of his people.

Just then, Brita came from the back of the hall, too, hurrying towards her. 'Wren, Earl Ingrid is up and dressed. She has asked to see you.'

Wren grimaced, looking between the two women. She did not want to see her ruler! Not after all the harsh things Earl Ingrid had said to her in front of everyone the previous evening.

'If it helps, she is in much better spirits than last night,' Brita added kindly.

Wren nodded, getting to her feet. She actually felt stronger today, ready to face anything—and it was all thanks to Knud and the way he'd made her feel last night. Since she'd met him, she'd felt her inner strength building. He'd helped her to like herself, to start to feel her own worth again. Perhaps this wouldn't be so bad...

She made her way across the hall, past the fire, stealing a grape from the bowl of fruit on the table and popping it in her mouth, before heading to the back rooms and finding the one Earl Ingrid was occupying. She took a deep breath and knocked.

'Come in.'

She pushed open the door to find Earl Ingrid looking a lot more herself—better than she had in days.

'Ah, Wren, there you are.'

Straight away, Wren knew Earl Ingrid had forgotten her insubordination from last night—or had perhaps decided to let it lie. And today, Wren felt a little more willing to forgive her ruler, too.

'I am glad to see you are feeling better, Earl Ingrid.'

'Thank you. And I have noticed you're standing taller, too, Wren. I do believe all the excitement and fresh air of the past few days has put the colour back in your cheeks and I've noticed you're sharing your thoughts and opinions more readily. I don't know what has brought about this change—the journey you made must have been good for you. Seeing this change in you, it has led me to come to a decision about your future.'

'Oh?' Wren said, biting her lip, suddenly unsure where this was heading.

Earl Ingrid steepled her hands in front of her, as she always did when she was about to say something important. 'Wren, you have served me well these past winters and I am grateful for your service. We have had some good moments together, have we not? But I have decided that you are ready, at last, to be a free woman.'

'What?' Wren gasped, her hands flying up to her chest, her heart clamouring beneath. Had she heard the other woman correctly?

'I am releasing you from your bonds, Wren. After tonight, you will no longer be my bond servant.'

She could scarcely believe what she was hearing. She felt as if her heart would burst into a thousand little pieces, ready to take flight. To be set free. She clasped her hands together in delight. How could it be that all her dreams were coming true? First last night with

Knud and now this. 'Thank you, Earl Ingrid. Thank you so much. But why?' she asked.

'Well, if I am being honest, you have Jarl Knud to thank for it. He arranged it. He made me see the error of my ways. And he is right—after saving my life, you deserve to be free.'

Wren felt the tears well up in her eyes and she couldn't stop them from overflowing. She was so grateful to Knud. She couldn't believe he cared so much that he'd arranged this for her. How would she ever repay him? She had never thought this day would come, but he had saved her life once more. 'But what about the others?' she asked, delighted for herself, yet concerned for those who might still be trapped in the same life as she had been.

'Jarl Knud has agreed to put on a freedom feast tonight, for you and the rest of my thralls, where you will all serve me one last time and then we shall remove your collars. I hope that you are happy with all this?'

She nodded, racing towards Earl Ingrid and wrapping her arms around her ruler, her companion of old. 'I am. Thank you, Ingrid. Thank you.'

Wren scoured the beach, hoping to find something she could give Knud—a gift of appreciation to repay his kindness. But each shell or shiny pebble she picked up seemed too dull, too insignificant a thing for the likes of a man such as he. Perhaps she would just have to give him her body instead…would that be enough?

Against the beautiful sunset, the villagers were slowly making their way from their farmsteads and into the hall and she felt apprehensive. She didn't know what to expect from tonight's ceremony and she fingered her collar, her trembling body getting the better of her. Would she feel any different when it was removed? Would she be treated as a normal person—one of them—straight away? And what would it mean for her life after tonight?

Suddenly a whole world of possibilities was opening up to her. Would she be welcome to stay here in Nedergaard as a freedwoman? Would Knud ask her to do that? She had gone in search of him earlier, after leaving Earl Ingrid's room, wanting to tell him the news, to share it with him—and to thank him. Yet he was nowhere to be found. But she knew he would be in the hall for the feast tonight and her heart began to beat faster. She was desperate to see his face again.

She couldn't believe he had succeeded in making it happen, as he'd promised her he would, and she wondered how much he'd had to pay in coin to recompense Earl Ingrid for the loss of her thralls. She determined she would find out and somehow pay him back, no matter how long it took.

Her worries from earlier, at how he'd treated her when he'd seen her across the hall, now seemed to disappear like dark clouds on a summer's day. He must care for her if he'd done this for her. She knew she shouldn't get carried away where he was concerned—after all, she'd told him herself that their lovemaking was just for one night—but things were changing so rapidly...

Now everything in life seemed possible, even marriage and children—things that she'd deemed unthinkable before because of her status, not willing to inflict this life upon anyone else. But now it was all within her grasp for the first time. Knud had given her hope back to her.

Making her way to the longhouse, she was made to remove her boots and change into a plain white tunic along with the other thralls, leaving nothing on beneath. They were led into the hall in a line, paraded before the villagers and the folk from Boer, and brought before Earl Ingrid, who was seated next to Jarl Knud in a second grand chair that had been moved on to the platform.

Wren had waited a lifetime for this moment and she couldn't believe it was finally happening, and with Knud here to witness it. She stole a look at him and, when his brown eyes, almost black in the firelight, collided with hers, her heart began beating frantically, but he quickly glanced away. He seemed so guarded, his arms crossed over his chest, but she felt sure his eyes returned once or twice to rake over her body in her flimsy gown and wondered what was going on beneath his watchful gaze. What was he thinking?

When the vibrant pagan priest, the speaker for the gods, began his ritual, the thralls were all asked to kneel. It felt absurd, being here, everyone witnessing this. His words seemed to go on for ever and she could feel the trembling in her thighs as finally, one by one, he began taking off her companions' collars—and her mind flew back to just days before, after the fight in the market, when Knud had tried to prise hers from her neck in desperation. Would he be just as relieved as she was tonight to see the heavy metal finally cast aside?

At long last, it was her turn and she began to panic. What if it wouldn't come free? She stood tall on her bare feet, holding her head up high. Was she imagining the silence in the room, as if everyone was holding their breath? Or was that just her? When the *gothi* swept away her hair to turn the key in the lock and the metal sprang free, she felt overwhelmed. Her hand came up to clasp her bare throat and her eyes sparkled with joyful tears. The collars were moved to the necks of various farm animals and Wren turned her head so she didn't have to watch as they were slaughtered as a sacrifice to the gods. She silently thanked the creatures for taking her place.

Next, the freed people were asked to serve Earl Ingrid, the Chief of Nedergaard and the people in the hall for the last time. As Wren poured Earl Ingrid her ale, her old ruler nodded her thanks and took a sip of the amber liquid. Then Wren moved to Knud's side. She leaned over his shoulder to fill up his cup, breathing in the alluring, all too familiar scent of him—saltwater and leather and spice—and her fingers shook as she poured the ale.

She willed him to look up at her, to say something kind, or to make her laugh to break the tension, anything. She didn't care if anyone saw the affection for him in her eyes—she couldn't hold it in any longer. She thought she loved him and, now she was free, maybe there was a chance—a possibility—that they could be together if he felt the same? But even as she reached the top of his tankard, she couldn't reach his gaze.

Wren felt wounded and unsure all at once. He must have known what her freedom meant to her. And she had wanted to share this joyous moment with him. She had wanted to thank him, but he seemed to have retreated from her, withdrawing into himself, blocking her out.

Goose pimples prickled along her skin. Something was very wrong—she knew it. He seemed quieter, more reserved than usual. Was he simply worried about Forsa's imminent attack and the safety of his people? Even so, surely he'd have the space in his heart to talk to her—or at least acknowledge her after they'd spent the night being so intimate with one another? But then, she'd set the ground rules, hadn't she? He had said he didn't want to take advantage of her and she'd said one night together was all she needed, so why was she expecting more now?

Then a thought lanced her. Did he regret what had happened between them? Was what Rebekah had said true—that he couldn't get over the loss and love of his late wife? Wren realised now she didn't even know the woman's name.

She bit down on her cheek as she worked her way around the tables, swallowing down the hurt, her throat raw.

Many of the people from Nedergaard thanked her for the ale and her heart went out to them, feeling loyalty and kinship towards them for being so accepting. But it wasn't their kindness she was craving. It was their chief's.

* * *

Finally, after the meal had been served and everyone in the hall had eaten, she and the other freed thralls were told they could join the rest of the people at their tables.

She made her way over to Brita, who hugged her, as did Rebekah and some of the others around their table, but her gaze couldn't help swinging back to Nedergaard's Jarl, sitting in his grand chair on the raised platform with Earl Ingrid at his side. What she would give to see that slow smile build, or just one wink, letting her know he still cared.

Instead, she tried to focus on the people welcoming her into their group.

'It seems you and I have a lot in common,' Rædan said as he embraced her.

'Yes.' She nodded. 'Jarl Knud told me your story.'

'He saved us both,' he said. 'I knew he'd do anything to achieve your freedom—even give up his own.'

'What?' she said, her brow furrowing. 'What do you mean?'

Then, Earl Ingrid and Knud were there, Ingrid turning Wren around by the shoulder to face them, her old ruler wrapping her up in an awkward hug. 'I shall miss you, Wren. You have been a close companion my whole life. But I suppose I shall have a husband to do all my chores now,' she said with a rather coy smile. 'We have set a date for the wedding—a moon cycle from today,' she announced, turning to address the table. 'And we can't wait to celebrate with you all.'

Chapter Eight

Wren felt the betrayal rip apart her heart, like a nettle weed rising up through cracked soil and sprouting forward, destroying all that was beautiful and good. Images of Knud and Ingrid together, saying their vows, rolling about in the hay, flashed into her head and jealousy burned.

No!

Earl Ingrid wasn't good enough for him. She couldn't make him happy. Not the way Wren could...

Wren simply couldn't believe it. She had thought he cared for her. Even though she'd told him she only needed one night with him, she had thought them going to bed together had meant something to him, as it had to her. And she couldn't believe she'd been so foolish as to think him in love with her. To want more than their one time together.

But while she had been thinking of him all day long, daydreaming about their future, even going as far as to contemplate marriage and children, he had been getting engaged to another woman, and the pain sliced deep. She was sure everyone must see the agony etched across her face and she felt humiliated all over again.

He had got what he wanted from her—what all men seemed to want from her—and now he didn't need her any more. Yes, of course, he was never going to marry her. She felt like such a fool. Marriage to a former slave would no doubt be considered undesirable. Unacceptable. And she gasped as she realised he hadn't turned Ingrid into his concubine after all…but *her*—the words she'd heard him utter at the tidal pool that first night now mocking her. She swayed on her feet and Knud caught her by the elbow.

'Are you all right, Wren?'

It was the first time he'd looked at her properly all evening, his brow a dark line, and she stared up into his concerned brown eyes.

No, she was definitely not all right. Her heart felt as though it was shrinking, crumbling to dust. So how was his touch still sending flames flickering across her skin?

She reeled, berating herself for misplacing her trust in him—in anyone other than herself. She should have known better. Yet, at the same time, how could she be angry with him? What had Rædan said? That Knud was doing it for her—giving up his freedom to set her free. She shook her head. She didn't want him to! She'd never asked him for this. And yet he'd done it anyway. He had given her her life back. Only she wasn't sure she wanted it with him not in it with her.

She felt a flash of anger in her stomach. None of this

was fair! She took a deep breath and forced her legs to obey her. Snatching her arm out of his grasp, she fought to get her breathing back under control. She stood tall, despite still feeling like her legs might not carry her.

'Congratulations,' she said at last. 'I'm very happy for you both. It is a good match. A happy alliance for your settlements. But if you would now excuse me, I think the excitement of the evening has become a little too much.' She pulled herself up, gave them both a last look, and turned and worked her way through the crowd, leaving the noise and laughter in the bustling hall behind.

Outside, in the cool night air, she bent double, feeling queasy. How could this be happening? How could he agree to marry that woman so soon after taking her virtue last night? He had stripped away her doubts and her fears, gently removed her clothes and made love to her twice, their naked bodies touching so intimately everywhere. And he'd cradled her as she slept, whispering compliments and words of affection into her ear. He'd made her laugh and he'd seen her cry. How could he do all that—and then do this? She felt like weeping.

Did he even like Earl Ingrid?

She suddenly had the desire to run, to get far away from this place. From the two of them. And why shouldn't she? There was nothing stopping her—she was a free woman, not beholden to anyone, not him, not Ingrid, not any more. Determination stole through her. There was no way she could stay here and see them together every day. She could not stay and celebrate their wedding and watch and wait to see how their marriage turned out—it would be more than she could bear. And she had far more pride than that.

She headed in the same direction as the way they came into Nedergaard the day before, along the beautiful moonlit beach, the soft sand sinking beneath her bare feet, following the curve of the bay round the fjord. She stopped briefly to scoop up some water in her hands to clean her bare neck, scrubbing away the dirt that had gathered beneath her collar over the winters she'd worn it.

Then she clambered over one of the new embankments and took the little winding path through the bracken and up towards the forest, ignoring the needles and stones hurting her bare feet. It was so peaceful out here. She had no idea where she was going, and no belongings to her name, but she didn't care. She would find another village and work for her keep. Anything was better than staying here and suffering this pain and humiliation. She had never felt so crushed.

All of a sudden, her arm was pulled backwards. 'What the—?'

'Where do you think you're going?'

Knud.

She struggled against his hold. 'For a walk. I have to get away…'

'At this time of night? Dressed like that? I don't think so!'

'What does it matter to you?' she snarled, trying to wrestle her arm out of his tight grip.

'Stop it!' he growled. 'You shouldn't be out here

alone.' He seemed angry, but she didn't care. She was angry, too!

'*You* shouldn't be here, you mean. Shouldn't you be back down there, celebrating with your wife-to-be?'

He ignored her, instead manhandling her out of the edge of the forest and trying to walk her back down the path.

'Let go of me!' she spat, wrenching her arm from his hand.

And perhaps because she seemed so livid, he let her go.

He blew out a breath, placing his hands on his hips, glowering at her. 'Look, I'm sorry you had to find out like that. I should have warned you. I should have come and spoken to you today, told you before this evening. But I was always going to marry her, you know that.'

It was true, she had known it. He had never kept it a secret. And she'd fallen for him and let him make love to her anyway. She was to blame for thinking it had meant anything to him. She was at fault for hoping that what they'd done together might have changed his mind about marrying Ingrid…

'But I need you to know that this marriage has never been about what I want,' he continued, raking a hand through his hair. His eyes bore into hers in the darkness. 'You've known my thoughts on it right from the start—from when you overheard me and Rædan talking at the tidal pool.'

Yes, she had, but it didn't make it any easier to swallow.

'I spoke to Earl Ingrid this morning and she agreed

to bring her army under my control. Her forces will help to fortify our new walls when Forsa's men come. They will keep my people safe. That was always my aim.'

She shook her head, feeling miserable. 'I understand. I can't enhance your position. I can't help you save your people... But why do you have to marry *her* to achieve it?' she threw back at him.

'I didn't... Her army had already arrived. I told her there was no need for us to wed, that we were two very different people. But then she promised me something better—she said she would release you and the others from your bonds if I agreed to marry her...' he said, taking a step towards her.

'And you said yes,' she said bitterly, her eyes cold and flat. 'So you were busy proposing to her this morning while I could still feel the things you'd done to me—while I could still feel you inside me?'

His eyes lifted up to the dark night sky and he cursed, turning away for a moment before coming back to her. 'Wren... If me being her husband can buy your freedom and provide you with a home here and keep you safe, then that is a sacrifice I'm willing to make.'

She shook her head fiercely. 'I don't want you to marry her. Don't I get a say in this? It's too high a price to pay for my freedom. And you think I want to live here now, to watch this happen? To see you two together day after day?' She shook her head. 'I can't do that.'

'No price is too high for your freedom,' he said, reaching out and tucking a strand of her hair behind her ear, and she shivered at feeling his fingers on her skin again. 'I cannot—I will not—compromise yours or anyone else's safety for my own happiness.'

She didn't understand what he was saying. Was he saying he didn't like Earl Ingrid? Was he admitting that he could be happy with Wren, but he was giving her up, simply to set her free? She frowned. Then she definitely didn't want her freedom.

'And I cannot be here to watch you do this,' she said, turning to go to stalk back towards the forest.

'So you're leaving me? Just like that?' He gripped her arm again, spinning her round, pulling her up against him. She could hear the anger in his voice. But there was hurt there, too.

She would gladly go back down there, walk into the longhouse and put that slave collar on again if it meant he wouldn't marry Earl Ingrid. If it meant she could be his.

Standing there, looking up at him in the moonlight, he looked just as he had that first night at the tidal pool, when he'd been deep in thought, the weight of the world on his shoulders. And she so desperately wanted to take away his pain.

But did she have the ability to do that? Could she make him see this was madness? That he had made a mistake and he should change his mind? She didn't think so.

Slowly, she raised herself up on her toes, leant up and kissed him softly on the lips one last time. His lips lingered longer than they should on hers, his body swaying towards her. But then she pulled back.

'What are you doing?' he choked, his voice strained.

'Thanking you, for all that you've done for me, Knud. And saying goodbye. Don't you see? I can't stay here, not now.'

She turned to go again, but he grabbed her hand. 'Wren, you can't kiss me like that and then walk away from me...'

'How can you kiss me like that and expect me to carry on?' she said quietly. 'When you've promised yourself to another?'

Knud pulled her closer, resting his forehead against hers, wanting to be in this moment more than anything. He didn't want to acknowledge his past or his future, all he knew was that right now, he didn't want her to leave him. He didn't want to be anywhere else but here, with Wren, and he had to show her how he felt before it was too late.

He bent his head and kissed her, claiming her mouth with his, his arms coming around her back to hold her tight to his body, scared she'd try to leave him again. But she was responding, her arms coming up around his neck, pressing her body closer to his. And he thought he must be losing his mind. He was wild with need for this woman. Suddenly his lips were everywhere—on her mouth, her neck, accessing the bare column of her throat that he couldn't reach before because of that metal cuff, nipping and licking her skin.

'I was so glad to see the back of that damn collar,' he whispered. 'My heart was in my mouth when the *gothi* was removing it.'

Her hands came up to hold his head, drawing his mouth down to her breast before she frantically began untucking his tunic from his trousers, as if she was just as desperate for him as he was for her. He groaned, wanting to be inside her, now.

'I didn't think you cared,' she whispered.

'I did. More than anything. I couldn't breathe, watching his hands move around your neck.'

His lips came back to hers and he ravaged her mouth once more before tugging his tunic over his head, discarding it on the ground. She started placing little kisses all over his chest, driving him crazy, and his eyes closed, savouring the feeling of her mouth on his skin again, banishing all thoughts of anything else. This was all he'd wanted, all day long, Wren, back in his arms again.

When he'd left the longhouse and reached the beach, looking for her, he'd been panic-stricken. He'd seen the hurt in her eyes as she'd heard Earl Ingrid's words and he'd wanted to stop her pain, knowing what she was feeling because he was suffering it, too. He'd felt like someone had put their hand inside his chest and was trying to rip out his heart.

Then, when he'd spotted a figure in a flimsy white tunic walking up the path towards that clifftop, his blood had run cold. In an instant he'd known he had to stop her, he had to reach her, before it was too late, not caring if anyone would be missing him in the hall, wondering where he'd gone.

His heart had pounded, the muscles in his legs burning as he'd raced to get to her, his breaths coming in sharp bursts. But now she was here, safe, wrapping her arms around his neck, kissing him fiercely, wanting him just as much as he wanted her, and he was walking her backwards, until her shoulders came up against a large tree. He pushed his knee roughly between her thighs, rucking up her tunic to her waist, bunching it up into his hands, and his excitement soared as he realised she wasn't wearing anything beneath.

'When I saw you come into the hall wearing this, I didn't want to worship any of the gods the *gothi* was speaking of, I just wanted to worship you. I couldn't look at you, because I was so sure someone would know what I was thinking.' He sank to his knees before her, his eyes full of intent, glittering up at her. 'I want to worship you now if you'll let me.'

She stared down at him, watching him, biting her lip, wondering what he intended to do. She nodded anyway. And as he pressed his open mouth to her moist heat, she gasped, her thighs trembling, and he hooked one of her legs over his shoulder, giving him better access to all her secret places.

His hands came up to hold her bottom, tugging her closer, while he set to licking her and kissing her so intimately. Her breathing changed into quick gasps and moans and her hands stole into his hair, holding his head in place at the centre of her world. His tongue trailed over her nub, circling it, before delving between her crease, pushing inside her, and he couldn't get enough of the sweet taste of her. He sucked and kissed her until she began to come apart, throwing her head back and quivering against his lips as she cried out her swirling climax.

He pulled her down into his arms, wrapping her up, cradling her in his lap as he kissed her hair and stroked her limp, trembling body.

'I'm sorry I stayed away from you today, Wren. I think I knew if I got close to you, I'd want this to happen,' he whispered.

She pulled away from him a little so she could look up into his face. 'And what's so bad about that?'

He smiled slowly and it seemed to light a new flame inside her. She reached out to tug the waistband of his trousers loose. He kneeled up to help her push them down and do away with them. Resting her forearms on his shoulders, she brought her knees up and over his thighs to straddle him.

'It seems we're destined never to do this in a bed!' He laughed, sliding her tunic up her thighs.

She ruthlessly took his cock in the palm of her hand, as he'd shown her how to hold him last night, and he groaned, their foreheads touching.

'I've thought about nothing else but this all day,' he said.

'Me, too,' she whispered.

'I knew I'd be helpless to stop it if I came near you.'

She guided the tip of him to her entrance and then lowered herself down on top of him, impaling herself on him, taking control of the depth and speed as she held his face in her hands, looking into his shimmering eyes. And as she began to ride him, rotating her hips, quickening her pace, he clutched her buttocks, trying to keep a grip on her and his spiralling feelings, until she ground down on him, harder and faster, taking him inside her so deeply he lost all control and exploded, fastening her body to his, never wanting to be parted from her, never wanting her to leave him again.

They sat cross-legged facing each other, under the stars of the Norse god Aurvandill, their breathing not long having returned to normal. Wren's tunic was pooled around her waist, exposing her breasts to him, and his glorious chest was still bare. He kept leaning in to kiss her neck, as if he was fascinated by the new expanse of skin available to him.

'Rebekah said you were married before.'

'Did she?' he said, his fingers circling over her bent knees. 'But you knew that already.'

She could tell the subject made him uncomfortable— that he didn't want to talk about it. But she did. She wanted to truly know him and all that he was keeping from her, to better understand him, to see why he was so adamant to go ahead with his plan to marry Earl Ingrid and make himself miserable. Perhaps there was a way to help him? To show him that this wasn't the only way? Maybe, if she could just prove to him how good they were together, that he could trust her with all his secrets, he would see that he'd made a mistake and change his mind.

'Will you tell me about her?'

'Do you really want to talk?' he said, his hands running up her thighs, his thumbs finding her soft, intimate folds, trying to distract her from discussing his past.

'I really want to talk,' she said, covering his hands and slowly moving them back to her knees.

He sighed. 'What do you want to know?' His mouth was chasing down her breast now and she pushed him back up to sitting.

'How did you meet?'

He swiped a hand over his face, as if resigned that he was going to have to talk to her about this. He studied her for a moment, before taking a breath, before beginning. 'It was an arranged marriage by our parents. An alliance between Nedergaard and Hvallatr—a settlement in the north.' His voice was gruff and she knew he was keeping the details to a minimum, trying to tell her as little as possible. But he knew all about her. Was it so bad that she wanted to know more about him in return?

'Did you care for her?'

He nodded. 'Yes, we were lucky. Even though we were young, we were well suited and, over time, we fell in love. She was a good person—kind, strong, pretty.' He stroked her hair, tucking it behind her ears again. 'A lot like you.'

Wren squeezed his other hand, encouraging him on. She knew what it felt like to lose a loved one and felt bad for bringing it to the forefront of his mind, drawing a cloud over their lovemaking, but she wanted him to know he could share his pain with her, as she had with him.

'What happened to her?'

He turned her hands over on her knees, his thumbs stroking her palms. 'I was away raiding in England and I left her in charge here.' He frowned. 'She'd wanted to come with me, but I'd refused, saying it was too dangerous. We rowed and we parted angry with each other.'

She curled her fingers around his, trying to remind him she was here, that he could find her if he got lost amid his dark thoughts. 'I was gone far too long, trying to build up a settlement there. It was an obsession at the time. I thought there was no better way of making a name for myself than having land both over there in England and here. But when we eventually came home for the winter, we discovered Nedergaard had been attacked. Farmsteads were burnt to the ground and there was barely anything left of the longhouse. Many people had been slaughtered... And my wife, Annegrete, she'd been taken.'

Wren gasped. 'Like me?'

He nodded. 'Yes.'

She felt sick. When she'd told him her story that night in the hut in Boer, it must have stirred his memories, brought back his pain. Was that why he'd been inclined to help her? To help all thralls, she thought. That explained a lot.

'She was taken and forced into slavery?' Wren asked.

His lips twisted. 'The worst kind.'

Wren placed a hand on his arm. 'I'm so sorry,' she said.

'The settlement was...in the most part, destroyed.

Many had lost their lives…women, children… And I was to blame. It was my job as chief to keep them safe and I hadn't been there to protect them. As well as wanting to build it back up, to make amends to my people, I became consumed with finding Annegrete—tracking her down. I travelled the length and breadth of Denmark, visiting every settlement I came across. I never gave up. But when I did eventually find her, she was all but destroyed, too.' His voice cracked and Wren gripped his hands tighter, offering him comfort.

'You don't have to tell me any more if you don't want to,' she said. 'I'm grateful you've told me this, so I can understand you a little better.'

But the words were flooding out of him now, like the dam had burst, setting his words and his grief free. 'I tried to negotiate for her freedom and the tribe leader eventually agreed—for all the treasure I had returned from my raid with. But when Annegrete came home to Nedergaard, she was a different person. I couldn't reach her, no matter what I tried. She wouldn't leave her room, she wouldn't talk to me or anyone else.

'And then, one day…she told me she was going for a walk. I was pleased she was taking in some fresh air. I encouraged it. That hill up there? The one you were heading up earlier this evening? She just walked right up to the ledge and stepped off the cliff, falling down to the rocks below, taking her own life. She didn't even talk to me, tell me what she was thinking. She didn't even say goodbye.' He shook his head. 'I thought I'd saved her, but I was too late. The damage had already been done.'

'I'm so sorry,' Wren whispered, her heart breaking for him. She released his hands to hold his handsome face, pressing her forehead against his.

'I blame myself for not being here. I should have taken her with me to England, or not gone at all. I should have been here to protect her and my people. Instead, I let them all down.'

Wren shook her head fiercely. 'You weren't to know what would happen. You didn't know Nedergaard would be attacked. It wasn't your fault.'

'It was, Wren, it's all my fault. If I'd been there, she wouldn't have been taken. I've often thought that perhaps the gods were punishing me for all the things I did on those raids in the west. And the seer, she warned me. She foretold that something like that would happen to me, but I never fully understood what she meant until our ships sailed into the fjord and I saw the smoke billowing up into the air. Until I held Annegrete's lifeless body in my arms. Then it all became clear. And after that, I wanted vengeance. You don't know the worst of it. What I did afterwards...'

'You can tell me.'

'I went back to that settlement, where I found her, and I did my absolute worst. I went in there wearing just my bearskin, no armour, and made those men pay for what they did to her.'

She swallowed. She could imagine. She'd seen the way he fought, almost in blind fury. No wonder he had such a formidable reputation.

'In my anger, I became just like them and I'm not proud of myself. I've been trying to atone for it ever since. I've been determined to make up for all my past failures. I vowed I'd never go raiding again, that I'd never leave my people alone, vulnerable to attack.

'When I heard about Forsa's imminent attack on the coastal towns, I knew I had to act, to do something to protect my settlement, or more people would die. I can't have any more blood on my hands, Wren. I promised myself that, for the rest of my life, I would keep them safe.'

'And you have. You are.'

'I also vowed I'd never take a bride again,' he continued. 'Promising to uphold Annegrete's name. But then I realised I'd have to break that vow if it meant I'd be able to protect my people...'

'So here you are, agreeing to marry Earl Ingrid.' Her skin erupted in goose pimples.

'I like to inflict pain on myself as penance,' he said, but his smile didn't quite reach his eyes. And she realised with a reciprocal pain in her heart that, while he was jesting, deep down he didn't think he deserved to be happy.

Then, a thought struck her. 'When I first saw you fight—and again in the market at Hafranes—I felt as if you had a death wish. That you didn't care if you lived or died...'

'I admit I used to feel like that. Sometimes I willed death to come for me in battle, to take away the pain...'

She nodded, finally understanding. Perhaps it wasn't Ingrid, but his self-loathing for all he felt he'd done wrong that was preventing them from being together.

'And now?'

* * *

Movement among the trees startled them and Wren raced to cover her breasts, pulling up her tunic, while Knud curled up to stand and reached for his sword. Had someone from Nedergaard come looking for them and caught them in a compromising embrace? But it was much worse than that. Suddenly, they were surrounded by a group of men and Knud recognised some of them from the market in Hafranes. His blood chilled.

It was Forsa's men—the very danger they'd been trying to evade for days. He'd been so absorbed in Wren and telling her about his past, hoping she wouldn't think the worst of him, that he hadn't noticed the precariousness of their situation, out here beyond the borders of his settlement. Now, after all they'd been through to get back to Nedergaard safely, Forsa's men had chanced upon them.

'Well, well, what do we have here?' the men said to each other, sniggering. 'We've been tracking you for days, but now you've made this much too easy for us.'

'We'll have a piece of that,' one of them said, drawing closer, trying to reach out and grab Wren.

'Get your hands off her!' Knud said, brandishing his sword. 'I am the Chief of Nedergaard and I demand to speak to your leader. You do not need the woman, so let her go.'

They chuckled. 'I don't think so, she is quite a prize.'

The man lunged for her again and Knud instantly disposed of him, but then a savage struggle ensued as the rest of the men pounced, crowding round him, and he swung his sword this way and that, holding each one off as they tried to get near him.

But, as if all his worst fears were coming true, he watched as one of them grabbed Wren and tried to bundle her away. Yet, like the strong woman that he'd come to know and care for, she wasn't going without putting up a fight. With her usual grit and determination, she began to lash out, struggling in the man's arms. She managed to swipe his knife from his belt, warding off his thrusting sword.

Knud didn't care what happened to him, but he couldn't tolerate them laying a hand on her. He could not let her down, as he had Annegrete, it would be more than he could bear.

Never before had he felt so protective of a woman. Never before had he wanted to make love to someone over and over again, as if he couldn't get enough of her. And he had never been interested in sharing confidences or his weaknesses before, laying himself bare. But this woman…she made him want to tell her everything.

He fought back harder—with everything he had. For Wren. He would die trying to save her. His blade jabbed and thrust, still fending off the men, with one eye on Wren and the other man still in the middle of their skirmish. His heart was in his mouth when he saw her lose her blade and the man picked her up, throwing her over his shoulder, holding her fast. She kicked and struggled, but he threw her over the side of one of their horses, slapping her to keep her down, before ruthlessly binding her wrists.

He continued to hold off his five attackers, even as he sank to his knees, gasping for breath, his arms tiring, blood pouring from his arms and chest. And he wondered if this was it—if this was how his life was going to end.

Wren had been astute, recognising that he'd been waiting for this moment for a while—after losing Annegrete and many of his people, there had been so many moments when he had willed the end to come, when he had thought he'd been ready to die, to be taken to Odin's Great Hall. But right now? His gaze was drawn back to Wren. She had brought joy back into his life again. Now he definitely wanted to live.

In the moonlight dappling through the trees, he took in the men's armour, their banners…and with stark realisation, he saw the symbol on their shields. He didn't know why he hadn't noticed it before, perhaps because it had been so subtle, or because he hadn't been taking that much notice. But now his eyes were fully open.

'Take me to your leader,' he demanded, spitting out the blood in his mouth as he continued to hold the men off, injuring each of them in turn. 'I have much to say to him. And if, afterwards, he wants me to bend the knee, or run me through, I swear I shall not put up a fight. You shall have your glory.'

And finally, tiring themselves, the men seemed to relent, one by one stepping back from the fight, in awe of his skill as a warrior, not having the heart to finish him off. Realising they were in the presence of someone truly great, they pinned him in place with their extended swords as they halted their attack.

'You have my word I shall come with you and the woman,' Knud said again. 'I shall put down my sword, but you must allow me to speak with your ruler. I have something to say that I think he shall want to hear.'

The men looked between themselves, and Knud slowly placed his sword on the ground, lifting his hands in the air. He sought out Wren and saw she was watching him from her position folded over the horse, her stormy grey eyes widened in fear. He hoped she would forgive him for what he was about to do.

The tip of their swords pressing into his back, the men dragged Knud to his feet and bound his wrists with rope, then began nudging him along the track through the forest, making their way to Forsa's camp. Knud was still bare-chested, his skin covered in gashes from their swords, and his body was weary from his and Wren's vigorous activities and then the brutal fight.

It took all his will to keep going, to see this through—for her. He wanted to reach out and reassure her, to offer her words of comfort. He knew this would provoke an onset of memories for her—that she would fear having her freedom stolen again, her control taken away. He felt sure she would be imagining the worst, wondering how she would be used by these men. But he would not allow it to get that far. He would do whatever he could to protect her, only this time, he might have to use his words instead of his sword. He just needed to focus on what he was going to say to the Earl of Forsa when they arrived.

* * *

They reached the large camp by dawn, on the other side of the pine forest, halfway to Hafranes, and Knud realised with a slow trickle of dread that Forsa's forces would have been upon Nedergaard today. Perhaps it was a blessing that he and Wren had been discovered in the forest instead. If he could only speak to the man in charge, he might be able to prevent an attack. He might be able to save Wren and his people.

Their captors bundled him and Wren towards the main tent in the middle of the camp and, once inside, forced them to their knees on to an exotic-looking rug, holding them at sword point. His shoulder brushed against Wren's and he could feel her body trembling.

'It will be all right,' he whispered, trying to reassure her. 'I have a plan.'

'We have quite the prize for you, Lord. This here is the Chief of Nedergaard,' one of the men he had fought in the forest said to his ruler, while he held his bleeding arm with his hand. His leader, taking note of all their wounds, rose from his seat and stepped forward to assess the captives.

Knud studied him back with interest, through his blackened eyes and bruised face. He had heard much of the destructive power of Forsa's forces, raiding settlements and claiming them as their own. But he didn't know much about the man in charge, apart from that he was ambitious and ruthless. Looking up at him now, the Earl was a tall man with long, dark hair in rope-like knotted strands, his skin almost completely covered in blue tribal ink, and he had penetrating grey eyes. Knud and his enemy were evenly matched in height and size, he thought, although he had the advantage of youth on his side, for this Earl was much older. But then again, right now, he was lacking a weapon. Not that he wanted to fight him—he hoped it wouldn't come to that. Not after this man heard what he had to say.

'And the girl?' the Earl said, barely glancing her way. 'Who is she?'

'Nobody of importance. We found them out in the woods on the borders of Nedergaard.'

'Then take her away—enjoy the spoils of your discovery,' the Earl said.

Knud heard Wren gasp as one of their captors gripped her arms to pull her to her feet.

'You don't want to do that,' Knud said hastily, as he watched Wren struggle against the man's hold, her beautiful face draining of colour. He, too, struggled against his bonds, wanting to get to her. 'She *is* of importance to you.'

'I don't think so.'

He had to get this man to listen.

'Stop—look at her right shoulder if you don't believe me.'

Wren's eyes widened, lancing him, but he focused on the Earl, needing the man to hear him. And slowly, the man's wrinkled brow creased further, suddenly taking notice. Yes, now he'd got his attention. The Earl nodded to his warrior, who roughly tore Wren's tunic away from her shoulder, revealing the unusual mark she had shown Knud at the stream in Hafranes. The one he'd been fascinated by ever since, wondering what it meant.

'My Lord,' the man said suddenly, stepping away in shock. 'I think you should take a look at this.'

Wren's eyes widened, as did the Earl's. And a woman, who had been stood behind the grand chair in the back of the tent, came forward, hesitant. Her interest had been awakened and she took her place at her husband's side. 'Orm...?'

Wren's head shot up as the Earl crossed the distance towards her and carefully studied her shoulder, then her face. And Knud watched as this imposing man's serious grey eyes filled with tears and he turned and nodded at his wife. She gasped before she flew forward towards Wren, embracing her in her arms.

'My child.'

Knud's heart was lodged somewhere in his throat as he locked eyes with Wren's over the woman's shoulder, a million questions in her hurt and confused gaze.

'Neva?' the woman asked. 'My child, is that you?'

'Mother?' Wren's voice sounded hollow and Knud could tell she was in shock, her face growing paler still.

Tears streaked the woman's cheeks. 'We wondered if we'd ever see you again.'

One of the guards stepped forward and, using his knife, cut through the ropes around her wrists, freeing her, and Knud watched as Wren swayed slightly, folding her arms over her stomach. He fought against his bonds to try to get to her, knowing she needed his support, that she was struggling to comprehend all this. And he wondered if she would ever forgive him for putting her in this position.

She fell to her knees, her arms by her side, as the woman sank to the ground, too, and held her.

'We were so afraid we'd lost you for ever,' the Earl said, coming down on his haunches, drawing Wren and the woman into his arms. 'Our Neva.'

Wren looked between the man and woman— complete strangers—staring down at her, feeling light-headed as she struggled to understand what was happening. Was Forsa, who she'd thought was her enemy, the settlement of her family? Could it be true? Wrapped up in their unfamiliar arms, she gave a slow, disbelieving shake of her head.

'Neva. That was your name. Do you remember? Do they still call you that?' the woman asked, pulling away from her slightly to take her chin in her hand and study her face, her hair, turning her this way and that.

She shook her head. 'I remember,' she whispered. 'But now they call me Wren.'

Looking up into the woman's face, seeing the curve of her smile, her once dark hair now grey but still braided, Wren knew in her heart this was her mother. She was alive. She had not died the day Wren had been taken—she had survived. Wren had not got her killed. And fifteen winters of guilt and sorrow, thick and raw, rose up inside her and she reached for the woman she'd missed so desperately when she was a child. Feeling overwhelmed, she broke down in tears for the heart-ache and loss they'd all suffered that day.

'What happened to you? Where have you been?' asked the man with strange blue warrior paint over his body—her father. 'We looked all over the country for you. We never gave up hope of finding you, not wanting to accept you were lost to us for ever. We checked every woman with a collar, knowing you had probably been taken as a slave…'

How strange life was, she thought—that on the morning after she'd had her metal collar removed, she'd come face to face with her parents, but her father hadn't even looked at her twice when she'd been brought into the tent, not believing she could be his daughter as she wasn't wearing the bonds of a thrall.

'The Chief of Boer took me as a gift for his daughter. I have been a thrall, serving them at their settlement all this while.'

'I shall kill him,' her father spat.

'He died a long while ago,' Wren said. 'And it is all right. I am unharmed,' she said, knowing it didn't even begin to explain everything that had happened over the years that had passed.

She could understand her father's wrath after the torment they must have been through. Just like Knud when another tribe took his wife. She glanced over at him, down on his knees, his beautiful body that she'd come to cherish covered in more wounds. His hands were tied behind his back and he was watching the scene unfold.

She was glad that he was here to witness this, the man who had built her up and brought her back to life. And yet, she couldn't understand how he had known she was the Earl of Forsa's daughter. When had he discovered it? A fresh wave of betrayal ripped through her. If he'd known where she came from, why hadn't he told her? Surely he hadn't waited till now just so he could use her as a means to escape, or to make a deal?

The Earl, sensing they had an audience, and seeing Wren looking over at Knud, delivered a flurry of instructions to his men, demanding they all leave the room and tend to their wounds, to give them some privacy.

'And take him away,' he said, motioning to Knud.

Wren's breath hitched, her heart torn. Memories of her being beaten in Ingrid's stead when she was little came back to her and moments ago, if they'd tried to harm him, she knew she would have begged to take his place. But now? Now he'd revealed he knew who she was, using her as a way to get out of this… Now she didn't know what to think. She suddenly felt as if she didn't know him at all.

She went cold as she watched her father's men bundle Knud to his feet, pushing him in the direction of the doorway. He'd lied to her about who she was, when he knew that, of all things, that was what was most important to her. That for too long she had felt as if she didn't belong anywhere and she desperately desired to know where she had come from—that she dreamed of finding her home and her family. How could he have kept something so important from her? Had he intended to use the information for his own gain?

Still, despite her doubts, she found herself needing

to protect him. She reached out and gripped her father's sinewy arm. 'Please. Don't harm him,' she whispered.

Wren spent the morning sipping tea and picking at fruit out of a giant bowl as she sat with the Earl of Forsa and his wife in their grand tent, adorned with hunting trophies, weapons and furs thrown over benches—and it felt so peculiar, knowing they were her parents and yet not knowing them at all. They were strangers to her.

She also couldn't marry together the images of them looking after her when she was little, with love and affection, with their army attacking Boer so ferociously the other day, leaving a trail of bloodied bodies in their wake. It was hard to come to terms with. What did that make them? Were they parents or monsters? And what did that make her? What kind of blood flowed through her veins?

Having regained her composure, they talked at length about the day she had been taken. Wren shared how scared she'd been and how guilty she'd felt for not listening to her mother, finally getting to apologise for the behaviour that had haunted her all these winters.

In return, they explained how vulnerable and bereft they had felt and how the attack had hardened their hearts. Afterwards, grieving for their loss, they had built up their settlement once more, turning it into a fortress, and had begun their search for their child, ransacking villages to try to find her, then claiming them as their own.

'We realised we couldn't go on as we had done before, living in peace. We knew from then on we had to fight to stop people taking what was ours,' her father told her. 'It was kill or be killed.'

It was how they had become such a force in these lands, yet Wren hated the thought that she had been the cause of so many other deaths, so much tragedy.

'After so long searching for you, we were starting to think we might never find you, but we never wanted to truly believe you were lost to us for ever...' her mother said. 'Searching for you has kept us alive.'

They asked her questions and listened to her talk of her time in Boer, wanting to know how she'd been treated and how she'd spent her days. And she told them everything—all that she'd told Knud before them—of Earl Ingrid's ruthless father, her brother, and of Ingrid, too.

There was much weeping and embracing and, by the end of the morning, Wren felt quite wrung out. She was completely exhausted—after all, she hadn't slept much the past few nights, as she'd been in the arms of the Chief of Nedergaard. Not that she was going to share that with them.

They offered her a tent to rest in and she accepted it gratefully, too tired to think about what would happen next. But she made her father promise not to harm Knud while she was sleeping, explaining that he was the man who had released her from her bonds and she needed to speak to him when she awoke.

As she lay on the makeshift bed in the little tent, the mellow amber glow of the sunlight filtering through the woollen walls, she found herself wondering how bad Knud's wounds were. He had fought fearlessly out there in the forest and she didn't know how he'd kept going. She and her father's men had been in awe of him. And yet she could tell on their journey here he had been in a lot of pain. Should she go to him and tend to his wounds? But why did she still care?

She was still furious with him for putting her in this situation without any warning. She kept going over his deceit in her mind. When her parents had first held her, she'd been too stunned, too numb to return their embrace. She was still wrestling with her feelings of discovery even now.

This new development had changed everything— her thoughts about who she was and where she fit into the world. How could he not have told her who her family was? He didn't know what kind of people they were—all he knew of them was how they had behaved like barbarians in Boer. And she fell asleep, wondering if she could rely on or really trust anyone, especially the man in the tent next door with the molten brown eyes. For each time she had trusted him with her thoughts and her body, he had let down her heart.

Knud, tied to the pole in the middle of a small tent, rested his head back against the wood. He knew he needed to sleep, to try to regain some of his energy, as he wasn't sure what lay in store for him now—not that he really cared about his predicament, as long as Wren was safe. He closed his eyes, wondering how she was dealing with the revelations of the morning. Was she coping all right?

Her face had turned white with shock as the realisation had dawned that the Earl of Forsa and his wife were her parents and he wondered if he'd made the right decision, revealing who she was to their enemy, before he'd even told Wren what he'd discovered. He knew he should have warned her, but when he'd seen that man put his hands on her—go to remove her from the tent and his proximity—he hadn't had a choice. He knew he had to speak out to save her.

Now, sitting here, waiting to find out his fate, his chest bare, his wounds smarting, he berated himself about all the wrong turns he'd taken these past few days. He didn't think he'd made one good decision since he'd met Wren at that tidal pool. He hadn't been himself at all. But the worst thing he'd done was make love to her the other night, taking her virtue, and then agreed to marry Earl Ingrid, hurting Wren badly.

He still didn't know why he'd done that. Had Rædan been right? Had he realised he was falling for her and panicked because he was scared? Because he was afraid she was getting too close? Because he knew what had happened the last time he'd loved and lost? He had promised himself he'd never marry again—to honour Annegrete's memory. He'd vowed he would never replace her, the guilt all-consuming. But by marrying a woman he didn't care for, was that worse? Was he making a mockery of himself, as well as his late wife? And Wren?

Like the fool that he was, knowing she was hurting, he'd gone after her when she'd walked out of the freedom feast, stripping away her anger and defences once more, claiming her body as his again, and now look where it had got them—they'd been discovered by the enemy and he'd even handed her over to them. But everything he had done, he'd done to keep her safe. To protect her. And he couldn't bring himself to regret his bedding of her.

When he'd seen the symbol on those men's shields, he had known with a sinking heart that she didn't belong to him. That she could never be his—not until she had gone back to her roots and discovered who she was. It was what she'd always longed for. To find out about her home, her heritage—and to see her mother and father again. He had to hand her back to her family, so she could know her true self and then make her own decision about what to do next and who she wanted to be with.

It had felt good to open up to her in the forest, to share his pain with her at last. Rædan had been right about that. But now what? Now they knew where she was from, what did that mean for the two of them?

He wondered what she had told her parents about him. Had their captors told the Earl about what they'd seen between them in the forest? If they had, he was pretty sure the Earl of Forsa would be coming for him, wanting his head. He probably deserved it. And if he was honest, he wasn't sure he had the stomach to take on Wren's father.

And then she was there, pulling aside the canvas door to the tent and stepping inside. Wren had come to see him. He didn't care that her eyes glowered down at him, her lips pressed into a hard line, he was just pleased she was here, that she was all right and she hadn't forgotten him—yet.

'How's the happy reunion going?' he asked, trying to sit up a little straighter, his body stinging and aching all over, his mouth dry. But his wounds he could cope with—it was the pain in his heart at looking at her, knowing she was angry with him, that could break him.

Her pale grey eyes narrowed on him like shards of ice. 'If you knew they were my parents, how could you not have told me who I really was and where I was from?'

She was still wearing that flimsy white tunic and he knew she wasn't wearing anything beneath, but now she had a woollen blanket wrapped around her shoulders, keeping her warm. He thought he could do with one of those, especially when he heard her frosty tone.

'I couldn't be sure,' he said, stretching his bent knees out in front of him. 'It wasn't until I saw the symbol on their shields that I remembered...'

'But you suspected?'

'I knew I'd seen it before—the mark on your skin...'

'So when? When did you first realise?'

'I don't know.' He shrugged. 'I thought perhaps you were someone of importance in the marshes, when you told me your name. I knew it meant leader of the tribe.'

'And you didn't think to tell me?'

'I wasn't sure what good it would do. I thought keeping quiet about it was a way of keeping you safe until I could learn more.'

'Or of keeping me down? Of keeping me feeling like

a nobody,' she said, lashing out, her jaw clenched, her stance closed off. 'Keeping me beneath you...'

'That's not true,' he said, shaking his head. 'When you showed me the mark, I suspected it meant something important. But I still hadn't pieced it all together. It wasn't until I was fighting those men in the forest that it dawned on me that they bore the same symbol on their shields that you had branded on your skin— that you must be connected to Forsa somehow.'

'And still you didn't warn me. You didn't think I might need a little time to prepare before you announced it in front of everybody?'

'When exactly could I tell you? When we were seized and marched down here?'

'Instead you picked your moment perfectly, didn't you? Sacrificing me for the greater good. To save your own skin.'

'And how do we think that's going?' he said wryly, shaking his bonds above his head. But this time his attempt at being funny didn't make her smile—her face was blank, emotionless.

'You saw what they did in Boer and you just decided to throw me to the wolves.'

'Those wolves are your parents, Wren, and, knowing that, I knew they wouldn't hurt you. They probably behaved that way in Boer because of what Earl Ingrid's father did. If he had taken you from me, I would have burned down his home and everyone inside it, too!'

'They didn't even know I was there then. They didn't know Earl Ingrid's father was responsible for taking me!'

'No, but they treated every settlement they invaded as if they were responsible for taking you. Grief and loss do strange things to a person… It strips away all your decency. I know because it happened to me. I realise it's hard for you to understand that because you're different. You're not like that, Wren. That's what amazed me about you when I met you. After everything you've been through, all that you've suffered, how have you remained so pure and good?'

Well, she had been pure before he'd laid his hands and his body on her.

'Everyone has their breaking point,' she snapped. Had she reached hers?

'What I'm trying to say is don't be too harsh on them, Wren. They may have responded in hate all these winters, but it was probably a reaction to fear. And don't forget they were searching for you because of love.'

'Oh, please! What do you know of love?' she said, attacking him.

His eyebrows rose at her harsh words. 'Wren…'

But he could tell she'd hardened her heart like stone against him.

She knelt down and, taking a knife from inside her blanket, she tried to cut the rope around his wrists. 'You set me free and I will now do the same to you,' she said, her voice firm. 'But you'd better go quickly, before they realise what I've done. I don't know what my father, Earl Orm, intends to do with you.'

'Earl Orm? That's the name you remembered, wasn't it—from your childhood?'

Her grey eyes widened, startled he'd remembered.

'But this is goodbye,' she said, finally cutting through the last of the rope, releasing him. 'Don't you think I've been through enough? From now on, I don't need people in my life I can't trust.'

'Wren…'

'Please. Just go,' she said again, turning to leave and walk out of the tent. 'You have a wedding to plan, after all.'

Chapter Nine

It had been a whole moon cycle since Wren's shock reunion with her parents. A whole moon cycle since she'd walked out of Nedergaard, leaving her life of thralldom to Earl Ingrid behind. And a whole moon cycle since she'd seen Knud.

She had convinced her parents not to go after the Danish Jarl that day, when they'd realised in horror that she'd set him free. At first, they had been angry, rallying their forces, ready to charge after him and track him down. But she had pleaded with them not to go. And fortunately, they had listened and believed her when she'd reiterated that the Jarl of Nedergaard had helped her escape her bonds, so he deserved the same treatment from them.

She had even managed to talk them out of their plans to attack his settlement—for now. Delighted just to have their daughter back, it seemed they, too, had lost some of their will to fight, so they had packed up their camp and turned around, making the three-day-long trip back to Forsa.

At first, Wren had been excited to return to her childhood home. As they'd finally crossed the little stone bridge over the stream, returning to the settlement, memories began to filter back to her, more vividly than ever before. Although the place was much changed, she recognised the edge of the forest and the stream that wound its way down to the rocky little beach and water's edge.

Now a grand wooden fortress was at its heart, but with sprawling farmsteads dotted around the outskirts. And as for the people, they were kind and welcoming— not at all the evil enemy she'd imagined. Many approached her, saying they used to play together when they were younger, and did she remember this or that, and she'd been delighted to be reacquainted with them all again. She was desperate to fit in, so wanting to belong, trying hard to blend back into their way of life. But fifteen long and difficult winters had passed since she'd been here. It was proving difficult to adjust. She had been just a child back then, but now she was a woman with thoughts and feelings of her own.

It was harder than she'd believed it would be to suddenly be a daughter again, with parents who wanted to cherish her, and although she was now a free woman, she felt beholden to their wants and needs. She felt as if she had to make up for lost time and please them, rather than think of herself.

She was also struggling to reconcile those who were her family with the people who had slaughtered her fellow villagers in Boer that day. How could her own flesh and blood have behaved that way? And yet, she had fought back so brutally, too, not realising who they were, wanting to protect her people. What if they had come up against each other at Nedergaard? She shuddered. It didn't bear thinking about.

Putting those images as far out of her mind as she could, she'd spent her days getting to know her mother and father again. Questions she'd carried around with her for years had finally been answered and she felt as if a chasm in her heart had been healed. Yet where that one had been sealed up with love, another crack had emerged, lying open and causing her pain, for Jarl Knud of Nedergaard had hurt her more than she'd first thought. And despite wanting to hate him, she could not forget him, no matter how hard she tried.

Life in the large settlement of Forsa was surprisingly peaceful and she attempted to distract herself from thinking about him, keeping herself busy with activities, helping her mother to cook her spicy stews, weave, or she'd enjoy long rides along the coast and hunting with her father. Yet she found herself constantly wondering what Knud was doing—whether he was busy planning his wedding to Ingrid and laying with her at night.

She couldn't seem to shake the feeling that a part of her was missing. There was a thick lump in her throat that never seemed to go away, a gaping hole in her chest.

Then, one morning, word came from Nedergaard via a messenger on horseback. Wren recognised the man, but she did not know him by name, and she watched with interest as he spoke with her father. And then came the blow. She saw it in her father's face, which had turned a deep shade of purple.

Earl Ingrid was demanding Earl Orm meet with her to discuss the reclamation of her stolen family's fortress—and suddenly all hell broke loose. Earl Orm flew into a rage, saying Ingrid should be offering him her fortress as atonement for her father taking his child all those winters ago and that he would die before he ceded the stronghold of Boer now. He swore vengeance would be his!

How foolish Earl Ingrid was, Wren thought with dismay. She had everything a woman could want, surely? So why was she doing this, stirring up Earl Orm's desire for revenge once more? Why couldn't she just enjoy her life in Nedergaard with her new husband and let things be?

Earl Orm rallied his troops once more and instructed they head back up north, to charge on the settlement of Nedergaard, and this time he would not listen to his daughter's pleas for peace. He wanted his enemies silenced once and for all.

He commanded that his wife and Wren stay behind, along with the rest of the women and children, but Wren insisted upon joining him, fearful for both Forsa and Nedergaard's people. She hoped that if she went with him, she might be able to intervene—to prevent this fight from ever taking place. And she couldn't deny a part of her wanted to see the Danish chief again.

The season was changing as they set out on their journey, the brighter days fading away, leaves dropping from the trees and crunching beneath their feet. The darker, colder phase was coming and she was grateful for the new cloak her father had given her. She wondered what fur it was around the neck, reminding herself she must ask the Earl which animal he had hunted to make it, and her thoughts returned to Knud lending her his own cloak to sit on back in Boer and the joke they'd shared about what it was made from.

She didn't know how she would feel upon seeing him again, this time on opposing sides of a battle. She was surprised by him, that he had allowed his new wife to send such a confrontational message to her father. But then, hadn't the terms of their marriage been that he would help Earl Ingrid reclaim her fortress? Still, how many strongholds did they need between them?

She had never thought greed was one of his attributes, but then he'd already proved she didn't know him as she'd thought she did. She braced her heart against him again.

When they re-entered Boer a few days later, it felt strange to be back and every sight and sound stirred a memory. The way the settlement was run and the faces of the people were different. As she looked round the square, she wondered if some of the men on the ramparts had been the ones to shoot arrows at her that day. Had any of them been among the group of men who had come looking for them out on the mudflats, forcing them to hide in that crevice? Did they feel any remorse?

Her thoughts returned to the last time she'd been here, with Knud, and how he had stayed behind to help her in the face of the enemy. He had made her feel safe, despite everything that had been going on around them. In fact, he had made her feel alive for the first time in her life. She wondered if she would ever feel that way again.

She thought back to the last words she'd spoken to him—when she'd asked him what did he know of love? Hurt had clouded his eyes. Had she been too harsh on him? After all, he—and Rædan—had told her he was suffering the bonds of marriage again so Wren could be set free... If that wasn't devotion, what was?

She walked down to the tidal pool, wanting to see her place of sanctuary again, to see if it still held the same solace for her now. But when she looked into the water, all she could see was his eyes staring down at her that night, as he'd approached the pool, the weight of the world on his shoulders. Now she understood what he'd been feeling back then, that he didn't deserve to feel joy, so he was planning to sacrifice his own happiness and marry someone he didn't love for the sake of his people.

He had finally opened up to her and told her about his wife and she knew that he had both loved and lost, and the pain had been immense. As he'd held her hands in the forest, she'd realised he was afraid to love and be loved again, scared of the agony it could cause. And suddenly she felt sick, as she realised she had done the worst thing she could have done.

She had been so hurt, thinking he'd kept the truth from her and betrayed her, for using her to get out of their predicament, that she'd abandoned him—just as his wife had done when she'd jumped from that cliff—making all his fears come true. She had been so blinded by her anger and mistrust, she hadn't fought for him at all, she hadn't stayed with him when he'd needed her. Instead, she'd sent him back to Earl Ingrid's waiting, open arms. And by now they would be married.

Wren thought how cruel the gods were, that Knud had thought he needed Earl Ingrid's army to keep his people safe from Forsa, when all along, if Wren had known who she was and where she was from, she could have been able to protect them by bringing Nedergaard and Forsa together. She could have tried to get Jarl Knud and Earl Orm to see eye to eye, because they were so alike in many ways.

They were both so proud. They were both formidable warriors who were willing to die fighting for the people they loved and their homes. And they had both had loved ones taken from them and suffered tremendously as a result. She also cared for them both a great deal.

But now that her father had received that message from Earl Ingrid, all hope seemed to be lost. Would he want to make peace with Nedergaard now? And would she have to choose a side—between the man she loved and her father? Because she did love Knud, she realised that now. That was why she'd been so hurt by his actions.

Staring into the water, in the place where she'd first met him, everything was starting to become clear. Perhaps he had behaved the way he did because he cared for her, too. But had she ruined everything? Was she too late?

Even if she was, there was still something she could do to help. She might have lost Knud for ever, but perhaps she could still save his life. Yes, she could warn him. If she spoke to him, maybe there was a chance she could make him see reason, for the sake of his people, and he and Earl Ingrid could renounce their claim on Boer before it was too late.

So while her father and his men spent the night in her old home, she left the fortress under cover of darkness, slipping out through the palisade walls, this time finding a horse in the stables and taking the mare with her. She knew Earl Orm would be livid if he found out she had gone to Knud to warn him. He would see it as a betrayal. She hoped if it came to it, he would one day forgive her—that he would realise she had done it not to thwart him, but to save lives. Lives of the people on both sides that she had grown to care about.

The journey to Hafranes had been a lot quicker on horseback and, as she passed the little stream she and Knud had bathed in, memories flooded her, both good and bad. Galloping through the rows of sleeping market stalls, she remembered their encounter with the slave trader and those terrible men, but it was all drowned out by the passion and wonderment of her first kiss with Knud. But she didn't have time to stop and reminisce, she had to reach him. She kicked her heels tighter into her horse's sides, spurring the animal on.

When she finally reached the clifftop above Neder-gaard, where she now knew Annegrete had died, she read the carved rune symbols again on the stone under the light of the moon. *Free in death, if not in life,* Knud had told her it said—and she determined that would not be her fate, not now he had saved her. In return, she would save him.

Looking down on the settlement, she had thought maybe it would seem smaller than she remembered now she had spent a month in the vast city of Forsa. But Nedergaard hadn't diminished since she first saw it. It was still as beautiful as ever. And she wondered when she saw Knud again whether she would feel the same about him.

The warning horn reverberated over Nedergaard and Knud and Rædan looked at each other across the table in the longhouse, putting down their tankards and rising to their feet, readying their weapons. The rest of the settlement had gone to bed, it was only them and the guards who were still up. They raced out of the hall and glanced up at the warning tower through the heavy pattering of the rain.

'What is it? Who is it?'

'A single rider, heading this way—and fast.'

They looked at each other again. So not quite the army they'd imagined might be at their door when they'd first heard the sound of the alarm. Good, they'd had far too much ale this evening as they'd talked long into the night. They tucked their swords back into their belts.

'I know that face! It's Wren,' Ivar shouted down at them.

Knud's heart jammed in his chest. Wren? *His* Wren? Surely it couldn't be her, this late at night? Had something happened? he thought in alarm. Or had she come back to him? He wondered, hope blossoming in his heart. But he instantly crushed it. Maybe Ivar was seeing things?

'Yes, it is Wren. And she looks good, too,' Ivar added.

'Open the gates,' Knud demanded urgently, not liking Ivar raking his eyes over her again.

He and Rædan stood there, getting drenched by the storm, as the new tall wooden gates they'd erected in haste, in preparation for Earl Orm's advance on the coastal towns, slowly began to open.

He tried to brace himself for what he might find on the other side, but his heart was hammering beneath his tunic. This was worse than hearing any enemy was at the gates. An army—a fight—he could cope with. But seeing Wren again? It had him feeling a lot more unsettled.

'Are you all right?' Rædan said from beside him.

'Ask me again later.' He grimaced.

And then the gates were open enough for them to see the lone rider through the driving rain and Ivar had been right—it was Wren, all by herself, sat elegantly astride a white horse, and his throat constricted. She was even more beautiful than he remembered, despite her damp clothes and her wet braided hair plastered to her face. It had grown since he'd last seen her.

But what was she doing here?

Knud and Rædan hurried forward, Rædan helping her down from the horse while Knud took the reins.

Envy burned at seeing Rædan's hands on her skin, but Knud tried to mask his annoyance, knowing he had no reason to be jealous of his friend. 'This is a surprise. Is everything all right?'

'No, not really,' she said, shaking her head. She bent over a little, resting her hands on her new breeches, trying to catch her breath. 'I rode all the way here at speed. My father's army is on the way. They mean to attack Nedergaard. I've tried to talk him down, but he's not having it. He just won't listen, not this time. I thought I'd better warn you.'

'He plans to attack us now? After all this while? Why?'

'Because of Earl Ingrid's messenger.'

His brow furrowed. 'What messenger?'

'She sent word that she wanted to reclaim Boer... and after what her family did to me, it did not go down well with my father.'

Rædan and Knud shared a look and Knud cursed.

'You did not know Ingrid did that?' she asked, glancing between them.

'No,' they said in unison.

Her concerned grey eyes swung to look at him. 'My father—he took it as a slight, now knowing it was the Earl of Boer who took me from him. And he means to take revenge on you all, many long winters of wrath waiting to be unleashed through his army of men.'

'Thank you for warning us, Wren,' Knud said, his eyes glittering down on her. 'How many of them are there?'

'A hundred, maybe more.'

He nodded, raking his eyes over every inch of her, wanting to consign the sight of her to memory again. She wore her hair in a longer, more elegant style, half of it braided on top of her head, and her new clothes suited her—woollen trousers teamed with a dark red tunic, a leather vest buttoned up over the top, fastened tightly around the waist. She looked both fierce and stunning, and he swallowed hard. 'You're soaked through. Come inside, warm yourself by the fire.'

She shook her head. 'No, I must get back, before they realise I've gone. I was hoping you could persuade Ingrid to change her mind—she'll listen to you,' she said. 'I will continue to try to convince my father not to fight. I promise I'll do all I can from my side.'

She went to mount her horse again. 'You're not leaving,' Knud said, reaching out, gripping her wrist, almost for his own sanity to check she was here, to feel if she was real. He could not bear for her to leave him again so soon, not now he'd seen her again after all this time. 'Not by yourself. Not in the middle of the night. A storm is coming.'

Her eyes narrowed on him. 'I must. I am.'

'Then I'll come with you, to see you safely back. Let me just ready my horse.'

'No!' she said, adamant, shaking her head. 'My father—you know what he's capable of. He will kill you if he finds you alone with me. Especially after...' She blushed.

Did Earl Orm know about them? About what they'd done together?

'He is not feeling particularly merciful right now.'

A loud rumble grumbled above them and they looked up. It seemed the sky was alive with Thor's chariot, thundering across the heavens.

'I'm not afraid of him,' Knud said.

'You should be.'

The flash of lightning came next, forking through the sky, illuminating her face. She was so beautiful.

His brow furrowed. 'Have they been kind to you, treated you well? I hoped you'd be safe with them.'

She nodded. 'Yes, don't worry about me, Knud. It's your wife you should be concerned about.'

And before he could say anything, she was throwing herself back into the saddle, tugging on the reins, rearing up the horse and turning the animal round. Then she was off, galloping up the path from whence she came, leaving him again, and he rubbed his hand over his chest where his heart hurt.

'She looks well,' Rædan said blandly.

And Knud rolled his eyes. 'Don't start,' he muttered.

His friend grinned. 'But she does, doesn't she?'

'Yes. She looks better than well.'

'And it was good of her to come all this way and warn us…'

'It was.'

'She must care a great deal…'

He groaned. He had gone too long without a woman. But the trouble was, he didn't want any woman but her. She had ruined him for anyone else.

As they re-entered the square, they headed for the longhouse to go in search of Earl Ingrid. What the hell was she playing at? She was going to bring war to their lands and Knud was furious with her. He hadn't spent all these many winters trying to build up his settlement, trying to keep his people safe, only for her to destroy it now.

How absurd it was that the woman he'd decided he should marry to keep his people safe was the very person who was now putting them in such grave danger. They were going to have to try to convince her to back down on her demands to Earl Orm of Forsa, to retract her message and apologise, but knowing Ingrid, that wouldn't be easy.

He couldn't believe Wren had come all this way to alert them of the impending danger. Rædan was right—a part of her, deep down, must care about him, about his people, and the thought spurred him on. It had been so good to see her again, although briefly.

He didn't like the idea of her riding alone at night, but she had been certain he mustn't return with her. He had to trust that she knew what she was doing. She was free to make her own choices now. But damn, he wouldn't be able to settle until he knew she was all right. And ridiculously, he almost hoped Forsa's army would come now—if only to see her again to check that she was all right.

The warning horn sounded again as they saw the first signs of Forsa's forces come over the hill the next day, in a snake-like trail of men. The people of Nedergaard were finally prepared for this—they were ready—as they raced to take up their positions on the ramparts, the embankments or in the trenches. Every man, woman and child knew what they needed to do to help. Each of them was important.

From the lookout tower, Knud and Rædan tried to assess how many of them there were, if Wren's estimate had been right, and what kind of weapons they had—and all the while Knud kept a watchful eye out for her. He hoped her father hadn't caught her on her way back to Boer and reprimanded her. She must be exhausted if she'd travelled all that way and back again. That is, if she was even here. He really hoped she was. Yet he did not want her fighting, especially not on the opposite side to him. He didn't think he could do it.

Then he saw her, coming down the path, travelling alongside her mother and father. His heart was in his mouth. How could he be expected to fight against her? There was no way... And he was livid with Ingrid all over again for putting them in this position.

But part of him was also glad, for her sending that messenger had brought Wren back to him. And now that he'd seen her again, determination had set in—he had a second chance to put everything right. This phase without her had been hell. He had been able to find no joy in anything and his feelings of inadequacy and self-loathing had returned with force. But now she was here. Now there was hope once more.

He'd had time to think about everything Wren had said to him in that tent—and time to think about the way she made him feel. He had left her, giving up the one thing he wanted most of all, because that was what she'd wanted, and he was ashamed he'd let her down.

But this past moon cycle, he had started to remember his childhood and the love his parents had shared, and how he'd always wanted that and had tried to emulate it with Annegrete. He'd wanted a family, but when she had died, so had his dreams of having children. Of ever being happy again.

But he was starting to think that that was no longer the case, if he could just allow himself to be. Was he really going to deny himself all that love and joy just because he was fearful of losing it again? It would be such a waste.

He had tried to make Ingrid see reason earlier, to get her to help with this dire situation, but she was being churlish, saying he'd brought this on himself, for not sticking to his end of the bargain. And she was right— to an extent. He had promised her he would help to reclaim Boer, but that had been back before everything had changed. How could he help her when the fortress now belonged to Wren's father?

He closed his eyes briefly, trying to recall Annegrete's face, wondering if she was looking down on him right now, but he couldn't picture it as clearly as he used to. And he realised it was because she was part of his past. He kept pushing himself to remember, trying to hold on, but she was gradually fading from view. She would always be there, a memory in his heart, but when he opened his eyes, he saw everything he wanted in his future, riding down the track towards him.

He no longer wished for death to come in battle— the time would come when he would go to the Great Hall of Valhalla, but right now, he just wanted to be with Wren. He knew it was an inopportune moment to be thinking like this, with an army at his gates, but at least he now knew what he had to do. And he couldn't mess this up. He had a lot depending on this encounter—his people, his home and his heart.

It seemed to take an age for them to reach the gates and Wren's hands gripped the reins of her horse in fear. It was the second time she'd approached the newly fortified settlement of Nedergaard, but this time, she was arriving with an army. An army who meant to fight the man she loved. She was relieved she had made it back to Boer by first light and had re-entered the fortress without being seen.

She was shattered and saddle sore, her legs aching from the ride, her skin cold and damp, but it had been worth it. She was pleased she had warned her friends. It had given them a chance to think about surrendering, or at least revoking Earl Ingrid's demands. And she was pleased her father had listened to her pleas not to charge and storm the settlement and instead try to talk through his demands first. It was something, at least.

As they approached the new gates, she saw Knud and Rædan standing on the bridge. Knud stared down at her and their eyes collided. She swallowed. Would she always feel this way when she looked up at him? she wondered. Like that very first time in the pool when he'd taken her breath away?

He was still the most magnificent man she had ever seen. His blond hair was tied back and he was dressed in the chainmail he had lent her back in Boer—protection against her family's men. But where it had swamped her small frame, it hugged his muscled chest. A hard chest made of solid muscle, but which encased his tender heart.

How could it have come to this? she wondered. How could they be on opposing sides of the battlefield?

When he had put his hands on her last night to try to stop her from leaving, that all too familiar heat had rushed up her arm, making her heart tremble. His fierce grip had turned into a gentle caress, his fingers circling her wrist, and when he'd asked her to stay, it had taken all her strength to decline his offer and get back on her horse, for she'd wanted nothing more than to stay and curl up in his arms by the fire.

But despite how he made her feel, she must not lose sight of where her loyalties lay and who he was now married to. Yet, even knowing this, she felt her heart skittering under his gaze. She was glad of the blue warrior paint her mother had drawn over her face—it would go some way to hiding her feelings.

'Earl Orm of Forsa,' Knud acknowledged him from the bridge. 'Welcome to Nedergaard.'

Her father took in the man on the bridge and the recent defences that had been put into place. 'Jarl Knud,' he said, tilting his head. 'I'm sure you know why we are here. I should very much like to speak with the woman who calls herself Earl of Boer, the Lady Ingrid, as our dealings are with her.'

Knud nodded. 'I understand. Although I'm afraid that's not possible right now. Is there anything I can help you with?'

So he was going to protect his new bride, Wren

thought bitterly. Of course he was. But he wouldn't have been the man she'd fallen in love with if he had given up one of his people.

'We came here for Earl Ingrid and we won't be leaving until we've spoken to her. If we have to break these gates down to do so, then we will. I have only given you the courtesy of not doing so already because my daughter has spoken well of you. Had she not been here, I myself would have smashed through them by now.'

Knud's eyes narrowed on him. 'I'm glad you haven't. I'm sure we can settle whatever dispute you have with us in a friendly and peaceable manner. Perhaps I could invite you and your family in while you wait? I have some fine ale you can sup. I promise that no harm shall come to you or your men while you're here. I mean only to talk. You have my word.'

Earl Orm turned to his daughter, as if to check if Jarl Knud could be trusted, and she nodded in response.

'Very well,' he said. 'We shall come in and wait.'

It felt ridiculous, Wren thought, as she and her father, her mother and two of her father's best men entered the gates, passing some of the people she knew and cared for while growing up in Boer and some of the more recent acquaintances she'd made in Nedergaard. She wanted to reach out and embrace them, find out how they were, but she didn't dare. Her father was watching her and he would not approve.

She kept her head down and followed Knud and Rædan across the square, past their warriors lined up in a shield wall, no doubt ready to fight if they must, and into the empty longhouse. Her heart was in her mouth. What was Knud thinking? Was he going to try to talk her father down? To stop Earl Orm from waging a war against his wife?

'Please, sit,' Knud said, motioning to a table near the central hearth.

And they all sat down, pulling up benches, as Brita, who gently squeezed Wren's arm while no one was looking, poured them some ale.

She could almost slash the tension in the hall with her knife—and she felt like laughing and crying. She was glad to be back here, despite the strange circumstances, and with her family. She didn't know what to make of it all. She wanted to introduce her father and Knud properly, knowing they'd get on if they just gave each other a chance. And she wanted to give her mother a tour of the beautiful fjord and the beach. But instead, she remained silent.

She didn't dare look at Knud again, thinking that everyone would see how she truly felt for him, the love shining out of her eyes. The intensity of her feelings alone were probably enough to start a war.

She looked around the longhouse. So where was Ingrid?

'Let us not play games, Jarl Knud, we are both far too sensible for that. Why don't you tell me where your wife is and we can settle what we came here for.'

'I have no wife, Earl Orm.'

Wren's head shot up. What? Had he and Ingrid not married?

Her father frowned. 'I was led to believe you wed Lady Ingrid recently.'

Knud nodded. 'You're right. At one stage that was the plan, but it did not come to pass.' He did not glance Wren's way as he was talking and she desperately wanted him to. She wanted to ask him why? What had happened? Her heart clamoured to understand, her throat thick with emotion.

'So is Earl Ingrid even here?' Wren's father frowned.

'She is. But I fear this has all been a grave misunderstanding. She never meant to cause you offence, Earl Orm. I believe it was me she was trying to retaliate at for cancelling our nuptials. She hoped by sending you that messenger you would retaliate, hurting me and my people in return.'

'So she does not want the fortress of Boer back?'

'She did. And I admit I had initially promised I would help to reclaim the stronghold as part of our marriage agreement, but then, well, everything changed...'

What? What had changed? Wren wanted to scream.

'Earl Ingrid found she no longer had my support in the matter. She was angry and sought revenge. That is the truth of it. However, having seen your army come across our border, I believe that she has now seen the error of her ways and no longer wants to wage a war to achieve what she wants. In fact, she told me she means to make amends to you and your family for her past wrongs. If that is acceptable to you, I shall send for her now.'

There was a long silence before the older man spoke. 'I am willing to listen to what she has to say,' the proud leader said.

Knud nodded and inclined his head at Rædan. But

then an almighty noise erupted from the square, startling them all, and within moments they were all on
their feet, racing towards the door to see what was
going on. Outside, it was carnage. Boer's army were
shooting down Forsa's forces with arrows and Earl
Orm's men were scaling the walls, trying to infiltrate
the square, fighting the soldiers on the ramparts at
the top.

Earl Orm's face erupted in anger and he immediately unsheathed his sword. In defence, Knud did the
same.

'I thought your word was to be trusted, Jarl Knud.
Clearly not.'

'This is not my doing, I swear.'

He glanced up to the battlements again and saw Earl
Ingrid instructing her men. He cursed. Damn Ingrid
and her quest to cause all-out war.

'I do not wish to fight you, Earl Orm,' he said, as the
older man lunged towards him. 'Stand down.'

'Never,' the man said. 'This is a slight on my honour
and my men. I shall have your head for this.'

Wren knew she had to do something. But what?
Her father and Knud were circling each other and she
knew this was serious. Neither man was likely to back
down—they were both far too proud, too ambitious.
But at what cost? There had been fifteen winters of
bloodshed, started by Ingrid's father. Where did it all
end?

All around her men and women had taken up arms.
It was the battle of all battles—what each warrior had
been preparing for their whole lives. A huge fight be-

tween three different tribes, each giving everything they'd got to achieve their supremacy. Everywhere she looked, weapons were slicing through the air—axes hacking, swords clashing, spears being thrown—and Wren felt as if she was witnessing the end of her world as she knew it. How had it come to this?

The courtyard where she had felt so content just a month before on their arrival at this beautiful place was now covered in blood. Bodies from all sides lay strewn about, people writhing in pain. Children stood on the sidelines wailing and loose animals were tearing about the place…it was the scene from her childhood, coming back to haunt her, and she knew she had to put a stop to it, once and for all. Had none of them learned anything?

'I don't want to fight you, Earl Orm,' Knud was saying again.

But her father, probably reminded of his own memories of the attack on his village and his family, jabbed at Nedergaard's chief, who knocked back his blade in defence.

They continued like this—Earl Orm thrusting his weapon forward, slashing the air, trying to strike his foe, while Knud dodged and lunged in response, trying to block the older man's blade from slicing through his skin, but not responding with attacking blows, no doubt unwilling to injure her father. Wren, unable to bear it any longer, leapt between them, needing to put an end to this madness.

'Stop!' she cried, shielding Knud's body with hers,

but not before the tip of her father's sword pierced the middle of her shoulder.

'Wren!'

Both men looked on in horror as she gripped the wound, blood pouring from it, thick and fast. Everyone around the settlement saw her sink to her knees and each fighter from every side—Boer, Nedergaard and Forsa—halted their weapons in shock.

They heard Earl Ingrid's high-pitched wail as she saw her lifelong companion, the only person she had ever truly cared about, even if she'd struggled to express it, collapse on the ground.

Earl Orm, seeing his daughter's blood on his sword, the crimson mark spreading across her tunic, paled as he released his weapon in grief and agony. 'I can't lose my child, not now I've found her again after all this time.' He cried.

And Knud instinctively dropped to her side, gathering her to his chest, cradling her limp body in his arms, revealing to everyone in the fortress just how close they really were. He pressed his lips to her forehead, whispering his words of apology, cursing himself for allowing things to get this far.

'Wren?' he whispered.

'This is what the seer must have meant when she saw my blood in the middle of a triangle,' she whispered. 'You must stop this fighting. All of you. Before anyone else gets hurt,' she said, looking between Knud and her father.

'Violence must be met with violence,' her father

declared shakily, although for once it didn't sound as though he entirely believed what he was saying.

'I used to think so, too...' Knud responded, his voice breaking. 'But violence can also be met with love. It is much more powerful. Your daughter taught me that. I believe we have much in common, Earl Orm, and most important of all is that we both care greatly for your daughter.

'I vow to you that I did not know Earl Ingrid meant to fight your forces today. I do not wish to do battle with you—it is peace and prosperity I want. Can we not try to resolve our differences in another way? It was my intention to ask you for your daughter's hand in marriage...'

It was the last thing Wren heard before everything went black.

Chapter Ten

Wren slowly opened her eyes, the brightness of a new day making her blink as she adjusted to the light. Where was she? Looking around the room, she couldn't be sure of her surroundings. And then Brita's face swam into view, smiling. 'You're awake!'

Wren tried to move, but the pain in her shoulder was too great. And then she remembered—she'd been wounded in battle when she'd stepped in front of her father's sword, trying to protect Knud from his wrath.

'Don't move, just rest,' Brita said. 'You've taken quite the blow to your shoulder.'

'Is everyone all right?' she whispered, her throat feeling coarse. 'What happened? Where am I?'

Brita perched on the edge of her bed, handing her a cup of water.

'Do you remember anything at all?'

She shook her head, trying to recall all the details. 'I remember the gates opening, seeing you in the long-house…the battle descending into chaos. I remember my father—Earl Ingrid…the seer's vision came true.'

And then Knud's words came back to her, the last thing she'd heard him say, and she gasped. Had he really asked her father for her hand in marriage? How had her father responded?

'What happened after—?'

'After you were wounded? We carried you into the hall. Everyone was so worried about you, Wren. Everyone gathered round you. You single-handedly put a stop to the fighting. No one had the stomach for it after that.' She shuddered.

Well, at least she had achieved what she'd set out to do when she came here.

'Knud was out of his head with worry, shouting at me to stop the bleeding, to save you. The whole of the fortress felt the force of his anger.

'And Earl Ingrid—he rebuked her thoroughly for starting the combat and she was so ashamed when she saw your seemingly lifeless body. I think she was also shocked when she saw Knud take you in his arms—many people were, seeing how much he cared about you,' Brita said, lowering her voice. 'Between you and me, I don't think she much liked it, yet it was clear she felt guilty that she had brought this upon us. Upon you. She has relinquished her claim on Boer, bending the knee and swearing an oath of fealty to your father. She said she would spend her days making up for her own father's failings.'

'And my parents? They are all right? Are they still here?'

'Yes, they stayed. Your father, well, he has been quiet for days... He feels responsible, of course, as you fell under his blade. It will take a while for him to forgive himself, I expect. But he spoke with Knud and they are trying to resolve their differences. They are rather alike in many ways, I think.'

Wren nodded, smiling. But she was waiting, holding her breath, hoping Brita would share more details—she was desperate to ask what her father had said about Knud's proposal. And her heart soared again in disbelief that he hadn't gone ahead with his wedding to Ingrid. She couldn't believe it. And she couldn't believe he'd announced that he intended to marry her—without even discussing it with her!

Was he going to ask her for her thoughts on the matter? Or had he merely been saying it in the heat of the moment, to stop the fight, to protect his people, to form the alliance he'd wanted from the start? After all, now knowing who she was, she had some value, some use to him now, didn't she? As the daughter of the Earl of Forsa, she could enhance his position, offer protection for his people, share trade routes…all the things he most desired.

She shifted on the bed, trying to get comfortable. So was her father going to say yes? To offer her up in marriage to form an alliance, or in exchange for peace? Did she get a say in it at all?

'Where is Knud?' she asked quietly.

'My brother? Well, he has barely left your side these past few days, until I forced him to go and wash and change a few moments ago—he was starting to leave quite a stench around the place! Perhaps that's what woke you in the end.'

Wren smiled. She realised Brita shared her brother's lively sense of humour.

'You're in his room, by the way. In case you were wondering. I wasn't sure if you knew where you were... if you'd seen it before?'

Wren shook her head, feeling her face heating under Brita's gaze. She couldn't believe it had taken getting stabbed to make it into his bed, she thought wryly.

'No, I should have known. He never lets anyone in here.'

Wren looked around, taking in the large, simple space. The bed was covered in a collection of animal furs and the wall was decorated with the head of a huge bear. There was a chair in the corner strewn with a few of his belongings, but it was the messy pile of trinkets in the corner that caught her eye. Jewellery, runes, clothing. She frowned.

'They belonged to Annegrete,' Brita said. 'It was like a shrine to her not so long ago. No one was allowed to touch anything. He moved it all out of the way when he brought you in here.'

Wren was touched, but she hoped he didn't feel he had to dispose of his trinkets and memories because of her. It really wasn't necessary.

She attempted to sit up, but Brita pushed her back down. 'You should rest now, Wren. I shall let them all know you're awake. They'll want to see you. Is there anyone I should send for first?'

But then the door was pushed open and her mother and father were there, rushing towards her, delighted to see her awake. They wrapped her up in a huge embrace and her father began to make his apologies—she could tell he felt awful. She told him all was forgiven and he mustn't feel guilty.

By the time afternoon came, Wren was weary from her many visitors, who had all popped their heads round the door, wishing her well, telling her how her injury had stopped the fight and that she'd saved them all. And she was truly delighted to have been of use, to have helped.

But despite being pleased to see them all safe, she hadn't seen Knud all day. The one person she desired to see most of all had not come to see her. He had been sat by her side for days, Brita had said, but now she was awake, did he not want to talk to her? She couldn't understand it. Surely they had much to discuss? Had she imagined the words he'd said to her father out in the courtyard, while he held her in his arms? Had she dreamed them up?

Wren struggled up to sitting and carefully swung her legs out of bed, not wanting to make any sudden movements, wary of her wound. She placed her bare feet on the cold floor and padded to the door. If he would not come to see her, then she would just have to go in search of him. She couldn't wait any longer.

She didn't know what she was going to say to him, she just knew she needed to see him again after everything that had happened. But pulling open the door, she gasped, for Knud was standing right there, outside the door, pacing, his head bowed, muttering to himself and scowling. When he saw movement in the doorway, he looked up, their eyes meeting, and her heart hitched.

She knew he felt he was to blame for her injury—it was etched all over his face. Was that why he hadn't come to see her? Was that why he was hovering outside the room? She felt her legs tremble and she faltered, but he didn't miss a beat. He cursed, scooping her up into his arms, chastising her for getting out of bed, and he carried her back into his room, kicking the door shut behind him. Seemingly reluctant to let her go, he sat down on the furs, leaning his back against the wall, cradling her in his lap.

'How are you feeling?' he asked.

'A little sore, but I'm on the mend. I'll be fine. And you?'

'Better than I deserve. I've been so worried about you, Wren,' he said, his voice cracking. 'I'm so sorry you got hurt. It was the one thing I was trying to prevent. When I saw that blade slice through your skin, when I saw all that blood... I thought the worst.'

'I know,' she said gently. 'I must have given you all quite a fright.'

He shook his head. 'I thought I'd lost you. It was more than I could bear.'

'But I'm all right. I'm fine now.'

'I'm sorry I fought your father...'

'He didn't exactly give you much of a choice.' She smiled wryly. 'You know you're very alike...'

'Both stubborn, you mean?'

She smiled. 'That and the rest.'

She leaned her head against his shoulder, breathing him in, so glad he was here. She was relieved to be alone with him, back in his arms. But she had so many questions…

'Knud…why didn't you marry Ingrid?'

He shifted her in his arms, drawing her closer. 'I never wanted to marry Ingrid. You know that.'

'But you were always prepared to go ahead with it anyway.'

'I thought it was something I had to do for my people. And later, for you, to ensure your freedom. When I left you at your father's camp that day, when you sent me away from you, I knew that I had hurt you. Badly. And in doing so I hurt myself. I realised I didn't want to spend my life being unhappy, being miserable married to a woman I didn't care for. All I could think about was you.

'I knew then that I had to try to make it up to you… and the first thing I had to do was to break free of the vow I'd made to Ingrid. You had saved me from having to stick to my promise, in a way. Even though we weren't together, you had taken your father's army away, lessening my need for Ingrid's forces.

'I also knew when I discovered your heritage—that you were from Forsa—I could no longer help Ingrid reclaim her fortress. It would mean going against your father—your family. *You.* That was something I wasn't prepared to do. I knew if I did, I would never get you back. So I had to sit down with her and tell her that the marriage alliance was off.'

'How did she take it?'

'Not well, as you can tell from all that has happened

since. But in a way I'm glad she sent that threat to your father, as it set in motion a chain of events that brought you back to me. I wasn't sure you ever wanted to see me again, but when I saw you at the gate that night, when you came to warn us about your father's army coming to attack us, it gave me hope—it made me believe that maybe you still cared for me, as I did for you.'

'I do care, Knud,' she said, turning her face to look at him, bringing her hand up to rest on his cheek. 'Those things I said in the tent that day... I didn't really mean any of them. I was just hurt. I regretted sending you away from me. I have missed you every single day that we've been apart. I feared that I'd pushed you into Ingrid's arms. I was so afraid you'd married her.'

'How could I ever have gone through with it, when I'm so in love with you?' he said, resting his forehead against hers. 'Despite what you might think, I do know a thing or two about love.'

She closed her eyes and opened them again, as if to check she wasn't dreaming. Had he really just uttered the words she'd been waiting so long to hear?

'And it was because I'd loved before, I was scared of doing so again. I felt guilty... The feelings I had for you were so strong, more than I've ever felt for anyone. And if it had hurt when I lost Annegrete, I thought the pain of losing you would be too much to bear. I was unwilling to face that kind of grief again. And then the worst happened...and I lost you anyway.'

'The pain, the grief, it is a positive thing. It shows how much you loved her,' Wren said. 'And you don't have to stop caring for her, just because you also care for me. You don't have to rid yourself of your memories. You have a great capacity for love, Knud, and I'm sure you have room in your heart for both of us.'

His mouth came down on to hers, placing the softest, most tender kiss on her lips, and she wrapped her arms around his neck, holding him tight and never wanting to let go.

They all sat around a table in the bustling longhouse— her mother and father, Knud, Brita, Rebekah and Rædan. All the people she cared most about in the world. Wren was back on her feet and everyone was busy making preparations for Earl Orm of Forsa's departure later that day. Taking in the view of the grand hall, everyone eating and drinking merrily, the fire roaring in the centre of the great room, she felt as if she belonged here. She had missed this place when she'd been away—she had missed Nedergaard's ruler. She wanted to be by his side, always.

So how could it be that she was leaving him again today? Her heart felt as if it was slowly crumbling, the pain ripping her apart from the inside, yet no one could tell she was suffering. On the outside, she was trying to hold herself together.

Knud had visited her many times in his room over the past few days and he had told her he loved her. They'd spent long mornings and afternoons talking, him holding her in his arms, but not once had he mentioned his offer of marriage out on the battlefield. Had he thought she hadn't heard and changed his mind, thinking better of it? What was holding him back?

Or had her father refused to give Knud his blessing, declining giving him his daughter's hand, wanting to keep her in Forsa after having lived without her for so long? She didn't understand.

They had shared many soft kisses on his bed, wrapped up in his strong arms, but when she'd gone to take things further, he'd halted her hands, telling her she needed to focus on getting better, making her furious.

When she'd asked him to stay with her last night, to hold her while she slept, he had said she'd needed her sleep, leaving her alone and frustrated in his room. It was infuriating! Did he not want her the way she wanted him? It was all she could think about. She would give anything to make him agree to be her lover again.

She glanced across the table at him, trying to catch his eye. He looked incredibly handsome, his damp hair pinned back, his beard neatly trimmed. Had he been for a swim in the fjord? But he didn't glance her way— he was too busy toying with his tankard, staring solemnly into its depths. What was he thinking? What secrets was he keeping from her now? Did he not care that she was leaving soon, probably for good this time?

Her shoulder had healed well and Brita had declared that Wren was finally ready to make the journey home. *Home.* She had so many places she had lived during the twenty winters she'd been alive…was Forsa where she really wanted to be? She had spent most of her days in Boer and she knew that settlement best of all, but it was here in Nedergaard where her heart lay, where she truly felt at home. Because this was where the man she loved was. This was where she wanted to be, if only he'd ask her to stay.

Her father stood suddenly, tapping his knife on his cup, meaning to make an announcement. And Knud turned, the whole table quietening down, wanting to listen. She felt Knud's gaze on her at last as she looked up at her father. Goose pimples erupted along her arms. What was happening?

'I wanted to thank our hosts for having us,' Earl Orm said. 'For their food and their ale and for taking care of my daughter after everything that came to pass here. Today we start out on our journey back home to Forsa, where we shall spend the winter, but know that you are all welcome to come and see us when the days turn brighter once more. In the meantime, Jarl Knud and I have agreed to share trade routes and send messengers often. I also have an announcement to make. My wife and I have decided to bestow a great honour on our daughter...'

Wren's head shot up.

'We have decided to gift her with a fortress.'

She gasped.

'We understand it was hard for her to settle back in Forsa after many winters away and she has grown into her own person, strong and wise and compassionate, and deserves a home of her own. So from now on, our Neva will be the Earl of Boer. And you will all be welcome in her great hall, I'm sure.'

A rush of breath left her, as her eyes met Knud's

over the rim of his tankard, while cheers and boots stomping on the floor erupted around the longhouse.

Was this why he hadn't renewed his proposal? Had he known her father was going to do this? Her chest shattered that little bit more. Had he kept a great secret from her again? She knew she should be overwhelmed by this decision of her father's and that it was a wonderful gift, an honour. It was more than she could have ever dreamed of. She should be delighted, so why wasn't she?

She stood on trembling legs as her father came around the table to embrace her.

'I don't know what to say, Father. Thank you.'

'We shall travel together to your stronghold this afternoon and get you settled. Then your mother and I shall depart for the south in a few days.'

She nodded, but instead of sitting back down, she grabbed her cloak, telling everyone she wanted to enjoy one last walk on the beach before she had to leave, as she exited the hall. She needed to get some fresh air, as it was stifling in there, so she crossed the square and followed the path to the bay. Like always, the view of the fjord and the striking longships lifted her spirits. She often wondered where they had taken Knud, imagining what adventures he'd had aboard them, making him the man he had become. What adventures lay in store for him next? she wondered. And did they not include her?

She truly did love him with all her heart, she thought, and the emotion tore through her again with the wild intensity of the waves tumbling on to the shore and the wind howling through the trees.

She continued down the beach, unsure how she should be feeling, the turbulent weather matching her thoughts. She came across the little hut where Knud had made love to her that first time and she stole inside, sheltering from the whipping wind. She went to stroke the horse in the corner, feeding him some hay. What secrets this animal knew of her passion and her heart, she thought, stroking its long nose.

A noise behind her startled her.

Knud.

He stepped inside the hut, closing the door behind him, before leaning his back against it.

'Don't make me go back to the longhouse,' she said miserably, shaking her head. 'I can't face it. Not yet.'

'I'm not going to make you do anything,' he said gently.

'Then what are you doing here?'

'I followed you.'

'I can see that. Why?'

'I wanted to know what you thought about your father's offer. You disappeared from the longhouse pretty quickly.'

'It—it's more than I could ever have imagined,' she said evasively.

He nodded. 'And yet you don't seem that pleased about it.'

She shrugged. 'How could I not be? It is everyone's dream, is it not, to have a fortress, people to rule over, riches…'

He stepped towards her, stopping halfway across the room, the howling wind ripping across the roof. 'It is a prize indeed, to have your own fortress. A home to make your own.'

'You think I should accept it?' she said, her chin tilted forward.

'If it will make you happy,' he said, his voice strained. 'And after everything you have suffered, you deserve this, Wren. You deserve to choose your own future. I cannot make those decisions for you.'

And she wondered…could it be that this was why he'd held back from proposing to her again? Because he didn't want to stand in her way of having this title, this fortress? Was he once again putting her needs before his own, not wanting to get in her way?

Yes, that was it. She was certain of it. He was allowing her to choose her own path, her own future, after being denied a choice in life for so long. But to choose, she needed to know all the options available to her. Was he one of them?

She took a step towards him, meeting him in the middle of the hut. 'To own my own fortress is indeed a great prize, but it's not the prize I most wanted, nor the future I have come to yearn for.' She pressed herself up against him.

'No?' he asked, his eyes glittering down at her.

As if she needed to make it even clearer, her arms came up to wrap around his strong shoulders, and she kissed him, crushing his mouth with hers. When she lifted her head away, she left him breathless.

'No,' she said. 'I have never coveted a title, possessions… Only love. *Your* love. That is all I want, Knud, if you still want me in return.'

* * *

Knud had been holding back from Wren all week, not daring to claim her body again, knowing the plans her father had in store for her. He wanted her to make the decision on her own—he didn't want to persuade or influence her in any way.

When he'd asked Earl Orm for her hand in marriage that day on the battlefield, he had meant it. He wanted to make her his. But later on that evening, with the mood sombre, and everyone worried about Wren, her father had refused. He'd said he and his wife had just got her back, that he wasn't willing to part with her again so soon. They had come to a truce anyway, he, Earl Orm and Ingrid, that they would no longer invade each other's lands. They had agreed Earl Orm would keep Boer and he had revealed his plans to Knud for Wren to take over the running of the fortress.

It was an incredible gesture and one Knud thought Wren deserved. So he had agreed to stand back, promising to keep his distance, giving her the chance to make up her own mind on whether she accepted it. But he couldn't believe it—here she was, standing before him, telling him she didn't want it.

She was telling him that all she wanted was him, making all his dreams come true. The feelings rushing through him were no less than ecstasy and he didn't think he could stay away from her for a moment longer. It had been enough of a torture staying away from her all week.

He hauled her closer, pulling her right up against him. Her hands splayed out across his chest, her stomach pressing into his hardening groin, and he hoped she could feel just how much he wanted her now. And the way she was bunching up his tunic, tugging down his own trousers in desperate urgency, wanting him naked, he thought she must be feeling the same way, too, and he laughed freely, delighted by her eagerness.

He unclasped the brooches holding up her pinafore and it pooled to the ground, then he gripped her tunic in both hands, stripping away the material quickly, wanting her naked. He had thought about nothing else for many days and nights. Then he turned her round in his arms, holding her back against his chest. He rested his head on her shoulder, one of his hands skating over her stomach and coming up to cup her breast possessively while the other smoothed over her thigh.

She whimpered and wriggled backwards, his rock-hard cock nestling into the crevice of her buttocks as she raised her arms, lifting them over her head to clasp behind his neck, fastening him to her. She held him against her, clinging on as he ruthlessly parted her legs wide with his own, his fingers stealing between her thighs, finding her already soaked with desire. And his potent touch made her gasp and her legs buckle.

'I wanted to claim you from the moment I saw you in that tidal pool,' he whispered. 'But I never thought you'd let me. That's why I fought for your freedom that day, so you could be free to one day choose to be mine.'

'I love you, Knud. I did from the first moment I saw you. And I want you to make me yours again now. Please,' she whispered. 'Please take me now.'

And he needed no more instruction. She was surrendering herself to him and he could wait no longer. Curling his hand around her neck, he gently pushed her down, bending her over a bale of hay. He brushed her silky long hair aside and trailed his palm over the ink on her shoulder, the symbol of her heritage, and down over the raised silver markings on her back, the scars that represented her fifteen winters she spent as a thrall.

But these marks were nothing compared to what he was about to brand her body with—the intensity of his love. He drew his fingers down the crease of her buttocks, curling beneath her, making sure she was wet and ready for what was to come. She moaned, raising her bottom towards him a little, showing him she wanted him, that she couldn't wait any longer, and neither could he as he positioned himself at her entrance.

Taking her by the hips, pulling her towards him, he drove inside her from behind, sliding all the way in in one wicked thrust, making her cry out in intense pleasure. She had asked him to take her completely and so he had complied, surging inside, needing to be close to her, to be part of her again. And she felt so good. Too good, as though she was made solely for him. He glanced down, wanting to see where they were connected, where he was buried so deep, and in doing so he had to fight to keep control of himself.

He saw her fingers curl into the hay, trying to hold on to something, to prepare herself for his next taking of her, and incredibly she spread her legs wider, wanting more of him, everything he could give, and as he dug his fingers into her hips, holding her in place, he thrust inside her again, roaring out in wonder at the soaring sensations she was creating.

He lowered his head to kiss the top of her trembling back, as his hand stole round between her legs, wanting to touch her intimately as he took her with his body, and his fingers stroked through her hair, curving over her as he impaled her again, rocking her mound into his hand, his fingers stoking her tiny nub.

She began to pant out her pleasure and he knew she was close. And so was he. He wasn't sure how much more of this euphoria he could take. He saw her grapple with the hay again, her body yielding beneath his, and then he thrust into her harder than ever before, slamming his groin against her buttocks, and, as she screamed with pleasure and her release, he came apart inside her.

It took a while for him to come to, to lift himself off her back and remove himself from her body. He tugged her up on to her feet, turning her around to look at him, checking she was all right. Her cheeks were a beautiful pink colour from the intensity of their love-making and her legs seemed decidedly wobbly. Knud stood before her, in all his naked glory, and his hand came out to stroke her hair behind her ears, taming it.

'You're trembling,' she said.

'You always have that effect on me,' he admitted.

'Is it always that intense?' she asked.

'No, just with you.'

And then, fiddling with his rings on his finger, he removed the one his father had given to his mother, which had been passed down to him, and he got down on one knee. He stared up at her, his brown eyes shining with love, the way he'd looked up at her that night in the forest, beneath the stars, telling her he wanted to worship her.

'Wren, will you marry me?' he asked. 'If you say yes, I promise I will spend the rest of my life trying to heal your wounds and make you happy, as you have done for me. You rescued me, Wren…'

'And you me,' she said. 'Yes, of course I'll marry you, Knud.' And she sank to her knees and took his face in her hands, kissing him, deeply, before he pulled her against him, bringing her naked body down with him on to the floor, holding her close.

'If you marry me now, you'll get the alliance I heard you speak of that first night in Boer…you'll get your legacy,' she said, teasing him gently.

He grinned into her hair. 'I don't need a legacy, Wren. What I need is love. Your love.'

'Is that so?' She smiled, wriggling her bottom back against him, nestling into his groin. 'I thought you said you didn't need love.'

'I was scared,' he said, propping himself up on his elbow, looking down into her eyes. 'I thought it was better not to love anyone else only to lose them all over again…but I did lose you regardless and it was worse than anything I've ever been through. And now you've said yes to being my wife, I'll probably spend the rest of my days worrying something will happen to you and trying my utmost to protect you.'

She smiled. 'No one is ever truly safe, Knud. Not really. That's why we have to make the most of the moments we have. It's why we have to hold those we love as close as we can.'

And he took her in his arms again, taking her advice. He rolled on top of her, parting her thighs with his legs, wondering if it was too soon to take her again. His need for her was insatiable. But when she eagerly brought her arms up around his shoulders, bringing his lips down on to hers, he knew he had his answer.

'My first marriage was arranged by my parents,' he said, kissing her lips, her cheeks, her jaw. 'My second was meant to be for the good of my people, for the freedom of a wonderful woman,' he said, trailing kisses down her neck. 'But this one—this one is for love and only love, and my heart is finally content,' he told her as he bent his head to take her nipple into his mouth. When he slowly thrust his cock inside her body once more, this time he took it slow, making it last.

Easing in and out of her unhurriedly, he thought back to his words on the mudflats that night and how incredible it was that Wren, the wild woman he had met out there, had been the one to patch up the cracks in Daneland, strengthen his borders and heal the wounds of his heart. And he felt so happy knowing he had all the time in the world to do this, to make love to her— and that he could do so for the rest of his days.

'Are you sure we won't be missed?' Wren whispered, laughing, as Knud carried his bride-to-be in his arms to his room at the back of the longhouse.

'I imagine they'll be celebrating the news of our engagement for a while longer yet. Rædan will make

sure of it. He promised to keep the ale flowing for us.'
He winked. 'And I promised you the next time we did
this it would be in my bed!'

They had returned from the hut this afternoon,
flushed and content, holding hands, not wanting to
let go of each other. They had gone in search of her
mother and father, who were readying their convoy to
leave, and Knud had pulled Earl Orm aside and asked
for his blessing for them to marry. At first, the Earl
had been shocked to learn that his daughter was re-
fusing the fortress of Boer, giving it up to stay here
in Nedergaard. But when he saw how happy she was,
and knowing she would be safe under the protection
of Jarl Knud, he soon relented, embracing her and the
Danish chieftain.

They'd all returned to the longhouse together and
announced the news to the people of Nedergaard, Boer
and Forsa—that the Chief of Nedergaard was to take
a new bride and everyone was delighted their new female Earl was the woman who had brought them all
together. They had all grown to love and respect Wren,
just like their leader had.

Wren's mother and father had quickly decided to
extend their stay until after the wedding, which would
take place imminently, Knud had said, as he wanted
to claim Wren as his wife as quickly as possible. And
then he'd demanded an all-day celebration, which had
gone on long into the night. They feasted and drank
to their heart's content, but then Knud had leaned in,
telling her he couldn't wait to be alone with her again.

Rædan and Rebekah had, of course, been delighted

to see them come together at last, knowing what it was like to find true love and happiness after so much suffering, and Knud had thanked his friend fervently for his good counsel. Brita had been overjoyed, delighted to discover Wren would be her sister, jesting she could now relinquish her role of having to keep her brother on the straight and narrow.

At some point during the festivities, Wren had spoken to her father about her plans for Boer and he had reluctantly agreed to her suggestion, not wanting to deny his daughter the peace she desired in her heart. So she had gone to find Ingrid in one of the little rooms and had offered her back her family's fortress, on the provision that she made it a place free from thralls.

To her surprise, Ingrid had thrown herself down at her feet, thanking her and begging her forgiveness for the way she'd treated her throughout those fifteen summers and winters. Wren had wrapped her hands around her old companion's arms and lifted her up, saying she had forgiven her a long time ago and that she wasn't one to carry hatred in her heart, only love.

The reinstated Earl Ingrid had thanked her, gratefully, promising to make Boer more prosperous and a place of peace, and she had congratulated Wren on her upcoming nuptials, admitting she had been jealous of the way Knud had looked at her from the start.

They had gone out into the hall and joined their people together, arm in arm, the way they had often done in Boer when they were little girls, and Wren had felt as if everything was right with the world again. Wren was pleased Earl Ingrid had accepted Boer, for she had no need of another stronghold—she had everything she needed right here in Nedergaard.

Knud carried her into his room and laid her down on the furs on his bed, peeling away her clothes, savouring the taste of her skin beneath his lips, telling her that he was going to make love to her with his mouth and then his body.

She tipped her head back in pleasure as he took her breast in his mouth, but his words had her thoughts drifting back to what he'd said about not wanting a legacy, only love. Could that be true? Surely it would be a tragedy for a man such as he to not have it all—to not have a family of his own?

'Do you want children?' she asked him, bringing a halt to his lips as he began to leave a hot trail of kisses down her stomach to the apex of her thighs. He lifted his handsome head to look up at her.

'Your children, yes. Do you?'

'Absolutely,' she said, thinking of a horde of little blond-haired warriors playing in the courtyard, or out on the longships on the fjord. She really did want that.

'Then we'd better not waste any time,' he said, sliding her undergarments down her thighs, stripping off his own clothes and settling himself between her legs. 'We'd better get started right away.'

Epilogue

Five winters later

Wren glanced across the bay, looking for her sons. Where had they run off to now?

As she scanned the horizon, her gaze fell upon her husband, standing in the hull of one of the longships, where he seemed to be acting out a story, shuffling forward and backwards with his feet as he waved his sword with fervour, fighting an invisible enemy. Perhaps this tale was of one of his raids and expeditions across the sea, or maybe even a Danish chief who rescued a lost girl from a life of thralldom.

Their twin sons, with longish dark blond hair tied back in matching buns, stared up at him in wonder, cheering him on, and she shook her head, smiling. She was so pleased the boys had each other. Aron had been born first, with Knud at her side, holding her hand, encouraging her on, and they'd been overwhelmed the gods had granted them a healthy son, revealing they had their approval.

But while they were cradling him in their arms, all of a sudden, her labour had started up again. At first, she had thought something was wrong and Knud had panicked, demanding his sister do something. But when she had gone on to birth a second child, Aki, they had felt blessed with plenty. It brought her great comfort to know her sons would always have a companion in life.

She made her way across the sand towards the jetty, her hands smoothing over her newly swollen belly as she walked. 'I've been looking all over for you,' she called, and her handsome brood all turned round to look at her. '*Morfar* and *Mormor* have arrived. Your grandparents can't wait to see you.'

Instantly, the boys leapt up, excited, clambering out of the boat and racing past her towards the beach, heading for the longhouse, and she rolled her eyes, amused. At the feast tonight, they were going to have the family emblem marked on their sons' shoulders in woad dye. Knud had agreed to using part of Forsa's symbol—the same one Wren had on her shoulder, as he knew how much it meant to her, for it had enabled her to find herself and her family. But their sons' family symbol would also feature the markings of a great bear.

'You shouldn't tell them of your tales and excite them so before the feast,' she chastised Knud gently.

'You're right, as always. I get carried away,' he said, putting down his sword and extending his hand for her to take.

'Which story was it this time?' she asked, allowing him to help her into the ship.

'My favourite adventure—the one that involves you.'

She smiled up at him. 'I like that one, too.' And he bent his head and planted a soft kiss on her lips.

The night was drawing in and the stars were beginning to twinkle up above in the inky sky.

'How are you feeling this evening?' he asked.

'Large!'

And he smiled.

'The baby's been kicking a lot today,' she said, and he stepped forward to place his hand gently over the curve of her stomach.

'She's going to be spirited, just like her mother.'

'She?'

He shrugged. 'You know I think it's a girl, to take after you, but I'll be happy either way. I've been thinking about tonight's ceremony and the symbols we're going to have inked on our sons' shoulders. I want to make a change to what we agreed on,' he said, taking her hands in his.

'Oh?' She looked up at him expectantly.

'I think we should include a wren, sat next to the bear...for he would be nothing without her. You know a wren is a symbol of rebirth—of freedom and happiness...'

She nodded slowly, tears filling her eyes. 'I like that.' She thought he might be right about them having a girl, as she was feeling things very deeply with this baby. *Helvete!* Who was she fooling? She'd been like this since Knud had come into her life...

'I suppose we'd better go and welcome your parents—and Ingrid,' Knud said reluctantly.

She had wondered if the alliances they'd made five winters before would last—if they would hold out over the longstanding feuds between their settlements— but they had. Indeed, they were stronger than ever, because family was at the heart of it. And looking up at the man she loved more with every breath she took, she knew the union between her and husband was the strongest of all.

He pulled her closer, pressing his lips against hers, his hand releasing hers to roam around and cup her bottom, tugging her into his hardening body. 'Unless we have time?' he whispered.

She laughed, throwing her head back, delighted he still wanted her, even though she was growing bigger by the day. 'If we're quick…' And his hands began to ruck up her dress. He was still as insatiable for her as she was for him. 'Where are we going this time on this longship of yours?'

'Our destiny,' he whispered.

He sank down on to the bench, tugging her with him, and she straddled his thighs, wrapping her arms around his neck. His fingers slid beneath her clothes, stroking and teasing her body, making her writhe beneath his fingers, bringing her to life. And he whispered that now he no longer went on raids and expeditions across the sea, her body was his new adventure and he promised he was about to take her on a new journey of discovery she would never forget…

She tugged him down on top of her in the hull of the boat and as he slid inside her body, making her gasp out her pleasure beneath the stars, she discovered his words were true. And she knew that in the winters to come, she would have many more adventures with this wonderful man by her side.

* * * * *

If you enjoyed this story, be sure to pick up
Sarah Rodi's Rise of the Ivarssons miniseries

The Viking's Stolen Princess
Escaping with Her Saxon Enemy

And why not check out her exciting Viking romance?

One Night with Her Viking Warrior

Get 3 FREE REWARDS!

We'll send you 2 FREE Books plus a FREE Mystery Gift.

FREE
Value Over
$20

Both the **Romance** and **Suspense** collections feature compelling novels written by many of today's bestselling authors.

HARLEQUIN
PLUS

Try the best multimedia
subscription service for romance
readers like you!

Read, Watch and Play.

Experience the easiest way to get
the romance content you crave.

Start your **FREE TRIAL** at
<u>www.harlequinplus.com/freetrial</u>.